MADDEN

BOOK FOUR

USA TODAY BESTSELLING AUTHOR

BROOKE O'BRIEN

MADDEN

Madden Cole is considered a rock 'n' roll god, and all the women want him. Except for me.

After working my butt off as a journalist for years, I've heard the rumors about him and his band and have read all about their dirty scandals in the headlines.

When I land a job as a writer for *Limelight* magazine, I'll stop at nothing to make a good impression. Even if it means agreeing to a sit-down interview with the bad boys of A Rebels Havoc.

They're making a name for themselves by soaring to the top of the charts with multiplatinum records and sold-out tours.

Madden is cold and closed-off, but the more I get to know him, the more he starts to open up to me. As hard as I've tried to resist wanting him, when he turns on his sweet-talking charm, all the walls I've built around me crumble.

They say what goes up must come down, and the band is forced to face the downside of fame. Rumors, lies, and blackmail threaten Madden's life and the career he and the guys have worked so hard to build.

He doesn't know about the secret I've been keeping.

And I fear when he finds out the truth, it could destroy everything.

Thank you for reading **MADDEN**! I hope you love Madden and Brielle's story as much as I do.

You can join my Facebook group, Brooke O'Brien's Rebel Readers Group, to discuss the series and get sneak peeks on future releases. Sign up for my newsletter to find out more about my new releases. To join, visit: www.authorbrookeobrien.com/followbrooke

Happy reading!

A REBELS HAVOC SERIES
READING ORDER

BRIX

a stepbrother, enemies to lovers, rock star romance

SINS OF A REBEL

a summer fling, brother's best friend, rock star romance

TYSIN

a brother's best friend, forced proximity, rock star romance

TREY

a surprise pregnancy, virgin heroine, rock star romance

MADDEN

a frenemies to lovers, journalist/rock star romance

Learn more and purchase your copy at:
www.authorbrookeobrien.com/arebelshavoc

DEDICATION

To you
Thank you for reading and supporting this series. It's changed my life in so many ways, and I can't tell you how much it means to me to live out my dream.

xoxo

CHAPTER ONE

BRIELLE

I can't fuck this up.

As we pass through the neighborhood, I peer out the window at the stunning homes behind gated entrances with stone pillars and statutes, each with freshly manicured lawns.

We pull up outside of a black wrought-iron gate, and Davis presses the button to the intercom.

"Hello?"

"Yes, it's *Limelight* magazine. We're here for our interview with A Rebels Havoc."

"I'll let you through. Please come to the front door."

The gate opens, and we pass through, down the long gravel road to the circular driveway and park.

Davis whistles when he leans forward to take in the beautiful home.

"Here I thought I've been saving myself for a hot shot financial banker or some successful real estate investor, when I should've been looking for a sexy rock star."

I shake my head. I'm not sure what I expected when we showed up here, but it wasn't this. Black shutters surround two large windows with a balcony on the upper level, a pillared entrance, and black and gray brick below.

I imagine taking in the view of the sunrise each morning with a cup of coffee and the sun glistening on the water.

"You ready to kill this thing?" Davis asks, bringing me back to reality.

He's overly chipper this morning. Something I'm not quite ready for.

I mumble, "Ready as I'll ever be," while mentally trying to hype myself up for what's to come.

It's just the two of us, and it's my first assignment. I can't believe my boss thought to stiff me with this interview on my first week.

"You have plenty of experience in the industry, Brielle. You'll kill it. I have all the faith in you," Sawyer sang, tapping on the doorframe before she disappeared out of my office.

She didn't give me a chance to protest.

Davis adjusts the bag on his shoulder and bumps his arm against mine.

"Let's do this damn thing." He grins.

We take the stone steps up the front walkway to the door. Davis hits the doorbell, and I clutch my bag holding my notebook against my side. I run my hand over my blazer down to my skirt to calm my racing heart.

While I may have years of experience, this job is something new for me entirely. I've never done a sit-down interview with anyone, much less the members of the biggest rock band in the country.

We stand outside, taking in the trellis of vines climbing up the brick exterior, waiting for someone to answer, but no one does.

"Where are they?" Davis peeks into the doorway, looking for any sign of movement.

"What the heck? Don't they know we planned to be here at two o'clock?" I grit out.

I've done my best not to let my distaste for A Rebels Havoc show. I've always thought of them as a bunch of arrogant, womanizing pricks.

"You'd think so," he says, shrugging. "Should I ring it again?"

I glance around, searching for any indication someone is even home.

"We have the correct address, right?"

"I mean, they have private security at the gate, and they did let us in? I'd assume they knew we were here." He huffs.

"No frickin' kidding." With a sigh, I reach across him and punch my finger against the doorbell again.

We wait another moment before we see a figure through the glass door. I can't quite make out the person; all I can see is a fury of purple rushing toward us.

The lock clicks, and the door swings open, and a woman who, from my research, is Kyla greets us. She's dating Tysin, their lead guitarist, and is the sister of their drummer, Madden.

We've been in touch through email over the past week, finalizing the last-minute details for their interview today.

"I'm so sorry to keep you waiting. I'm Kyla, the band's manager. Forgive me; I thought Madden was going to grab the door. It must've been a misunderstanding." She presses her lips together in a forced smile. She folds her hand against her heaving chest, out of breath as if she ran a mile to answer the door.

"The guys should be here any moment. They just wrapped up practice about an hour ago and were getting cleaned up."

She steps back, letting us in.

"Can I get you a drink?" she offers, holding her arm out to lead us inside.

"I wouldn't mind a water," Davis says, smiling.

"I'll have one too," I add.

"Great, I'll grab those for you. We thought we could do the interview over here in the sitting area. Madden displays their awards and mementos from over the years in there."

My heels click on the tile floors as we follow her into a room with a large sofa and two sitting chairs. The stone-blue walls have plaques, pictures, and awards covering nearly every surface.

"This works perfectly. I'll head back out to grab the rest of our equipment, and we'll get everything set up while we wait."

Kyla scurries off, and I turn back to Davis. He shrugs and shakes his head.

"If you want to figure out a setup, I'll get our stuff. You good?"

I nod, waving him off, and he disappears out the door.

Setting my bag down on one of the chairs, I look at all their achievements hanging on the wall.

Over the years, I've covered A Rebels Havoc, so I've heard the rumors swirling around in the media about them. They've had everything from drinking and partying too much to fights and rumored pregnancies splashed all over the headlines.

Their record label knew what they were doing by setting up this interview. They have a new album coming out in a few weeks, and even though there's no such thing as bad press, I'm sure this is their way of trying to smooth over their image.

Despite this being an incredible opportunity for me, I'm not exactly excited about sitting down and talking with them. They seem like nothing but a bunch of punks who only care about drinking and getting laid.

I brush my finger over the frame holding the multiplatinum disc from their breakout album. Not many have accomplished that incredible achievement, so it's cool to see their award in person.

"Fuck, baby, that feels so damn good." A loud throaty groan filters into the quiet space, and my whole body freezes. "Let me see those pretty eyes while you suck my dick."

I gasp, my mouth dropping open before I quietly slap my hand over it to muffle the sound.

Who the hell did I just overhear?

"Fuckkk," he moans. "Take it deep, sweetheart. Mmm, just like that."

My face warms at the sound of his words, heat spreading over my body. His deep voice has me rubbing my legs together.

I can't believe I'm standing here still listening, but I can't manage to pull myself away either.

"Let me hear you, baby," he mutters.

I finally force my feet to move, turning to glance out the large bay window overlooking the driveway. Davis still has the back of the SUV open, shuffling around to collect our equipment.

Kyla will likely be back in here any second. Where are the rest of the guys?

His loud, throaty moan interrupts my thoughts, and I lean against the wall next to a bookshelf, wrapping my arm around my waist and placing my hand on my chest.

She moans quietly, and the sound of her gagging filters through the air.

My chest heaves, my breaths coming out in pants. I can practically feel my heart beating against my palm. I move up, wrapping my fingers around the base of my neck, and lean against the wall.

"I'm close," he mutters. "I'm fuckin' close. Open your throat, baby, and take it all." He grunts, and the sound nearly has me melting on the floor in a puddle.

I'm embarrassed by how turned on I am listening to this go down. Even more, I'm ashamed I didn't walk outside with Davis and give them privacy to finish what they're doing.

I don't think I would've been able to leave if I tried.

I squeeze my eyes closed, imagining he's standing above me, and his arousing words are from my hands and mouth on his body.

It's felt like forever since a man has touched me.

Too long.

If I gave in and slipped my hand into my pants, I'd realize just how desperate I am to be touched again.

I swipe the back of my hand over my forehead where the perspiration dots my brow. I attempt to smooth over my hair, trying and failing to collect myself, when a door swings open. I frantically push off the wall and come face-to-face with a shirt-less Madden.

"Who the fuck are you?"

My mouth drops open, and I fumble over my words, not sure how to answer.

"Uh, yes, hi. My name is Brielle."

"What the hell are you doing in my house?"

I steel my spine and narrow my eyes.

What the hell am I doing in his house? What the heck does he think I'm doing?

"I thought we didn't have any hired staff here today?"

I'm tempted to tell him to fuck off. Is this how he talks to guests or people who work for him?

His eyes trail down my body, and the heat behind them causes my brain to misfire. How is it I just overheard him with someone else, and now I'm picturing I was her?

What the hell has gotten into me?

The faint sound of heels clicking on the tile floor moves closer and closer to us. A petite brunette appears, wearing a tight black tunic and a pair of distressed denim jeans.

I resist curling my lip when I notice her smeared lipstick, knowing exactly why.

She stops when she reaches Madden and glances back and forth between us. She sneers, her eyes giving me a once-over before turning to him.

"I'll see you soon?" she asks, running her palm over his chest.

I step back to give them space, hoping this is my out to go search for Davis and avoid this humiliating conversation.

Madden turns back to me and holds up his hand. "Wait, please."

I nod and grit my teeth, glancing away to avoid looking at them. He leans down into her ear and whispers, "Thank you," then hugs her.

"I'll text you soon," he murmurs.

She nods enthusiastically and presses a kiss against his cheek.

"Excuse me," she replies sweetly, moving to pass between us but not before she flashes me a devious grin.

I return hers with a forced smile, stepping back to let her by, and she disappears out the front door.

Madden's demeanor changes when he turns back to me.

"Back to what I was saying," he retorts. His voice drops low, without an ounce of caring. "I wasn't expecting any staff to be here today. In the future, when I have a guest over, I expect you to give me privacy."

I bite my tongue to resist telling him to fuck off.

He has every right to want privacy, except I want to throw in his face how rude it is to invite guests into his home and then treat them like shit.

I chuckle under my breath and shake my head. He takes the step separating us, leaving enough room for me to smell his woodsy cologne mixed with the smell of sweat.

Do not think about how delicious he smells, Brielle.

"Can I ask what's so funny?" He lowers his eyes to my chest.

I'm afraid to even check my own reflection right now because I know the heat flaming my cheeks gives away just how much he affects me.

Whenever I'm nervous or anxious, I break out in what looks like hives. No matter how hard I try, I've never been able to prevent it.

I shake my head and finally glance up, locking eyes with him. It takes everything in me to stay composed.

"I know you were listening to us, and judging by the dazed look in your eye, you liked it. So unless you're waiting for me to drag you into that room for round two, I'll need you to clue me in. Although, I could assure you that you wouldn't find it the least bit funny if I did."

My face falls, and my eyes widen.

Why am I not surprised? Only these guys would finish getting their dick sucked and walk out here minutes later to proposition me.

"I wouldn't let you touch me if you were the last dick on earth," I spit out.

As soon as the words are out of my mouth, I wish I could take them back.

"Um, excuse me, Madden?" A voice interrupts, and we both turn to find Kyla standing in the entryway.

The door opens behind her, and Davis enters, carrying a tripod along with another bag.

My eyes flick back to Kyla, and her face is solemn.

"Can I have a word with you, Madden? Please," she mutters coldly, her eyes wide with a scolding look that says, "You better listen to me right now."

What the hell just happened?

CHAPTER TWO

MADDEN

Fuck, I thought the interview was tomorrow.

"I told you earlier this morning," Kyla snaps.

"I didn't hear you. I swore you said it was tomorrow."

"Yeah, when I reminded you about it *yesterday*," she retorts. "I swear, sometimes you don't pay attention."

I want to fly off the handle with a remark like, "Oh, you mean when you were fuckin' my best friend behind my back?"

I don't, though. Instead, I grit my teeth and pace back and forth in the kitchen, massaging my fingers into my pulsing temples.

Kyla pulls out her phone. "Trey is pulling up now. Brix and Tysin should be here any minute, and you still look like you just got done practicing."

She's right; I need to get cleaned up if we're supposed to do this interview soon.

I'm still recovering from the fact the hot-as-sin woman I hit on is actually here to do a sit-down interview with us.

As if we don't already have enough fuckin' bad press to begin with, now I have to worry about this shit.

"I'm gonna go shower. I'll make it quick."

"Okay. I'll do my best to distract them while we wait, but hurry, will ya? The interview was supposed to start thirty minutes ago."

I clench my jaw and nod, walking past her back into the entry-way.

The woman, I think she said her name was Brielle, stands in the living area next to a tall, slender man busy setting up their lighting equipment.

Her big blue eyes flick over to mine, and her face heats when she catches me staring at her. Her hair is sleeked back into a bun and those red lips tempt me once again.

She looks out of place and uncomfortable, reaching to tuck a strand of hair behind her ear. Her eyes flick down to my bare chest before forcing them up to meet mine.

Something about watching the emotions play out on her face, along with her reaction to seeing me earlier, taunts me. She was listening and appeared to be turned on by it.

Then I went and opened my big fuckin' mouth and made the situation worse.

"We'll be ready to start in about five minutes. Ten minutes max," I mutter when I pass by them.

"No problem," the guy replies. "We're just getting set up now."

Brielle peers at me intently. I soften my face and nod as if it's some sort of peace offering, and she returns it by pressing her lips together in a forced smile.

The last thing I need is to start us off on a rocky foot with the stuck-up journalist.

After all the shit in the media over the past year, we hope to shed a different light on who we are with this interview. We're still the same rebels we were early on in our careers, even if the guys have settled down some since falling in love.

Except for me.

I would've thought I'd be the first one to find someone, but the further we got in our career, the harder I've found it to trust people around us.

Loyalty and trust go a long way, but it's crazy what money and fame can do to people. I only want to be surrounded by the people who ride for me, and if they don't, they can get the fuck out of my life.

I jump in the shower and clean myself up, still slick with sweat from our practice session earlier. We're so close to releasing our new album and will be going on tour again this summer.

I can't fuckin' wait to get back out on the road. I miss it so much.

Absolutely nothing is like going out on stage and playing in front of a sold-out crowd.

Playing the drums has always been an outlet for me. My parents never wanted this to turn into my career even though they were supportive and bought me my first set.

They thought it was a hobby I'd eventually outgrow. I still remember my dad's snide comments about getting a real job, refusing to accept this has always been my dream.

Since signing on with our label, he's cut the comments despite wishing I had gone to college and got a degree in business like he did.

I don't give a shit what he thinks anymore. I love what I do, and I'm not in it for the money even though it's definitely one of the perks.

Don't get me wrong, though; this life comes with a lot I wish I didn't have to deal with too.

A black leather jacket and denim jeans with a white T-shirt wait for me in my room. I grit my teeth, knowing Kyla has been getting everything lined up for this interview for a month now.

I slip my leather cuff back on and run some product through my hair and over my beard, trying to look as if I've got my shit together.

I hate these fuckin' interviews. The sooner I get this over with, the quicker I can get the gossiping jackasses out of my house.

Brix and Tysin stand at the end of the hall when I step out of my bedroom. Tysin nods in my direction, and Brix turns, his eyes flaring before he stalks toward me, meeting me halfway.

"Sounds like shit already started off on a bad foot."

I stare at him, deadpanned, and shake my head. "Don't even get me started."

"You don't have to tell me. Kyla already did," he retorts.

I clench my jaw, wishing I had a couple of minutes to give everyone a piece of my mind.

"I'm sorry to interrupt," a soft voice says, and we both turn toward Brielle.

She holds her hand up and dips her head.

"Forgive me; I just wanted to let you know we're ready to get started whenever you are."

Trey sits on one of the barstools behind the sofa, facing two of our chairs. Brielle circles to the other side, and I watch as she runs a hand over her blouse before taking a seat.

She crosses her legs and sits up straight, holding a stack of notecards in her hands.

I know our label cleared this interview and the questions we agreed to go over before they stepped foot in my house. Still, inviting them here doesn't sit right with me, even though the point was for it to feel more personal and intimate.

Too intimate.

I clench my jaw, hating how the sight of her legs captivates me.

Trey must notice and elbows me.

"What?" I grunt as I climb onto the barstool next to him.

"Nothin', just checking for signs of life."

"Shut up," I fire back.

Brix and Tysin take a seat on the sofa in front of us.

When we begin, we talk about how the band got started and what it was like bringing Trey into the mix before moving into our relationships.

Brielle manages to avoid looking at me for most of the discussion.

"Over the years, you've been known to have a way with the ladies. Would you agree?"

Brix and Tysin chuckle and Trey shakes his head.

"Over the years, yeah, I think that would be true. We're all still young and figuring out what we want in life," Brix says.

Tysin nods. "I'll speak for myself in saying I made some mistakes before Kyla came back into my life last year. You learn a lot about who you are and what you want in life when you get out, date around, and meet new people. After a while, though, I realized I was chasing the wrong things. Lord knows it got us into some trouble along the way too," Tysin adds.

"You guys have been talked about a lot in the media as of late," Brielle says, changing the subject. Her eyes move to each of us before landing on mine. "Is there anything you'd like to say about the rumors? Anything you'd like to clear up?"

"We've talked about this in previous interviews. It's starting to feel like the only stories that get attention are the ones painting us in a bad light," Trey shares.

"Before I started seeing Layken, I'll be the first to admit I wasn't going down a good path. I believe now that joining the band and seeing her again out on tour saved my life. I don't think the road I was going down before would've led me to a good place. I'll admit I made mistakes both before we were together and even early on. The stories about going to strip clubs and even the fight I got in back in Nashville were twisted in a way that almost seemed like they were intentionally trying to tear us apart and bring me down."

I nod. It was hard watching what Trey and Layken went through. We've had drama stirred in the media before, stories circulating about Brix stepping out on his relationship with Ivy, and even Kyla and Tysin, when Kyla's engagement to her ex, Canon, was ending.

He's in the media a lot too with his motocross career, so it added an extra layer of interest, focusing all eyes and attention on us.

Those stories were easy to shrug off. The stories about Brix were a load of bullshit. There's no way he'd ever cheat on her. Old photos resurfaced and were made to seem recent when they weren't.

As for Tysin and Kyla, it was bound to happen. News got out about Kyla's engagement ending, and it wasn't long before Tysin and Kyla were spotted together.

They fought against their feelings for years and weren't going to wait any longer. We all knew it was something we'd have to get through.

It was different for Trey and Layken. Every word posted online caused a lot of hurt between them.

"We've started to look at the people we have in our lives, who we trust and allow in our space," I add, and Brielle's eyes connect with mine. "Forgive me for how this may sound, but it's situations like this. Inviting you here, into my home, is like inviting you into my life. When you leave here, you could walk away and write whatever you want based on your opinion of us, and who knows what sort of effects that could have."

Brielle crosses her arms in her lap, her gaze roaming over my face. Something about her posture and her stoic look tells me I may have said the wrong thing.

"I'm here to do a job and do it well. Between all of us, I'm not here to get on your good side to squeeze information out of you only to smear it through headlines later. If I'm being honest, I have no interest in getting close to you at all."

She purses her lips, and my eyes lock on them. My dick hardens in my pants.

She looks like she'd get off on verbally sparring with men, destroying them into a million pieces and living off their remains for days.

Brix clears his throat, and Tysin chuckles. I want to knock their heads together and tell them to shut up.

"What's so funny?" She narrows her eyes on them, and they go silent.

"He's usually the one who manages to sweet-talk women. It's funny to watch him be put in his place for once by someone other than his sister."

"Will you shut the hell up?" I add, and Trey joins in, laughing with them.

The guy working with Brielle, I don't think I ever caught his name, leans down and whispers in her ear. She stares at the floor, as if taking in what he says, and jerks her head into a nod.

"I think that's all the questions we have for you today." She attempts to paste on a sincere smile, but I see through her phony facade.

"We would like to get a few photos of you together for the article, if that's okay?" the man says.

"Yeah, man, no problem." Brix reaches his hand out to shake his, and I hear him introduce himself as Davis.

"Actually, I'm sorry, but is it possible you could come by tomorrow instead? Something came up last minute and we'll need to wrap up." I cross my arms in front of my chest, never taking my eyes off Brielle.

She, on the other hand, looks ready to shoot daggers at me.

"We're only in town for the day. Our flight takes off tomorrow." Her jaw tightens. It's clear I'm getting under her skin.

"Great, we can plan for tomorrow before you take off. It shouldn't be a problem, right?"

Davis glances at me and over to Brielle, then back at me. I hear him mutter under his breath about how they could come over in the morning before their flight leaves.

Brielle snaps her gaze back to me. "Certainly," she replies sweetly.

Brix and Tysin snicker. Meanwhile, Trey stays silent. He's not like them and didn't grow up finding every way possible to dig in under my skin like they enjoy doing.

"We'll get packed up then and out of your way." She turns to grab a clipboard she left sitting on the chair beside her.

The guys file out of the room. I hang back, offering to help Davis.

"I'm gonna take this out to the car," Davis says, looking from me over to Brielle. "Should I meet you outside?"

Brielle nods, but I follow Davis into the entryway. It's not until he steps outside and shuts the door behind him that her voice drops low. Back to the tone she used with me when I first found her eavesdropping earlier.

"Oh, and Madden, make sure you're ready for us tomorrow. I have no interest in a do-over of today either."

CHAPTER THREE

BRIELLE

I didn't have high expectations going into the interview yesterday. Madden played right into what I expected them to be like.

Being someone who sticks to a schedule and likes a routine, the last-minute changes throwing off our plans are driving me crazy.

The photos for the article are important, but I'm annoyed it delays our trip home until tomorrow. The fact we started off late because they weren't ready, then couldn't get the photos we needed grinds on my nerves.

No matter my disdain for A Rebels Havoc, I won't let them ruin my chance at making a good impression with my new boss, Sawyer. She's put a lot of trust and faith in me, and I wouldn't let her or my peers at *Limelight* down.

Sawyer is the only person who knows the truth about who I am. When it comes to my job, I didn't want any connection to the Granite family name or Granite Industries.

Although my father has tried to convince me otherwise, I have no interest in working for him or following in his footsteps.

Becoming Brielle Silvers was a big step for me in distancing myself from that world. Up until this point in my life, I've managed to fly under the radar when it came to the media talking about my family.

They seem to care more about my father and two older brothers anyway. He's positioned them to take over his role, and it's been all about them from the day they were off the tit.

I guess there were benefits to being the only daughter. It played into their belief I wasn't being looked at as their equal. As much as it would bother me any other day, it helped me separate myself and focus on my passions.

Sooner or later, my identity is bound to come out, but for now, I'm keeping it this way.

"All right, you ready to go? Maybe if we wrap up early, we can head out of here and find something to do with our Friday night." Davis wags his brows and adjusts his camera bag under his arm, nodding toward Madden's house.

I release a heavy sigh and turn toward the sidewalk when the front door opens. I fully anticipate Kyla to welcome us or maybe his assistant, but not this time.

I'm once again forced to face Madden and his sinfully sexy smile.

He's barefoot, wearing a black T-shirt and denim jeans. He folds his arms over his chest and leans against the doorframe, tilting his head to us in way of a greeting.

I don't miss the way his eyes linger on mine. I grit my teeth and flare my nostrils, trying and failing to control my body's reaction to him. Maybe if I keep telling myself the butterflies in my stomach are from new job nerves and not the sight of his dimpled cheek, I'll be able to get today over without any further incidents.

It doesn't look like he's going to make it easy on me, though.

"Someone's lookin' a little happy to see you this morning," Davis whispers.

My eyes snap to Madden, whose gaze burns into me. I press my tongue into the inside of my cheek and attempt to breathe slowly through my nose.

My face flames when he catches me staring, and the edge of his mouth curls. I try to disguise the hitch in my breath with a cough.

Davis chuckles next to me, and I resist telling him to shut up.

"It's nice to see you both again," Madden says, never taking his eyes off me.

What's with the change in demeanor from yesterday? Gone is the snide, arrogant man I met.

He's trying to smooth over what happened, Brielle, using his charming smile and sexy dimple to swindle you. Don't fall for it.

Madden steps back and holds his hand out, welcoming us inside.

"I don't know what you have in mind for today, but we have a few places I thought would be good for the shoot. We can use the sitting room we were in yesterday or change it up and go outside. It looks like the weather will cooperate too."

He watches me but, this time, makes an effort to glance at Davis.

"Outside sounds perfect," Davis says. "If Tysin and Trey want to hold their guitars and maybe you could have your drumsticks, we can snap a few photos of you guys as a group. I also took some pictures during the interview we can use."

Madden smiles and nods, turning to lead us through the double staircase toward the large doors surrounded by floor-to-ceiling windows overlooking the small courtyard outside.

We overhear the sound of voices coming down the hall, and I glance over to see Tysin and Kyla heading down the corridor toward us, with Brix and Trey sauntering behind them.

"Kyla, would you mind showing them to the area we discussed earlier? We're doing the photo shoot outside. I'll join you in a few."

Kyla's gaze lingers on me for a moment. I wonder if it has anything to do with yesterday's incident or if there's more behind it. She smiles, shifting from one side to the other, before nodding over her shoulder to follow her.

"Of course," she croons. "Come with me. I'll show you the spot, and you can get set up while the guys finish getting ready."

When I move to pass by Madden, he quickly darts his hand out to stop me. My eyes snap to where his hand grips my wrist and then back to him.

Standing close to him again reminds me of how large and intimidating he can be looming over me. He's at least a foot taller than me, with broad shoulders and muscular forearms.

I refrain from letting my eyes roam over his body, taking in the scent of his cologne and the curve of his lip when he fights off his smile.

"Brielle, would you mind talking with me for a minute?" He motions across the room, away from where the guys huddle together, shooting curious glances our way.

Davis notices I'm not following him and turns to search for me. He and Kyla pause near the door. I hold my finger up to Davis to signal I'll be outside in a minute before turning back to Madden.

"Sure thing." I attempt to paste on a forced smile.

He presses his hand against the small of my back, leading me away from everyone. All the voices in the room suddenly stop, leaving only the sound of my heels clicking on the tile floor, making it painfully obvious they're watching us.

When we're away from their curious eyes, Madden turns to me and crosses his arms over his chest before dropping them to his side.

"I want to talk to you again about what happened yesterday," he starts.

I hold my hand up to stop him.

"Madden, it's truly okay. You don't have to explain yourself to me. This is your home. A beautiful home, by the way. Who you're dating and what you do in privacy is not my business."

He clenches his jaw and nods. I'll say whatever I need to say to end this conversation. I don't want to be reminded of the desire in his eyes when he walked out of the room to find me standing there overhearing what was meant to be kept between them.

As I said, it's not my business. Even if I kept replaying the deep sound of his voice and the dirty words he said when I was alone in my room last night.

I didn't, even for one second, think about what it'd be like in her shoes, on the receiving end of them.

"We're not dating. She isn't my girlfriend," he clarifies. "Just a friend, but you're right." He narrows his gaze. "I was referring to our conversation after."

My face is practically on fire from the heat of embarrassment. I admitted to listening to him again, and he wasn't even talking about that part of the hellish morning.

I want to crawl into a hole and die.

"I'm sorry for what I said after, though. I, uh... I was a jerk, and I know we didn't start off on the best foot. I hope we use today to start fresh and pretend it never happened."

"A fresh start." I nod. "I think a fresh start sounds like a good idea."

I can't change the mortification I felt when he caught me, but if he's going to give me an out, I'll take it.

He rubs his hand over the back of his neck and glances over my shoulder, shuffling his feet from side to side. I don't need him to say it, but there's more to the olive branch, and I'm falling into the bait of waiting for him to spit it out.

"This won't affect the article you're writing, will it?"

And there it is.

It makes sense. It's no secret there have been a lot of eyes on the band over the past year and not exactly for good reasons.

Women still flock to them, and they're still topping charts. They announced their upcoming tour earlier this year, and the tickets sold out in minutes. Most of the guys are in steady relationships, which you'd think would quiet some of the gossip swirling around them, but it seems to only be heating up.

I don't doubt he's worried about their public image. If I had to guess, I bet they're feeling the heat from their record label.

"I'm here to write an article about the band and your rise to stardom," I say.

He swallows hard. "I guess what I'm trying to say is a lot of bullshit gossip has been printed around me and my bandmates as of late. Some things are untrue, and others have been taken out of context. I'd like to squash this and leave it in the past."

"I have no intention of spreading misinformation or painting you in a bad light."

He claps his hands and rubs them together. "I appreciate it."

I force a smile and step away. "I should probably head outside and help Davis set up."

I notice the guys standing in a group out of the corner of my eye, watching us intently. When they catch me glancing in their direction, they duck their heads and turn away in unison.

My mouth goes dry when I turn to Madden, catching his eyes trailing down my body before they meet mine. The butterflies in my stomach return.

"Hey, um... before you go, we have a show tonight at Whiskey Barrel. It's the bar we started out at that we mentioned in the interview."

I nod, recalling them talking about their rise to the top and how Whiskey Barrel gave them a stage every weekend to play for their hometown crowd.

"We'll be introducing some of our new music. We like to get on stage and play our newer songs to thank them for getting us to where we are today. Anyway, I'm not sure how long you'll be sticking around, but you guys are welcome to come."

I hesitate for a minute. The voice in my head practically screams it's not a good idea. On the one hand, there's a chance it could give me more content and behind-the-scenes material to use in the article.

On the other, I'm apprehensive about putting myself in the position to be close to Madden again. The trip here is strictly business for me, but the fact he's inviting me to join them feels like we're at risk of mixing the two.

I can't let myself get close to him.

"We actually have an early flight to catch tomorrow..." I trail off.

"C'mon, it'll be fun. Take the chance, let your hair down and live a little."

He smirks, and I resist urge to tell him to fuck off. He has no right to be so goddamn sexy and tempting. It's almost infuriating.

"I'm sorry, I'll have to pass this time, but I appreciate the invite."

"It's your loss." He shrugs. "I was thinkin' you may want more photos for your article and a chance to tease what's to come, but I understand. You have more exciting things to do tonight and have to be up early."

I grit my teeth. He has a point about the photos. I may not want to join them. I'm not a big rock fan, and I've never been one to listen to their music, either. This is for my job, though. With it being my first submission at *Limelight*, I want to knock it out of the park.

This could give me a different side of the guys—a chance to get to know them on a deeper level they haven't shared before.

Or it could turn out to be a big mistake and a waste of my time.

Madden smirks as if he knows he's got me right where he wants me.

"I guess you sold me. Let me know what time, and we'll be there."

He grins. "I promise to make it worth your while."

I'm not sure what he means exactly, and that's what I'm afraid of.

CHAPTER FOUR

BRIELLE

After we stop for dinner, we make it back to our hotel around six. I drop my bag and purse on the dresser and collapse on the bed. With my arms stretched to the side, my heart rate slows to a steady pace for what feels like the first time all day, and I start to relax.

I hate how I'm attracted to Madden almost as much as I dislike him.

I lose track of how long I'm lying there when my phone rings from my purse across the room. I ignore it the first time, letting the call go to voicemail. The ringing starts again, and I wince, dragging myself up to answer it.

"Ugh, I'm too tired for this right now. Who could possibly want me?"

I blindly dig my hand through my purse, feeling my phone vibrate before pulling it out to see Serena's name on the screen. I click the answer button to accept the FaceTime call.

We couldn't be more different from each other if we tried.

Where I've been trained from an early age to stay poised and professional, she's loud and outspoken. You can't help but gravitate toward her, even if her bubbly personality puts you off.

"You should've known I wasn't going to let you blow me off. Get real." She smirks.

I narrow my eyes and shake my head. She props her phone up on her vanity while she looks in the mirror, rolling on her lip gloss. She blots them and puckers them together before turning back to me.

"You were ignoring me, weren't you?" She huffs.

"Not exactly. You caught me at a bad time. I just walked through the door and was about to doze off before I need to get ready for tonight."

Her brows deepen. "I thought you didn't fly back until tomorrow?"

Here we go.

"Well... I was invited to watch A Rebels Havoc play tonight." She whistles, and I try to ignore it. "At a local bar in their small town where they grew up playing. Madden invited me to come check them out."

I try to play it off and act nonchalant, but when she lifts her brow and smirks, I know I've failed miserably.

So much for being poised. She can read me like a damn book.

"He did, did he? How very sweet of him."

"I'm only going because I'm hoping to get behind the scenes of where they first started. You know, to help with writing the article and all."

She purses her lips together and nods slowly. "Uh-huh."

I roll my eyes, carrying my phone across the room to collapse on the bed. I undo the claw clip, and my hair falls, fanning around me on my pillow.

"Besides, I won't be alone. Davis will be with me. We're hoping to get a few photos too."

"Well, that's good. Otherwise, I'd think it was a date."

"No," I bark. "Could you imagine me dating one of them? I mean, Madden is the only one not in a relationship anyway. Trust me, I think he's already spoken for. At least judging by the little rendezvous I overheard yesterday."

I realize the error of my ways the moment the comment leaves my mouth.

She's going to force me to spill all the details, and I'm not sure I can repeat them without dying of embarrassment.

"What happened?"

I shake my head. "I shouldn't have mentioned it. Don't ask. Please, don't ask."

"Well, that's not happening now."

I take a deep breath, trying to figure out where to start.

"Promise me, no matter what, you won't repeat this to a soul."

Her eyes widen. "Of course, I wouldn't. Who the hell do you think I am, B?"

"I'm serious, Serena."

"I promise," she says, picking up the phone and pacing around her room.

I chew nervously on my lips, my mind filtering through the memories. I have no idea how to say this, so I decide to just come out with it.

"So the interview was at Madden's house, right? Well, we get there, and his sister let us inside to get set up. He has a beautiful house."

"You're stalling. You can tell me about his house later. Get to the good stuff."

My face drops, and I narrow my gaze, giving her one of my best "I'm annoyed with you" looks. She waves her hand, urging me to hurry up already.

I swear, if we weren't best friends, we would've ended up hating each other. She knows all the ways to get under my skin.

"Anyway..." I sigh dramatically. "We're getting set up when I overhear him and a woman."

She gapes at me. "Say what now?"

I nod, and she squeals. "Yep. Seriously, if you could've heard, I swear."

My face flames again. "Heard what? What did he say? I want to know."

"The noises he made. The dirty talking. Let me just say, I've never heard a man say anything like the stuff coming out of his mouth."

"Oh God, I'm so fuckin' jealous. I'd let that man slut me out in a minute."

"Serena," I balk, and we both burst into a fit of laughter. I slap my hand over my mouth, unable to contain it.

"I'm here to say what you never will, and we both know it."

She's not wrong. We grew up in two different worlds. It's something I envy about her. She's never been impressed with anything that comes along with my life. She'd still be here for me if I were broke without a penny to my name.

Word has spread about how when my father passes away, I stand to inherit over two hundred million dollars. Honestly, I'd trade it all in most days for a peaceful, normal life.

I've watched how money and greed ruin people. It's hard to find someone who is loyal and doesn't give a shit about your bank account. It's why she's one of the few people I will ever trust in this lifetime.

Hell, I think I trust her more than my brothers, and that says a lot.

They are true examples of what money and power can do to people. I'm glad they want to take over for my father because no chance in hell would I ever want to do it myself.

"I mean, you're there for the night, so if it happens, then let it happen. You damn sure could use some fun in your life."

"No way in hell would I ever let myself fall for a man like Madden Cole. Absolutely not."

"Why not? Who said you had to fall in love with him? This isn't about love, girlfriend. This is about orgasms. You can't tell me that man wouldn't dish them out like a goddamn buffet, too. He even looks like he'd be good in bed."

"What's that even mean?"

"You know what I'm talking about. His confidence says he knows how to put that thing down, flip it, and reverse it."

"I can't handle you right now. I'm gonna let you go and figure out what I'm wearing."

"Like hell you will. You can get ready with me. I want to see if what you're wearing is slut approved."

"I can't look at you right now. Listen to yourself."

I toss my phone on the bed and begin shuffling through my suitcase, trying to figure out what I could wear.

With a huff, I cross my arms. I hadn't planned to stay for an extra night, let alone hit up the town while I was here.

"Listen to *you*." She emphasizes the word you. "Don't act like you don't need an orgasm or two. Let me help you."

"I don't need your help. Okay? I'm perfectly capable of finding a man for myself."

"Oh, you mean like Mitchell?" She cackles.

I swipe my phone off the bed and flash her a warning look.

We had an agreement we wouldn't talk about Mitchell again. Not because of any residual hurt or feelings leftover from when our relationship ended.

She has valid reasons for not liking him. Ones even I can't refute or argue. He wasn't good enough for me and was a prime example of letting the wrong people in who only wanted to use me for what they could get from me.

We made a deal we'd leave him in the rubble of mistakes, never to be seen or spoken of again. She broke the rules.

She holds her hand up. "Listen, I'm sorry for bringing up *he who shall not be named*, but it had to be said. All I'm trying to do is look out for my friend."

"Looking out for me by interfering with my job and trying to convince me to hook up with a playboy rock star? How is this helping exactly?"

"We've already been over this." She shakes her head. "Orgasms. It all comes back to orgasms." She claps her hands, emphasizing each word.

"You know how you could help me? Help me figure out something to wear that doesn't look like I'm about to have a sit-down meeting with the president."

She screeches and drops her phone, but I'm left listening to her laugh at my expense. Usually, she's the one making the jokes. However, this time, I managed to hit her with one.

I start laying my clothes on the bed, trying to make sense of what to wear. I hit the button to flip the phone screen around and snap my fingers, ordering her to focus.

"Will you help me? What should I wear?"

I have two pairs of pants—one is the pair of Alexander McQueen black slacks I wore on the flight here, and the other is the Saint Laurent jeans I planned to wear home. For tops, I have a yellow chiffon blouse or a cobalt-blue peplum sleeveless top.

Neither of them is fitting for a night out at a small-town bar watching a rock band.

I rub my fingers over my forehead, massaging it. My backup plan is to come up with a way out of this night entirely.

"Go with the blue and your denim jeans. Wear your hair down with your black Louboutins. Maybe bring a clutch with you instead of your purse."

She's right. It's the best choice given what I have if I don't want to walk in there looking overdressed.

Two knocks sound on the door, and I quickly check the peephole to see who it is. Davis is standing on the other side, running his hand through his hair. I flip the lock and open it, noting he's wearing a pair of lounge pants and a white T-shirt. Judging by the look on his face, something's wrong.

"Is everything okay?"

He shrugs, dropping his hand to his side. "Honestly, no."

"What's wrong?" I ask, stepping back to let him into my room.

"I won't be staying long. I think I got food poisoning from the restaurant we ate at for lunch. I can hardly stand. I feel like I'm going to be sick again."

"Okay, that's fine. We can cancel for tonight."

I clutch my phone in my hand. I swear I can hear Serena yelling at me.

"No, don't," he pleads. "You should still go. I mean, at least one of us should, especially if we can get photos for the article."

He's right. "You said you know how to use my camera, right?"

I chew on my lip and nod. "It's no problem. I'll make it work."

"I'm sorry," he reassures. "I'm sure whatever photos you manage to get will turn out great, and we'll figure it out."

I mentioned my interest in photography. My only experience is from high school when I took photos for our school newspaper and yearbook. This is entirely different, though.

"I'll stop by on my way out to grab your camera. We'll figure it out, one way or another."

We both say our goodbyes, and I step back from the door.

My mind is a storm of worries, all bringing me back to reality when I hold up my phone, remembering Serena's still on Face-Time.

"Looks like you need a date with orgasms after all."

CHAPTER FIVE

MADDEN

"You mind tellin' me what the hell is goin' on out there?" Tysin asks, stalking into the back room at Whiskey Barrel. "I can't believe you invited her here tonight."

"What do you mean you can't believe it? She's in town to interview us about our album. We got off on a bad foot yesterday, and it's our fault we started late. She needs pictures for the article, so I figured she could come get some live shots of us playing."

I twist off the cap of my beer, feeling the intensity of his gaze burning into me.

I should've known they'd be on me for inviting her. I didn't expect her to show up alone. I wasn't going to be a dick to her, leaving her to sit by herself. So I offered for her to join us and introduced her to the girls.

"Don't act like I don't notice what you're doing." He narrows his eyes.

He has a lot of fuckin' nerve questioning me when he was hooking up with my sister behind my back.

"I'm sorry, you have a problem with what I'm doing?" I slam my bottle down on the table and pick up my drumsticks, flipping and twisting them in my fingers.

His nostrils flare, and he shakes his head.

"Yeah, I thought so." I smirk.

I couldn't believe they had kept their relationship a secret for as long as they had. I didn't see through their hatred toward each other to mean there were unresolved feelings between them.

Hell, I thought she despised him after he made a bet with Brix.

I felt stupid when I realized there was so much more I didn't know. I guess I could say the same for Tysin too, though.

We've both moved on, and they're as happy as ever. It's still weird as fuck to watch them together, but all I care about is that he treats Kyla right.

"We both know we can't afford more bullshit to be spewed about us in the media, okay? Like I said, shit got off on a bad foot with her yesterday, and I'm trying to make it right. Smooth it over. I figured if I came in, sweet-talked her a little, then maybe she would leave out the fact I yelled at her for being in my house like she broke in or some shit."

Tysin shakes his head, trying not to laugh.

Yeah, the guys had a good chuckle when they found out what happened. It's been stressful as hell lately, with our album dropping soon. Hanna stopped by after practice and helped me relieve a little tension.

Nothing is going on between us, but we've been hanging out more over the past few weeks. She's been coming to our shows for years.

It's nothing serious; she knows the score between us. She'll drop by my place, and we'll fuck around. We've never gone on a date, and she never stays over. It's just easy.

Although, if I'm being honest, I can't deny the immediate spark and tension I felt after being around Brielle for even twenty minutes. Not only is she beautiful, but damn if I didn't love her smart mouth. The attraction and pull are unlike anything I've ever felt.

I've been so focused on our music over the years I haven't let myself think about a relationship. Watching all my friends fall in love, get engaged, and start families has me feeling like I'm behind.

"That's all this is, then? You're just trying to get on her good side to make sure she doesn't write anything bad about us?"

I avoid looking at him, picking up my beer and downing the rest. We're about to go on stage, and I'm entirely too sober for this conversation.

"Yep," I reply curtly.

He nods slowly, clearly not buying it. I don't care, though, because he'll have to take it.

"Let's get goin'. We need to get on stage." I stalk out of the back room toward where our stage overlooks the packed crowd.

Standing off to the side, near the doorway, is Hanna. She's leaning against the wall, her arms crossed, waiting for me to come out.

When she spots me, she pushes off the wall and saunters toward me, her eyes lighting up.

"I was hopin' to catch you before you went on." She smiles, moving to stand against my side.

She runs her hand over my chest, and I nod, anxious for the first time, hoping no one spots us together.

I've never cared if my hookups saw me out, talking to other women, or even knowing if I took someone home with me. Hanna is one of the few people I've hooked up with more than once, but now that she's here and touching me, I'm hyperaware about Brielle being across the room and possibly seeing us.

It's not like she hasn't seen Hanna already, considering she was standing outside the room when she walked out after.

I don't want Brielle to get the wrong idea, though, and think anything more is between us.

"What's up?" I ask, twisting my baseball cap around on my head.

She drags her teeth across her lip, watching me, and I clench my jaw. I know the look, and I can only imagine what she's thinking in that dirty fuckin' mind of hers.

She rubs her breast against my arm, fluttering her long lashes at me.

"You doin' anything after your show tonight?"

"I'm not sure," I say, trying to sound noncommittal.

There's no way anything will happen with Brielle, but I can't lie and say the thought hasn't crossed my mind. It's just too damn bad she's enemy number one.

Even if she's attracted to me too, and we gave in to see where it could go, I'd never be able to fully trust her.

I've seen how people in the industry like her will do anything they can for a chance to make a quick buck, even if it fucks over celebrities. Whatever they gotta do to get clicks and attention, the more they'll have to line their pockets.

It's too bad, though, because, damn, I'd love to get my hands on her and crack her perfectly crafted exterior.

The thought of her on her knees, staring up at me, with tears streaming down her face while she sucks my dick into her sweet little mouth, makes my knees weak.

"Maybe, if you're up for it, I could stop by your place when you get home, and we can hang out for a bit."

She emphasizes the words "hang out," and we both know exactly what she means.

I nod. "I'll let you know, okay? I've gotta get goin'."

I spot Brix taking the stage, trying to catch Trey's and Tysin's attention to get their asses up here with us.

My eyes flick over to where Brielle sits with the girls at a table. Abel stands nearby, making sure no one bothers them.

A slow smile stretches across my face when I spot her looking over at us. She appears to be chatting with Ivy. Layken sits across from them with Kyla.

Trey and Layken just announced their engagement online earlier today. She's getting to be far along in her pregnancy. Only a couple more months or so and their daughter will be here.

Trey has been on high alert all night, making sure everyone keeps their distance and no one messes with her. The only way he chilled out about having her here tonight was knowing Abel would be by her side.

I can't say I blame him, though. It's packed, with people standing shoulder to shoulder, trying to get close to the stage. I wouldn't want my girl, carrying my baby, left without someone lookin' out for her, either.

Brielle's eyes connect with mine from across the room. She presses her lips together to fight off her grin when she catches me watching her.

I step behind my drum set and hold my sticks above my head, spinning them around my fingers.

"Are you ready to get this fuckin' party started?" Brix growls into the mic, and I take a seat on my stool.

I kick us off on the drums. With lights beaming down on me, I close my eyes and let the music take control, beating with every ounce of energy I have in me. I swear, nothing feels more right than sitting behind my drum set playing music.

It's been a form of therapy for me lately. Some days, when shit has gotten so stressful and out of hand, I'll sit down and play until I have nothing left.

We don't play a full set, only a few of our new songs and a couple of our old fan favorites. No matter where life takes us, I'll always love coming back here and playing at Whiskey Barrel.

It grounds us to remember where it all began. I love going out on the road, playing in massive venues we thought would only be a dream growing up. Hell, my entire life, my dad liked to tell me my music would never get me anywhere, and it's not something I'll ever forget.

Sold-out tours, packed crowds, multiplatinum records. None of it matters if we lose who we are in the process.

It's why we've insisted on staying in North Carolina and living in CB. This is who we are, where we're from, and it'll never change.

Between songs, Brielle disappears from the spot where she's been sitting next to Ivy, and I notice her off to the side snapping photos.

After we wrap up, I take the stairs near her. She's leaning against the wall, waiting.

"You guys are… incredible," Brielle says when I approach her.

Tysin and Brix trail me, and I hear one of them grunt. I assume it's Tysin, based on our earlier conversation.

"I'm glad you're having a good time," I say.

I lift my shirt to wipe the sweat dripping from my brow. I don't miss the way her eyes snap from my stomach to meet mine, or how her throat bobs when she swallows hard at the sight of my chest.

"You up for another drink?" I ask with a nod toward the bar.

I could use a beer, and she still seems tense and nervous around me. I'm hoping if she gets another drink in her, maybe she'll loosen up and get rid of this uptight, professional act she's putting on.

"Actually, I'm thinking about taking off for the night."

"Oh." I try to cover up my disappointment. "All right, well, give me a second, and I'll walk you out."

She nods, and I jog into the back room to toss my sticks on the table and grab a beer. I untwist the top and quickly down half of it, right as Brix and Tysin step in from outside.

"What the fuck is goin' on with you and that reporter chick?" Brix grunts, and I grit my teeth.

"Not right now."

Tysin shakes his head and crosses his arms over his chest.

"Tysin told me you're tryin' to butter her ass up so she won't write anything bad about us, but we both know she'll do it regardless. Pick someone else to hook up with, for fuck's sake. You're only going to make shit worse."

I quickly glance down the hallway to where Brielle stands, and her eyes meet mine. I'm worried she may have overheard him.

"I'll talk to you later," I say, taking another drink and stalking into the bar toward her, only now she's nowhere to be found.

I push through the crowd, spotting her platinum blond hair weaving through people up toward the front. Jayde, the bartender, waves her hand, asking if I want another, and I raise a finger to let her know I'll be back.

Brielle's hot on her heels, trying like hell to get out of here, and I know without asking that she heard Brix talkin' shit.

I want to kick them both in the ass because this is the last thing we need right now.

"Hey, Brielle, wait up," I holler.

Her footsteps slow, but she doesn't stop or bother turning around.

I jog ahead to catch up to her, and she spins around when she reaches the black SUV I saw her driving earlier today.

She holds up her hand. "I'll be good from here, but thank you for making sure I made it to my car safely."

I stop, caught off guard by the change in her demeanor. She's back to the feisty woman I ran into after I found her listening in on me with Hanna.

"Is everything okay?" I ask.

She presses her lips together, avoiding looking at me, appearing to consider her next words before she nods.

"Everything's fine. I'm tired, and I have an early flight tomorrow. Thanks again for inviting me. I think I've got some good shots, so we should be set for the article."

She pats her camera bag and reaches into her pocket to pull out her keys.

"It was great to meet you, Madden. Have a nice evening."

I grit my teeth, hating how quickly she's back to giving me the cold shoulder.

"Wait, don't go," I breathe out, stepping in close to her. She turns, and I press her against the side of the car.

"Why?"

"I don't want you to go yet," I admit, making the first move. "Maybe I'm reading this wrong, but I don't think you want to leave either."

CHAPTER SIX

BRIELLE

"Madden, please," I murmur, holding my hand up.

He takes another step toward me, only now I'm left with nowhere to turn. I jerk my hand away from his chest. I swear, I could feel his heart beating wildly beneath my palm, or maybe it's my own.

I refuse to think he feels anything for me. I overheard him talking to Brix. How could I have missed it? He was damn near shouting at him.

I took it as my sign to get the hell out of there. Of course, he isn't letting me go so easily.

His chest is damp with sweat, and I clench my hand into a fist, detesting how it only makes me want him more. I hate how my body reacts to him.

He and I are from two completely different worlds.

Whatever this is between us, I know nothing good could come from letting my walls down and getting close to him.

"Please, what?" he whispers.

The urge to look up at him grates on me until I give in, tilting my head back until our eyes lock.

He stares at my lips when I quickly dart my tongue out to lick the dry skin, causing his nostrils to flare. If I thought he was unaffected by me, he's proving I might be wrong about my assumption.

"Don't go," he adds. "Stay for a little while longer."

"I don't think that is a good idea." I shake my head.

"Why not? You said you were having a good time. Who cares if your flight leaves early? You can sleep on your way home."

"It's not what you think. I'm not tired, it's just..." My voice trails off.

"Is it what happened yesterday? Or what Brix said inside?"

So he does know I heard them talking. This isn't exactly something I want to get into again.

"It's not about yesterday, Madden. Like I said, what you do in your home has nothing to do with me. It's not about Brix, either. It's just, I don't think it's a good idea for us to do this." I motion between us. "I just started at *Limelight*, and the fact I landed an interview with A Rebels Havoc is huge. I want to make a good impression, and I think being with you could make things messy."

"Define being with me?"

"Madden." I grit my teeth. I hadn't meant for it to sound like it did, but he can't play stupid with me. Look at us right now. We both see what's happening between us.

"No one needs to know. Not if you don't want them to anyway."

He presses his hand against the side of the car, leaning in closer to me. I'm met with the subtle smell of his woodsy cologne mixed with the musky scent of his sweat.

I can't believe I'm thinking this, but damn if it doesn't entice me more.

"What do I need to do to convince you to stay?"

I suck in a sharp breath, tightening my fist around the strap of the camera bag.

"What if I told you I'm fighting so damn hard against the urge to kiss you, to see if you taste as good as I think you do?"

Oh God. There he is with his dirty talk again. Only this time, it's aimed at me.

How could we go from meeting the way we did yesterday to him pinning me against the side of a car and tempting me with a kiss?

I tilt my head back, inching closer to him, unable to resist. His warm breath feathers over my lips, and I dig my nails into my palm, trying to control myself.

He slips his arm around my waist, holding me against him, and grips my chin. The possessive move is intoxicating, and any doubt lingering in my mind seems to evaporate.

He groans against my lips, sliding his hand along my cheek, and deepens the kiss.

I fumble, not sure what to do with my hands, so I blindly reach out to grip the front of his shirt and hold him close to me.

When he swipes his tongue along my bottom lip, I release a low moan and open my mouth.

We already know he's good with his hands. God, now I have to wrestle with the thought of him being a good kisser. I don't think I'd be able to handle finding out what other things he's skilled at.

He pulls back, pressing his forehead against mine, and whispers, "Are you still gonna act like we don't feel this between us?"

"Even if I do, it won't change anything."

He shakes his head. "Who said it has to?"

I feel my resistance wearing thin.

"Come back to my place with me," he whispers. "You can head to your hotel in the morning."

He doesn't give me a chance to answer before he pushes my hair back from my face and lightly brushes his lips against mine.

No matter what either of us says, if I were to go with him, it would change things between us. How could it not?

I'm here for one reason and one reason only. I can't let it interfere with my job. Not when I have too much on the line to lose.

It's not only about making a good impression on my boss and proving I deserve this job. It's about showing I can make a name for myself apart from my family, and if I mess this up, I'll be proving them all right.

I haven't been with another man since I was with Mitchell. Even still, I know, without a doubt, there's no way he compares to what it would be like to share a night with Madden.

"Madden?" shouts a voice from across the parking lot.

I release his shirt and shove him away.

We both turn to where it's coming from, and I realize it's the girl I saw him with yesterday before the interview.

Seeing her again feels like a bucket of ice-cold water dumped over my head. It's a sobering and painful reminder of how giving in to him would add me to a lengthy list of conquests he has on his roster.

"I've been looking everywhere for you," she says, flicking her eyes over to me. Her lip curls, and she clenches her jaw. "Are you ready to head to your place?"

I swallow hard. *Head to his place?*

Did he make plans with her tonight, too? So what, he was going to try to convince me to come home with him, knowing damn well he already had her lined up?

Or maybe if things fell through with us, at least he had her as a backup.

"Hanna, now is not a good time. Can you give us a minute?"

She nods. "I'll meet you out back by your car."

Her voice cracks, and I notice for the first time she's fighting off tears. I wonder how long she watched us before she said anything.

Madden shakes his head, shrugging her off, and turns his attention back to me. She looks back and forth between us, quickly brushing her finger under her eye before she disappears.

I reach for my keys in my pocket, hit the unlock button, and quickly open the door.

"Wait," Madden insists, reaching for my hand. "Please don't go."

"This was a mistake."

His brow furrows. "No, it wasn't."

"Yes, it was. Listen, I know what you're doing here. I heard you talking to Brix inside. It all makes sense now. You think if you sweet-talk me and I sleep with you, it'll save you from having some garbage written about you in the article."

He sighs, shaking his head. "You weren't supposed to hear him, but it's not what you think. Okay? I swear, you have me all wrong."

"All wrong, huh? You want to explain to me what just happened, then? She was crying, Madden, and you just gave her the cold shoulder. How do I know you won't get what you want and toss me to the side too?"

He winces. "I need to talk to Hanna to clear things up, but I thought we were on the same page. I was honest with you earlier today. I'm not dating anyone, and she's not my girlfriend. Yeah, we've messed around and I think she's a cool chick, but there's nothing more between us."

I'm a fool for kissing him, and I'd be an idiot to believe him now too.

"Madden, I'm here to do a job and only to do a job. Not to hook up with a rock star who could have any woman he wanted inside." I shake my head. "I have no intention of smearing your name or making you and the band look bad, okay? I'm writing about your rise to fame, and even if I were to mention the bumps in the road along the way, I want no part in dragging you guys through the mud like others have done in the past."

I pull my phone out of my pocket and climb into the car, setting the camera bag on the seat next to me.

"I'll tell you what, though," I say, pulling out one of my business cards. "Here's my contact information. Email me so I have yours, and I'll send you a copy of my submission before it goes to press. Okay?"

He takes the card, studying it before peering up at me. His piercing eyes glisten beneath the parking lot lights.

"We got off on the wrong foot, Brielle. This isn't how I wanted it to go down. I'll be honest with you, the band, we've had a lot of shit said about us in the media over the past couple of years. Like I told you yesterday, I've learned the hard way who we can and can't trust. You'd be surprised at the lengths people will go to betray you if it means earning them a quick buck. It's the same reason you can believe me, though. I'd never lie to you."

He doesn't have to explain it to me. I already know, but I'm not going to tell him. It's for the best he doesn't know who I truly am.

To him, I need to stay Brielle Silvers.

Hell, if he knew who I was and the connections I have, I'm certain I'd see a different side of him too. I've grown sick of people using me too.

"You don't have to explain yourself to me. You can trust me when I say I understand."

He nods, pushing the door open, and steps into my side.

"Well, what do I have to do to change the way you're looking at me now?"

Somehow, the concern in his eyes and the vulnerability in his voice only makes it harder to leave.

I shake my head. "I need to go. I meant it, though. It was good to meet you and the guys, but this—what happened tonight—was a mistake."

He presses his hand against the side of my face, gripping my chin to lift my eyes to meet his.

"Don't lie to me, Brielle. I told you I'd never lie to you."

He brushes his finger along my lip before dropping his hand to his side and taking a step back.

"I wish things hadn't gone down the way it did, but it is what it is, right?"

I nod, forcing a smile, reaching for the seat belt to buckle myself in. It's the only thing holding me back from letting go.

"It was nice meeting you, Brielle," he says, reaching for my door. "Don't worry, though. You'll be hearing from me soon."

He waves the business card in the air and winks before closing the door.

He doesn't move when I turn the key in the ignition. His eyes stay locked on me when I back out from my spot. When I pull out of the parking lot, I glance in the rearview to find him watching me go.

The farther I get away from him, the more regret twists in my stomach.

Some may consider Madden Cole a god of rock 'n' roll with a long list of women falling over themselves for a chance at one night with him, but I refuse to be one of them.

CHAPTER SEVEN

MADDEN

Goddamn, that kiss.

I've been going out of my mind thinking about her and our kiss all week.

She told me she'd need time to work on the article, so I didn't want to reach out right away. It was hard watching her leave and even harder waiting to talk to her again.

I've fucked it up in every way imaginable since we first met, and I messed up by asking her to come back to my place with me.

I knew from the moment we first met she's not like other women I've been with. She's closed-off and hard to get through to, but damn if I don't want to make her as weak as she makes me feel.

Even if all I can have with her is one night, I'll take it.

Something about her has me going crazy. I can't stop thinking about her, imagining every way I can have her in my bed and at my mercy.

From: Madden Cole <maddrummer@email.com>
Date: March 17th, 2022
To: Brielle Silvers <bsilvers@limelightmag.com>
Subject: A Rebels Havoc article

Good afternoon, Brielle,

Thank you for taking the time to sit down with the guys and me. I hope you enjoyed your time in CB too. Do you have any updates on the article and when I may be able to read it?

Madden Cole

My finger hovers over the send button, debating if I should say something about the night of the show and our goodbye. I want to tell her how I can't get the sight of her out of my mind and how my lips still tingle when I think about our kiss. Hell, I'd even tell her how hard it was going to sleep that night, wishing she'd come back with me.

Except I remember what she said about just starting her job and wanting to make a good impression. What if someone saw the email and asked questions?

I quickly hit send before I overthink it any longer and promptly pocket my phone. The guys will be here any minute to start practice.

We haven't played much since we finished recording our album. Brix and Ivy are practically married, Trey and Layken will welcome their daughter any day now, and I don't even want to think about what the fuck Tysin does with my sister.

Things seem to be going well for them, though, and that's all I care about.

A door creaks open, followed by the subtle click when it closes. I lean my head against the back of the sofa in our studio, waiting until Brix turns the corner.

His brow furrows when he sees me. "Everything okay?"

"Why wouldn't it be?" I ask.

"I've seen the look on your face before. You look... moody." He shakes his head and shrugs out of his jacket, tossing it onto the chair.

He widens his stance and crosses his arms.

"You've been in a mood all week, come to think of it. Something's off with you. This have anything to do with the reporter chick?"

I roll my eyes. "Will you give it a fuckin' break already?"

"Answer the question."

"No, nothing is going on. I haven't even spoken to her. Though she is supposed to give me a heads-up on the article before it goes to press."

"Nothing is goin' on between you? Nothing at all?"

I push myself off the couch and stalk past him. I should've lowered my shoulder and checked him with a warning to mind his own goddamn business.

If I did, though, he'd know something was up, and I'm trying to get him off my ass.

"I told you nothin' was going on, which means nothin' is going on."

"Well, that's funny because Ivy saw Hanna outside of Whiskey Barrel that night, and she was upset. In tears, actually. She didn't say much, but she did tell her she saw you kissing another girl. I think her words were 'the blond bitch she saw at your house the other day.'"

I grit my teeth. *Fuckin' Hanna.*

I didn't see her again after she saw me with Brielle, despite saying she'd meet me by my car. She disappeared by the time I went back into Whiskey Barrel. It doesn't matter, though. I wasn't going to hit her up again, and I didn't want to face her emotions when I rejected her attempts to go home with me.

"She doesn't know what she's talkin' about."

"She doesn't? She must've seen something for her to be as upset as she was."

I flare my nostrils, keeping my back facing him, and grab my drumsticks from the caddy next to my drum set. I can feel his eyes on me when I turn to sit down, but I don't give a fuck what he has to say or what he thinks about our relationship.

"Stay out of my business."

"Oh, like you do with all of us?" He chuckles. I want to tell him to eat shit, but he has a point.

The difference between the rest of the guys and me is they don't ever seem to think with the fuckin' head on their shoulders. How many times have I been the one who plays cleanup crew when they get into trouble?

The only time I didn't was when Brix and Tysin had a bet going between them, which was different. Still, tensions were high between them for months after. It wasn't until Brix managed to get Ivy back that he finally chilled out and came around.

You want to know who busted their ass to smooth shit over?

Me.

So they can say what they want about Brielle and me, but it's none of their concern, and would stay that way if anything happened anyway.

I pull on my headphones and flip my drumsticks around my fingers, drowning out him and his bullshit. I close my eyes and go hard, not caring about finishing this conversation. As far as I'm concerned, it's over.

I don't know how much time passes before I cut and grab my water for a drink. When I glance up, Trey stands in front of me with his arms crossed.

"Is this a solo practice today? If so, I'd like to get the fuck out of here and back home to my woman." Trey drops his arms and shrugs.

Brix leans against the bar across from us, still looking pissed off from earlier. Tysin is in his own world, his face buried in his phone.

"I was just messin' around until we got started."

"Well, let's get the fuckin' show on the road then." Brix grunts.

Despite all of us being in a mood, we're able to let it go when it's time to get to work. Our album is dropping soon, and we'll be heading out on the road doing press along with a few performances. We need to get ready, so we don't look like a mess.

None of them stick around after we finish, which is fine with me, so I dip out to shower. I don't want to deal with their questions, and every one of them has their panties in a wad.

I take a deep breath through the steam-filled room and adjust the towel at my waist, stepping out into my bedroom, where I've laid out my clothes.

My phone lights up, and a notification flashes on my screen. Brielle's name immediately comes to mind, and I'm hoping it's her.

I've checked my phone every chance I got to see if she replied, and still nothing... until now.

From: Brielle Silvers <bsilvers@limelightmag.com>

Date: March 17th, 2022

To: Madden Cole <maddrummer@email.com>

Subject: Re: A Rebels Havoc article

It's good to hear from you, Mr. Cole. I want to thank you again for your warm hospitality.

My deadline to send it off to press is the end of this month, but I'll be sure to send you a preview next week.

Brielle Silvers, Limelight Magazine

My lip curls at the mention of my warm hospitality. I debate asking her to elaborate further on what she liked most.

Was it how turned on she looked when I caught her listening to me with Hanna? Or maybe it was the kiss in the parking lot after our show at Whiskey Barrel?

Or was she trying to be overly professional with me to make it clear she's not interested?

My eyes zero in on her signature, specifically the phone number at the bottom.

From: Madden Cole <maddrummer@email.com>
Date: March 17th, 2022
To: Brielle Silvers <bsilvers@limelightmag.com>
Subject: Warm hospitality

The pleasure was truly all mine, Ms. Silvers. I'm speaking candidly when I tell you I wasn't ready for you to leave.

I apologize again for the way we first met and hope we'll have an opportunity to see each other again soon.

Madden Cole

From our first meeting, I could sense she didn't give a shit about who I was or my career. She didn't seem the least bit impressed or interested in meeting me.

When she fired off about how this was an assignment for her, and she intended on doing a damn good job at it, something about her sass drew me to her.

From: Brielle Silvers <bsilvers@limelightmag.com>
Date: March 17th, 2022
To: Madden Cole <maddrummer@email.com>

Subject: Warm goodbyes

You don't have to keep apologizing to me, Madden. I don't intend to blindside you with a splash in the headlines, so you can stop sucking up to me now.

Brielle Silvers, Limelight Magazine

I suck in a sharp breath when her response comes through. This time, I don't hesitate when my finger hovers over her phone number. The call rings twice before the line connects and she answers.

"Brielle Silvers, Limelight Magazine."

"Brielle," I breathed, and I could've sworn I heard her gasp when she realized it was me.

"I'm sorry, who is this?"

"It's Madden."

The line goes silent. "Yes, hello, Madden. How can I help you?"

"I wanted to tell you personally, so you can hear me when I say, you're wrong."

"Excuse me?"

"You're wrong about what you said in your email. I'm not trying to suck up to you, as you continue to believe."

"Okay..." She pauses.

"Don't get me wrong, I was concerned by how we met and feared maybe it was going to fuck up your first impression of me, but not exactly for the reasons you seem to think."

She considers her answer. A subtle click sounds in the distance, and the line goes quiet.

I hold out the phone in front of me, checking to make sure we're still connected, and we are.

"What are the reasons then?"

"I think you have it all wrong about me. I'm not sucking up to you, Brielle." She sighs, and I continue. "I'm fighting for my life to forget that fuckin' kiss. The only sucking up I'm willing to do is to find a way to finish what we started."

"Madden, I—" she says, but I cut her off.

"I get it. Your job."

"Yeah," she murmurs, and it almost sounds dejected.

"I won't tell if you won't tell."

She snickers. "I don't doubt you won't."

I picture her sitting at her desk in her office. Those sexy-ass legs crossed, and her hair pulled up like she had the first day we met, wearing another one of her fitted dresses. The way they accentuate every one of her delicious curves taunts me, nearly bringing me to my knees.

"Are you seeing anyone?" I ask, holding my breath.

I want to tell her not to overthink it even though I know she is. She seemed to second-guess every word when we were together, almost as if she was holding herself back.

"I haven't dated in a while."

Who in their right mind would pass up an opportunity to get to know her? I sure as shit won't be.

"Good."

"Good?"

"Well, I'm hoping when I tell you I'm saving your personal number from your email, you'll tell me you hope I'll use it."

"Madden—"

"C'mon, Brielle. If anything, give me a chance to do a little more sucking up, only in my way."

CHAPTER EIGHT

BRIELLE

It took everything in me to climb into my car and leave Madden standing outside of Whiskey Barrel. My lips still tingled, and my body was like a live wire from his touch.

I convinced myself I'd made a mistake.

I've squeezed my eyes shut and replayed the kiss over and over in my mind, wishing I could go back and relive it while hating myself more for feeling this way.

The truth is I didn't want to tell him no. I didn't want to leave, even if I knew it was the right thing to do. I was there to do my job. Not fly in, hook up with a rock star, and leave thinking I'd ever be able to pull myself back together.

No matter how many times Serena tried to convince me I should take advantage of the orgasms, I didn't want to regret it later when I became another notch on his bedpost.

Another fling on a long list of conquests.

It hasn't escaped me how I haven't been able to stop thinking about him since I landed back in New York.

Just when I thought I started to forget the feeling, convincing myself it was all a fever dream, Madden's name appears in my inbox.

After hearing his sexy voice on the other end of the line this afternoon, it's been impossible for me to focus on anything.

The elevator to my penthouse dings, and my heels click on the hardwood floors, echoing around the empty space. I kick off my shoes, letting the cool floors soothe my aching feet.

After talking to him, I don't hesitate, heading straight for my wine cellar and pulling out a bottle of cabernet sauvignon. I grab a glass from my shelf and hastily pop the bottle open.

It's been a long and hectic week, and it's only Thursday.

I pour myself a glass and drag my ass to the living room, leaning against the back of my couch to gaze out the floor-to-ceiling windows overlooking downtown.

New York is beautiful when you take in the view from this high.

Originally, I had dinner plans with Serena, but they fell through at the last minute. Although, on second thought, it's almost a blessing in disguise.

I needed a relaxing night. I planned to fix an easy dinner, draw a bath, and maybe distract myself with a book before I crash.

My phone vibrating in my purse, which I left on the kitchen island, pulls me away. I glance down at my watch, noting it's already almost eight, and I'm only just now getting home from the office.

"Who could be calling me at this hour?"

I don't answer in time, but when I click on the number, the city displays as being from North Carolina.

Madden.

I quickly hit redial and the nervous excitement is back when I hear his deep velvety voice, sending a shiver through my spine.

Jesus. It must be the alcohol already because there's no way hearing this man speak can do this to me.

"Hi," I mutter.

"I hope I didn't catch you at a bad time. You busy?"

I glance around the room and shake my head. If he could only see me right now, he'd probably realize how lame I am.

"No, I just got home from work. Going to pour myself another glass of wine."

"Mmm, another? Guess I called at the right time."

I stop, holding the glass in front of my mouth. "Why is that?"

He chuckles. "Well, I guess I'm hoping it'll make you less nervous to talk to me."

"Nervous? You don't make me nervous," I lie. Even the words sound forced rolling off my tongue.

The truth is, he *does* make me nervous. His confidence, the way he carries himself, and how he doesn't hesitate to go after what he wants is both sexy and intimidating. He commands a presence, and you can't help but be drawn to him.

"Brielle," he says. The way he says my name gives me butterflies. "Don't lie to me, baby."

I squeeze my eyes shut and blindly reach for the counter, stumbling to set my glass down. It nearly goes crashing to the floor before my hand brushes the edge of the marble and my eyes fly open.

"Madden, we've gone over this. I think if you thought about it too, you'd agree nothing good could come from this."

"From what? Talking to me?"

I curl my lip. "You know what I'm talkin' about. Don't play coy."

He chuckles. "All right, you're right. Can I tell you somethin', though?"

"What?"

"I haven't been able to stop thinkin' about kissin' you again since you left."

I suck in a sharp breath and shake my head. This is what I was afraid of.

I know better than to think Madden Cole could ever want anything more than a fling.

He's a rock 'n' roll god in the music industry. He could have any woman he wants, and I've somehow caught his attention.

For now, anyway.

It's only a matter of time. He'll meet someone new out on the road or at one of his shows, someone who's there and ready to jump at the chance to give him what he wants, and he'll forget all about me.

This is exactly why I refuse to let this get between me and my career. My job at Limelight is everything I've dreamed of.

I'm finally doing what I've busted my ass to do, and I'm not about to throw it all away over a fling that won't mean anything to him after the article is published in a few weeks.

Still, it doesn't change how he knows exactly what to say, how damn attracted I am to him, or how badly I wish I could have just one night with him.

I've never had a one-night stand, but with him I want to try.

Even if it's kept between us, and no one ever finds out. There's no harm if my boss never finds out, right?

Except maybe when it's over, and I'm left trying to forget having his hands on me and those dirty words in my ear. I refuse to let him take my heart and destroy it, though.

It will be fine if I keep reminding myself it's all for fun. I could use a little fun in my life.

Hell, look at me. I'm sitting at home alone for the seventh night in a row with nothing but another glass of wine.

"I haven't been able to stop thinkin' about it either," I admit, dragging my lip between my teeth.

"Now that wasn't so hard, was it?"

I smirk, and for a second, I wish I could take it back. Until he releases a throaty sigh and the sound makes my heart and pussy flutter. It reminds me of the noises he made when we first met, and dammit if I don't wish those moans were for me.

"When I was talkin' to you earlier at work, all I could think about was you sitting at your desk. I bet you look beautiful in your dress, those killer fuckin' legs tempting me when you cross them, and your delicious lips begging for me to have a taste."

Oh God. I press my palm to my chest, feeling my heart rate kick into high gear. How can he do this to me when he's hundreds of miles away?

"I want so badly to dirty you up for me."

He makes me feel so sexy. Wanted. Desired.

I haven't felt this way with a man in a long time. Hell, maybe ever.

Heaven knows Mitchell never made me feel this way. I've always believed he was only in it for the money and connections. Which is why I like what I have with Madden; he has no idea who I am.

Something about the way Madden wants me is so addicting. I felt it from him the night at Whiskey Barrel. Like he'd give anything to haul me over his shoulder and get me alone.

"What you want is to ruin me," I retort.

"Is that what you think?" he asks.

I shake my head. I guess I don't know, but it's what I fear.

"I've been single for a long fuckin' time," he grunts. "Too long. I've spent time with women, but it's never developed into anything more. I have no interest in anyone, though..." He trails off. "No one but you."

"No one?"

"Nope," he emphasizes. "I've been labeled as a player. The media has made me out to be some womanizing prick. They've done it to all of us. Give me a chance to prove you have it all wrong about me."

"Well, how do you envision we do this when you're in Carolina Beach, and I'm all the way in New York?"

"I guess I'll have to find a way to get my ass to New York then, huh?"

I smile. "In the meantime, I guess I should get to know you a little. Let you get to know me too."

I pick up my bottle of wine, topping my glass off, and saunter into the living room. I climb onto the couch and curl my legs beneath me.

"Tell me something about you then," he murmurs.

I swallow. There are many things people don't know about me, but I'm not sure how I feel about breaking myself open and showing him the real me yet.

"I found out my ex-boyfriend was cheating on me," I admit.

"Damn"—he sighs—"I'm sorry."

"It's okay. He has no idea I know. Not many people do. Our families are close. I think they always hoped we'd end up together, get married, and have a family. You know, the whole thing. I found out he was cheating, though, and I ended it. I told him I didn't have the same feelings for him anymore when, in all honesty, I just didn't have it in me to fight for him. To care. He showed me everything I needed to know about him, and I was done."

"I don't blame you," he says sympathetically. "I guess it explains why you're so focused on your job. I've done the same thing, although for different reasons."

"What are your reasons?" I ask.

He's giving me an in, a chance to get to know him, and I'll take it.

"I just have a hard time trusting people. I'm sure you can relate after what you've been through," he says, and I nod even though he can't see me. "Once you've been burned in the past. Friends we've made, women I've started to see who sold stories to the media for money. It's hard not to build a wall around you. I guess I did it to protect myself, but I only pushed people away in the process."

"You're letting me in right now, though, so that has to count for something," I say.

"I guess you're right. I haven't in a long time, though." He exhales, and silence falls over us.

I'm starting to feel like I misjudged him in the beginning.

Anytime A Rebels Havoc was ever brought up, I'd curl my lip in disgust, shrugging them off as being a bunch of womanizers.

The bitter side of me, who's still hurt from Mitchell cheating, wants to believe Madden is exactly who I've always thought he was. Yet, the more I talk to him, the more I want to give him a chance. If anything, just to get back into the dating game again.

We sat on the phone for almost an hour. We talked about traveling and the band's upcoming tour. His energy changed when he spoke about how excited he was when they went out on the road for their first sold-out tour.

When I admit I haven't been to a concert in years, he scoffs as if it is the craziest thing he's ever heard.

The following morning when I'm sitting at my desk, unable to stop thinking about him or contain my smile, I click on the internet icon and quickly type out, "A Rebels Havoc tickets," and hit enter.

Their tour sold out months ago, so my only hope now is to snatch an overpriced resale ticket online. It's a few months away, but their first stop is in New York.

I throw caution to the wind and go for it, buying the ticket.

What's the worst that could happen?

CHAPTER NINE

MADDEN

I'm beginning to wonder if Brielle is blowing me off.

I sent her a text a couple of hours ago asking if she was at work. She read it immediately but never responded.

My lip curls on the edge, resisting the urge to pull my phone out of my pocket to check it again.

"What's the plan for tonight?" I ask, reclining on the sofa in our hotel room.

On nights like this, I hate being the lone wolf without a girl-friend. I miss the nights when the guys would hit up a nightclub or grab a beer with me.

Now they're all locked down, and if I have any hope of getting out of here, away from their sorry asses and the reminder of how single I am, it'll have to be on my own.

"We have an early morning tomorrow, so whatever you're thinking, don't overdo it because I'm not dragging your ass out of bed," Kyla sneers, and I roll my eyes.

She's the reason we keep our shit together these days. I guess I shouldn't complain because I know what it's like to be in her shoes. For years, I tried to keep Brix and Tysin in line. Of the three of us, I'm the only one with my head on semi-straight.

At least, that's how it used to be.

Ever since I met Brielle, my mind hasn't been able to stay away from anything but her.

When I found out we'd be in the city again doing press on our album *Come Hell or Havoc*, I was hopin' I could sneak away from the guys for the night to see her.

Brielle: Yeah, about to head out of here soon, though. Why do you ask?

I press my lips together to fight off my smile. If the guys caught me, they'd grill me about why I'm grinning like a kid on Christmas morning.

Me: You free tonight? I'm in the city and was hoping to meet up for drinks.

The bubbles on the screen appear and disappear again. The longer I wait for her reply, the more nervous I get thinking she's trying to find a way to get out of it. But then her response comes through.

Brielle: You are?
Brielle: Where?

I step out of the room and click on her name, dialing her number. She answers, her voice coming out breathy and sultry. I squeeze my eyes shut, my mind once again picturing her at her desk.

What is it about her in those sexy little dresses that makes me want to ravage her like an animal?

"You never told me you were coming to the city."

"We're only here for a couple of days."

"I see," she murmurs.

"I'm going to take off here in a few. I'll be waiting outside for you in about twenty minutes."

She's quiet for a moment, and I picture the wheels turning in her mind.

"Don't overthink it. We're just friends, right? Two friends hanging out and eating some food."

She giggles. "Is that right?"

"Of course. Why, what's goin' on in that dirty mind of yours?"

When her laughter picks up this time, I know I got her there.

"Only one of us is allowed to have our minds in the gutter, Brielle, or else tonight will end up going differently than I planned. I'm trying to prove I want more than to pin you against the wall and finish what we started outside Whiskey Barrel."

"Madden," she hums, her voice dropping low.

"Doesn't mean I haven't thought about how I wish I could bend you over your desk or how badly I want you on your knees for me."

She gasps. I roll my eyes closed, picturing her kneeling in front of me.

"Mmm. Soon, though," I whisper.

I imagine her soft skin flushed from the heat of my words, her chest heaving with the force of her heavy pants filtering through the phone.

"I'll see you soon, Brielle," I force myself to say, not wanting to end the conversation now.

"I'll be waiting."

Damn, I have it bad for this woman.

I stand in my room, rubbing my fingers over my eyes and thinking about anything I can to get the brick in my pants to go down.

I get to see Brielle again. The thought alone isn't helping.

"I'm gonna take off here for a bit. Maybe go grab a drink or something," I say, shutting the door to my room behind me.

I try to play it off cool, but I catch Trey and Tysin eyeing me for a moment.

"You want us to come with you? I wouldn't mind grabbing a drink," Tysin says.

"Honestly, I think I'd like some fresh air away from all the people. I wouldn't mind being alone."

Even the words sound like a lie coming from me. When have I ever turned down going out with the guys?

It's been a long day, and we've been on the go since we landed last night.

"You good?" Trey asks.

I nod. "Never been better."

He studies me, flicking his gaze over to Tysin.

For as much as these two hated each other in the beginning, they are thick as thieves now. I know they're both wondering what the hell is going on, but I'm not about to stick around and let them dissect it further.

"I won't be out late," I say, swiping my leather jacket off the chair and ducking my head, escaping out the door of our suite.

Abel's room is next to ours. We told him he could relax for a bit, but if I tried to leave without telling him, I'd only dig a deeper hole to bury myself under a heap of questions later.

I tap my knuckle against his door. The lock clicks before he swings it open. His brows deepen.

"Everything good?" he asks, on high alert.

"Yeah, I'm taking off. I was hoping you could give me a lift."

He nods. "Yeah, sure, no problem. Give me a second."

"I'll meet you downstairs. I have somethin' I need to do first," I say, taking off down the hall toward the elevator.

I didn't need him to follow every step I took. I was doing enough by asking him to come with me. He had the keys, and I needed the ride.

Now I need to do some sweet-talkin' to the hotel manager for what I have up my sleeve.

We meet downstairs in the front a few minutes later. He's wearing a dark pair of aviators, his gray polo, and black dress slacks.

"You wanna tell me what this is about?" he asks, following me outside. I could've waited until he pulled the SUV around like he'd prefer, but Brielle is almost off work, and I don't want to waste time fuckin' around.

"I'm meeting up with someone."

"You care to tell me who this someone is?" He glances over, his gaze burning into the side of my face.

"You promise me this will stay between the two of us?"

He's silent.

"For now. Please," I add.

He nods. "Yeah, you got it. What's going on?"

"You remember the girl from the interview a few weeks ago? The one who came out with us to Whiskey Barrel."

"Yeah?"

"I want to pick her up and take her out for dinner and a drink, but I'd like to keep it on the down low if we can."

"You do realize that wherever you go, there won't be an easy way of getting you in and out without drawing attention."

"I've got it figured out. I just need you to get me to the front of *Limelight* as soon as you can."

He opens the back door to the SUV, and I climb in.

As luck would have it, we ran into traffic on the way there but still managed to make it outside on time. Glancing around outside the front, I'm relieved she wasn't left waiting when she's nowhere to be found.

I keep my eyes trained on the front entrance. When she walks outside shortly after, her long blond hair down and swept over one shoulder, all the oxygen is nearly sucked out of the small space.

She's carrying a laptop bag on her shoulder, and her handbag hangs from her arm. She crosses her arms in front of her chest, glancing from side to side, searching for me.

I quickly reach for the handle and push the door open. Abel scolds me, telling me to wait for him, but I ignore it when her eyes land on mine.

She'll probably deny this later, but I could've sworn a smile was playing on her lips.

I let my eyes trail down her body, taking in her fitted black dress, her tan legs, and black patent heels.

We walk toward each other, and the closer we get, the more her smile forms. She drops her hands when she reaches me, lifting her eyes to meet mine.

"I can't believe you're here," she whispers.

I take in the subtle rise and fall of her chest and her hands fisted at her side.

"It's good to see you again," I say, fixated on her mouth when she bites on the corner of her lip.

The sidewalk is full of people, so when I reach for her hand to lead her to the SUV, she quickly jerks it away.

"I don't want anyone to see us," she mutters.

I nod, stepping in close behind her as I usher her toward the door.

Abel stands waiting for us, and I don't miss the curious look he sends my way.

I open the door for Brielle, and she climbs inside. As soon as it shuts behind her, Abel whispers under his breath, "Are you sure you know what you're doing?"

"Not right now, please."

He nods. I'm sick of everyone laying into me about Brielle.

We've had a long history of run-ins with the media. I'm trying to remind myself that while I've learned who not to trust the hard way, Brielle has had every opportunity to throw me under the bus since we first met.

She could've rejected me and told me to fuck off after our kiss in the parking lot at Whiskey Barrel.

She didn't, though. She may have a wall up and is hard to read at times, but I know without a doubt she feels this between us, and dammit if I'm not going crazy over how bad I want her too.

"Where are we going?" she asks when I climb in next to her.

"You'll have to forgive me. This all happened at the last minute. The hotel we're staying at is not too far from here."

Abel's eyes flick to mine in the rearview mirror, but I turn to Brielle, keeping my gaze trained on her. Judging by the look on Brielle's face, she has the wrong idea too.

"It's not what you're thinking. I'm just hoping to get you to myself without anyone around. As you can see, it's not easy for me."

She nods. "I like the sound of that too."

"I talked to the manager of our hotel, and she's agreed to let us have their restaurant to ourselves for the evening."

She tenses, her mouth snapping shut before she asks, "What hotel are you staying at?"

"Granite Hotel."

She flicks her eyes away and nods, forcing a smile. I reach for her hand between us, slipping our fingers together.

"Sound good to you?" I ask.

She stares down at our joined hands when I rest them in my lap, brushing my thumb over hers.

"Sounds perfect."

She gasps when I press a kiss to the back, watching my lips sweep over her skin.

Abel clears his throat. "Back to Granite then?" he asks, his voice more stern than usual.

"Please." I nod.

Brielle's eyes flick over to mine. When she drags her lip between her teeth, I reach over to trace my thumb along her cheek, fighting against the urge to kiss her again.

I've been thinking about it since I watched her leave Whiskey Barrel that night.

"In case you can't tell, I'm happy to see you again."

I glance from her mouth up to meet her eyes. She hesitates, checking if Abel is watching us.

"It's just you and me," I whisper low.

Her mouth curves at the edge. "Then kiss me."

I smirk, gripping her chin between my fingers, and press a soft kiss against her lips. She moans against my mouth, and I'm half tempted to tell Abel to pull over right now to give us a minute alone.

All I want is more of her in every way I can have her.

CHAPTER TEN

BRIELLE

Why does it feel like the universe is warning me I'm playing with fire?

It's been one bad thing after another since I woke up this morning.

First, I fell asleep early last night and forgot to charge my phone, which meant my alarm didn't go off. I managed to make it to work on time, but not without making myself look like a crazed lunatic running through the lobby of Limelight headquarters.

We had our important editors' meetings today, and I forgot to put my phone on silent. I got a text message from Madden followed by a phone call from my father within a matter of seconds, drawing the attention of everyone in the room.

I thought the day was turning around when Madden told me he was in town. Only now, here we are, finding out he's staying at none other than my family's hotel.

The same hotel he's rented out for the evening for us to be alone.

I grew up at this hotel. Most, if not all, of the staff knows who I am.

The entire drive there, I'm racking my brain trying to come up with a plan on what to do. I've busted my ass to keep my career away from my personal life, especially from my family.

As far as they know, I'm a freelance writer, but I've made every attempt to keep my name and identity separate from my work.

We pull up outside of the hotel. I spot Cedric, the bellhop I've known since I was a toddler, standing near the door. He steps outside to welcome us when Abel nods, signaling he's got it, opening the door to greet me with a forced smile.

"Thank you," I murmur, reaching for my bags.

"You can leave your things with Abel," Madden says behind me. "He'll make sure they're safe, won't you?"

"Of course, ma'am."

I hesitate for a moment, then nod, not wanting to lug it inside. I set it on the seat, and Madden climbs out first, reaching for my hand to help me.

"Let's go," he whispers against my temple, pressing his hand along the small of my back.

I duck my head, managing to get past Cedric without him noticing me. It all comes to a crashing halt when we step inside, and I spot Annabelle, the manager, near the front lobby.

"Mr. Cole, good to see you again." Her eyes shift from him over to me, brightening when she recognizes me. "Brielle, wow, this is a pleasant surprise. Your father didn't mention you'd be by today."

Madden glances between us, and I can almost hear the swirl of questions hitting him like a tidal wave.

"It's okay. He didn't know I would be here with my friend."

Madden drops his hand, the heat of his body disappearing, sending a chill of nervous energy through me.

"We've gone ahead, sir, and made arrangements to ensure you have the restaurant to yourself." Annabelle looks over at Madden and holds her hand out to gesture for us to continue.

Madden steps in close when we take the elevator to the rooftop bar. His gaze burns into me the entire ride up, the questions playing out on his face.

The restaurant and bar span the length of the twelfth floor along the front of the hotel. The back half has suites, nearly twice as tall.

The lights are dimmed with ambient lighting cast overhead. The bar covers the back wall, and shelves with liquor bottles reach the ceiling. The black marble booths and tabletops have smooth and sleek leather seats.

Madden leads me to the section of U-shaped booths. His hand returns to the small of my back, urging me to take a seat when we reach the one with a candle lit in the center.

I slide in, and he claims the spot across from me, giving him a direct shot of the door. I tell myself it's because he wants his eyes trained on the door in case anyone walks in and catches us, but I'm keenly aware he's doing it for our safety too.

"Does your father stay here a lot?" Madden asks, the questions from Annabelle's comments lingering in the air.

How do I answer this without lying to him, when I'm not ready to come out with the truth? At least not yet.

"He used to, although he doesn't much anymore," I say, which is the truth. My father has been slowly turning more control over to my brothers.

He nods, seeming to accept that answer, and I'm relieved when he doesn't continue his line of questioning.

"What are you doing in the city?" I ask, changing the subject.

"Press for *Come Hell or Havoc*." He leans back against the seat with his eyes fixed on me. "We have another busy day of interviews tomorrow before we fly out Friday morning."

Two nights.

He's in the city for two nights, and I can't deny I hope to spend them both with him.

"I saw you guys are killin' it on the top charts." I smile. "I'm happy for you."

The server, Diego, is not someone I've met before. He's younger, wide-eyed, and giddy when he approaches us. The first thing out of his mouth is how excited he is to meet Madden, followed by reassuring us he'd respect our privacy this evening.

I don't doubt Madden made it clear he wanted our dinner to be kept private.

Diego takes our drink orders and slinks away, leaving us alone again.

"Thank you," Madden says, lifting his water to take a drink.

I swallow hard at the sight of his throat bobbing, the cord of his muscles flexing in his arm as he does. I'm finding it hard to focus on carrying on a conversation with him.

"I have to admit it's not even the highlight of my day, though."

I press my lips together, hesitating to ask him what is before he answers.

"You. I wasn't sure when I'd get the chance to see you again. I've been thinking about what it would be like, though." His voice drops low.

I inhale a deep breath and nod. Only he throws me off when I watch him slide out of the booth to circle around to my side.

"Except I don't like this space between us." He leans in close to my ear. "So I'll have to ask you to scoot over so I can join you."

I lift my eyes to his, his mouth only inches away from my face.

"Don't tell me it's not a good idea, Brielle." He smirks.

I snicker and tilt my head to the side. "What if I told you I can't think straight with you so close?"

"Well, don't overthink it. Problem solved."

I flick my tongue against my teeth and nod, sliding over. He takes the seat next to me.

He rests his hand on my crossed legs beneath the table, brushing his finger along my thigh, causing me to tense.

Diego returns with our drinks, and I'm thankful because I need a second to catch my breath. He flicks his eyes over to me and gives me a look I'd expect Davis to throw my way if he saw the two of us together.

We thank him, and when he asks if he can take our dinner order, Madden sends him away, telling him we'll let him know when we're ready.

"I need you alone right now," he whispers, turning toward me.

I lift my glass of champagne to my mouth, taking a heavy gulp, and Madden's eyes glitter when he hears me sigh.

He tilts my head back, brushing his thumb along my cheek and over my lip, glancing down at my mouth.

I flick my tongue against his finger. He hisses and gives in, leaning in to crash his mouth on mine. All I can do is hold on for the ride.

"C'mere," he mutters, tugging me onto his lap.

"What are you doing?" I chastise him but don't resist.

I kneel on the booth seat next to him, and he leans back, trying to reassure me there's enough space.

When he catches me shimmying the bottom of my dress up to allow room to climb onto him, he reaches his hand down to skate up my thigh, and this time, I turn the tables on him.

I grip the base of his neck, tilting his head back against the seat, and fire blazes in his eyes. He shoots me a warning look and shakes his head.

"Nuh-uh," he growls.

He pulls his hand away but not before his finger brushes over my panties, and this time, it's me who's gasping.

His hand tightens on my hips, urging me onto his lap, and this time I obey. Once I'm straddling him, his hands slide up my legs, banding his arm around my waist and forcing me closer to him.

"I promise this isn't the only reason I asked you here tonight," he whispers against my mouth.

"Then what was the reason?"

He eyes my mouth, pressing his palm against the side of my face.

"I'm still trying to convince you I'm not the person you think I am."

I curl my lip into a smile.

"Two friends having fun, right?"

He leans in to kiss me again, pulling back to whisper, "If that's what you want to believe, I'll go with it for now."

I pull back, my brows deepening.

"Well, what is it you want?" I ask.

He exhales and seems to think about it. Something about sitting this close to him while asking such a serious question feels more raw.

"Do you mean with you or in life?"

"All of it," I say, seizing the opportunity.

I keep telling myself this is for fun. After ending things with Mitchell, I need to get back into the dating scene.

We live in two different worlds. At some point, I need to face the reality that despite what we want, it may not be possible with each other.

No matter how hard I try to slow down and live in the moment, I can't change who I am. I'm a planner and like to be able to see the path ahead.

This is what's terrifying about being with Madden. Everything about this feels so new and unfamiliar, and the future with him seems so unclear.

"I mean, I grew up living an ordinary life in a small town. In the summer, we spent much of our time at the beach or on the boardwalk. I think, on some level, I still want that life. I want a family and to raise my kids where I lived.

"On the other hand, I've been chasing this dream forever. It's my passion and what I love. I want to see how far A Rebels Havoc can go."

"You and I, we come from two different worlds," I say, admitting my fears out loud.

"Same world, baby, just different places. We're living in it together now. Stop lettin' your pretty little mind come up with every reason this will never work out."

He still manages to read me like a goddamn book.

He smirks, and I shake my head. "I'm right, aren't I?" he adds.

"I'm not overthinking anything. I'm being realistic. It's easy for you to live with your head in the clouds, Mr. Rock Star."

He catches me off guard when he wraps his hand around my throat and pulls me in to kiss him. Only this time, the heat between us turns all the way up.

His fingers dig into my hips as if he's holding me, not wanting me to stop him. He hums in appreciation when my body relaxes, his tongue brushing along my mouth until I open up for him.

It's easy to forget all the things that could go wrong when I'm here with him.

When he pulls back and I press my forehead to his, he whispers, "Live in the moment with me. Please."

He grips my ass, and I grind my hips against him.

Maybe this is living, but it feels like free-falling, and all I can do is hope he'll be there to catch me when it all comes crashing down.

CHAPTER ELEVEN

MADDEN

Our last day in NYC has been chaotic, jumping from one interview to the next. The only thing that helped me get through it was thinking about my date last night with Brielle and knowing I'll see her again tonight.

I don't bother sticking around when we get back to our hotel. After a quick shower, I change and slip out the door when no one is watching.

Abel meets me in the lobby.

"I'll text when I need you to pick me up," I say, meeting his eyes in the rearview mirror.

"What should I tell the guys if anyone asks where you're at?"

I tighten my hand into a fist. "Tell them you don't know."

He clenches his jaw and nods. I don't bother to wait around for him to grumble over it either, reaching for the door handle.

It's a cool brisk evening. A gust of wind swoops in, sending a shiver through me. I shove my hands into my pockets and pull the brim of my hat down to cover my face when I approach the front entrance. The sliding glass doors open, leading into the lobby, where a man stands behind a counter, ready to greet me.

"Can I help you, sir?" he asks, his eyes going wide.

He's dressed in a charcoal suit, his dark hair slicked to the side.

"I'm here for Brielle Silvers."

"Silvers?" he questions, glancing up at me from behind the computer screen, and I nod.

He clears his throat. "Yes, Ms. Silvers." He smiles. "She let me know she's expecting you. Her apartment is on the thirty-seventh floor."

I thank him and take off toward the bay of elevators leading up to her apartment.

With each floor I pass, I find myself growing more anxious to see her. We'll finally be alone, in private, away from anyone watching us.

She greets me as soon as the elevator dings and the door opens. She's dressed in a pair of black lounge pants and a cream-colored sweater, her arms wrapped around her waist. Her hair is pulled up in one of those messy buns, and she's wearing a pair of dark-framed glasses.

It gives her a studious look, and I can't help all the sinful thoughts swirling through my mind about corrupting her in every possible way.

"Hi," she says, her voice dropping low.

She lets her eyes trail down my body to my red T-shirt covered by my black leather jacket and dark denim jeans.

I've been dying to get my hands on her, to feel her soft skin beneath me.

I stalk toward her, shrugging out of my jacket. She reaches her hand out to take it from me, and I shake my head, hanging it on the coatrack near the door.

When I turn toward her, I catch her staring at my ass, but she quickly darts her gaze up to meet mine, and I grin, knowing I've caught her.

This time when I make my way to her, I don't stop until I'm standing an inch away.

"I finally have you all to myself," I whisper, lifting her chin, gripping it between my fingers.

Her eyes soften. "Isn't that what you wanted all along?"

I smirk. "You know better than to think that." I lean in, leaving our lips a hairsbreadth apart, but she gives in and wraps her arm around my neck, pulling me down to her. When our mouths crash, she moans against me, and I grasp her hip, lifting her.

She circles her legs around my waist. I groan when she grinds against me, realizing I have no fuckin' idea where the hell I'm going with her.

I saunter through her apartment and pull back to carry her into the kitchen, setting her on the counter. For the first time, I allow myself a moment to look around the space.

I'm not sure what I expected. Her apartment appears to take up the entire floor. It's nice, all gray and white lines, giving a classy yet modern feel.

She leans back, resting her palms behind her, and stares down at me when I step between her legs.

"I've been thinking about having you spread out like this for me since last night," I say. She tightens her legs around me, staring down at my mouth. "I want to know if you taste as good as I think you do and sound as sexy when you moan my name."

"Madden," she groans, and I growl.

"Yeah, baby, just like that."

Her eyes feather shut, and I lean in to kiss her again. Only this time, it's slow and full of passion. I rake my hands up her legs to grip her hips, dipping my fingers beneath the waistband of her pants.

Her body quivers when my fingers brush along her bare skin.

"Touch me," she whispers and leans away.

I nod, looping my finger through the drawstring and tugging on it until it unties. She has a dazed look in her eyes when I slide her pants down her legs.

I groan when I realize she's not wearing any panties.

"I think someone was hoping I'd have my face buried between their legs tonight." My nostrils flare at the sight of her bare pussy.

Her only response is a nod, confirming I'm right. I guess we've both been thinking about this night.

When I step back, she raises her heels to the edge of the counter and lets her legs fall open for me. I curse at the sight of her, not holding anything back.

"Madden, don't keep me waiting."

"Oh, sweetheart, I won't, but damn if I don't want to keep the sight of you right now forever ingrained in my memory."

She drags her hand up her thigh and reaches for the hem of her sweater, lifting it over her head. She drops it on the floor next to my feet, leaving her with nothing but the lace bra she's wearing underneath.

"Your turn," she mutters, and I quickly shed my shirt, unhooking my belt and unzipping my jeans.

My dick strains against the front of my boxer briefs. Her tongue darts out, wetting her lips.

I brush my finger along her inner leg up toward the apex of her thighs. She quivers beneath my touch, and I pause, lightly rubbing my knuckle over her clit.

"I want to see your body twist and turn as I explore every inch of you."

I do it a few times until she lifts her hips and mutters a low, "Please."

"Please what, baby? Tell me what you want."

I pull my hand away, and she replaces it with hers. I grit my teeth while I watch her rub her fingers over her clit before sliding down to enter her.

"Brielle," I mutter, and she rolls her eyes closed.

The sight of her pleasuring herself turns me on even more until the sound of my name passes her lips. It takes everything in me not to pull her to the edge of the counter and slide my dick home deep inside her.

I fight it off, pushing my jeans and underwear over my hips, and wrap my hand around my dick.

When she slowly blinks her eyes open, they zero in on my hand, and I tighten my fist, paying close attention to the tip.

"I'm dying to feel your tight pussy around me," I mutter, and she nods.

Yet when she pulls her fingers out and lifts her hand to my mouth, I squeeze the tip to fight off the temptation to fuck her hard and fast like I desperately need. She traces them over my lips until I open, sucking on her sweet fingers.

I tighten my hand around her wrist.

"Now you're just teasing me, Brielle," I grunt. "I don't particularly like being teased. One thing you should know about me is when we're together, whether it's in the bedroom or anywhere else, I'll be the one calling the shots."

She clenches her jaw.

"Do you understand?"

She hesitates for a moment, and I give in, brushing my finger over her clit. Only this time, I'm the one doing the teasing, dragging my finger through her folds down to her entrance.

I slip the tip of my finger inside her, and she lifts her hips, seeking more.

"I'm waiting, Brielle."

"Yesss," she hisses. "Yes, I understand."

"Who calls the shots?"

"Please," she mutters. I lean in and flick my tongue over her nipple, not giving her a centimeter more.

She drags her nails into my hair, holding me to her. When I suck her nipple into my mouth, she pulls my head up, locking my eyes with hers.

"You call the shots, Madden, but dammit, stop teasing me. I need more."

"Lean back, baby," I order, and she obeys. "Let me show you how much I crave you with my tongue."

I don't tease her, flicking my tongue over her swollen clit. She thrusts toward me, and I loop my arms underneath her thighs, holding her to me.

"Mmm," I hum, licking and sucking.

She grinds her pussy against my face, dragging her fingers through my hair and tugging on the strands. Her moans grow louder and throatier.

When I pull back to slip my finger inside her, she flings her arm over her mouth and moans into the crux of her elbow. I slowly enter her, turning my wrist to brush over the bundle of nerves inside her, and suck on her clit.

"Holy shit, Madden," she moans, her legs folding against the side of my head.

She cries out, her body trembling. She's close; I can feel it.

I flick my eyes up her body, brushing her finger over her taut nipple when I mutter, "Let me taste your sweet cum, Brielle. Give it to me."

She writhes beneath me, her breath sputtering when she crashes over the edge, her release flowing through her. She drops her arms to her sides, letting out a long, surrendering moan.

I don't give her a chance to come down from the high. I pull her to the edge of the counter, brushing the head of my dick through her wetness.

"I want my dick slick with your cum." I grunt, tightening my fist around my cock.

"Oh God," she mutters when she realizes what's coming. "It's okay; I'm clean and on birth control."

I stop, realizing the thought of grabbing a condom from my wallet completely escaped my mind. I've never been one to hook up with someone without one, but with Brielle, I want nothing between us.

"I'm clean too. I get checked often, I promise."

"I trust you," she whispers, pressing her hand over my heart.

Those words. If only she knew the weight of how much they meant for me to hear.

When I plunge in deep, I tilt my head back and squeeze my eyes shut, feeling her pussy grip me like a fuckin' vise. It's unlike anything I've ever felt before.

She's wet and fits me like a glove. Like she was made for me, and I was put on this earth to enjoy every inch of her sweet body.

I lean over, and she wraps her arms around my neck, her legs tightening around my waist, not letting me go. I lift her off the counter, changing our position.

"Hold on to me, baby," I mutter into her neck. "This first time, I need you hard and fast. I'm desperate to fuck you out of my system until my knees nearly give out."

She nods, and I adjust my grip to curl under her legs. She tightens her hold on my neck. When she starts to bounce on my dick, it takes everything in me not to let my knees buckle beneath me.

"Fuck, baby, you feel so damn good," I murmur. "This pussy, you, I want it all."

She tosses her head back, her long hair flowing behind her, never letting up. I set her on the edge of the counter again, moving my hand between us to brush over her clit. She arches her back as my hips piston into her like a freight train speeding down the tracks.

I don't give in or let up until she comes. Only this time, it's with her pussy clenching around me and my name on her lips.

"I'm not going anywhere tonight," I mutter, lifting my head after coming down from the high. "I haven't gotten enough of you yet."

CHAPTER TWELVE

BRIELLE

"Brielle? Brielle?"

It takes a second to separate my dream from reality. I shoot upright when I realize my father's voice originates from somewhere within my apartment. My body tenses.

"What the fuck is he doing here?" I mumble under my breath, looking down as the sheet falls from my chest.

A low grumble next to me brings me crashing to reality when I find Madden asleep.

He's on his stomach, his arm stretched out above his head, leaving his broad shoulders on display. He pries one eye open and stares up at me.

"Who's here?"

"My father," I grit through clenched teeth. "Please do me a favor and stay up here. I need to see what he wants and get him to leave."

He turns onto his side, dragging his hand through his messy hair. It's short on the sides and a little longer on the top, and the strands stick up from where I spent all night raking my fingers through it.

I fumble and nearly trip as I search for my clothes before it dawns on me that we left them downstairs in the kitchen last night.

"Shit, shit, shit," I mutter, padding to my closet. "Give me a second, Dad. I'll be right down."

"What are you doing still asleep? It's after nine in the morning." His deep voice grumbles, echoing into the high vaulted ceilings to my loft. "What's with this mess you left down here too? Crap is everywhere."

That's my father for you. I don't know how my mother put up with him for all these years.

The only thing higher than his bank account is his unmeasurable expectations for everyone, his family included. I came to terms with it a long time ago. No matter what I do, I'll never live up to his impossible standards or make him proud.

I quickly pull on a pair of jeans and shrug on a sweater. I glance in the mirror and find my hair is all over the place.

I don't even remember what time I fell asleep. Madden and I went a few more rounds, once on my couch, before we eventually stumbled our way upstairs.

He couldn't get over the view from my apartment and insisted we turn the lights off so only the sight of downtown New York surrounded us.

He's right, though. It's what sold me on this place. The floor-to-ceiling windows surround all three sides. You can't find a better view. While I didn't love how my bedroom was a loft overlooking the living area downstairs, this view made up for its lack of privacy.

Although I haven't found it to be a problem until this moment when I realize how likely it would be for my father to see Madden if he even tried to climb out of bed.

"I don't have my clothes," Madden whispers, sitting up when I turn around. His gaze drags down my body before finally meeting mine.

"It doesn't matter anyway. I don't want you to go downstairs until he leaves."

I smirk, and he rolls his eyes.

I need to get this over with and convince him to go. I jog down the stairs to where my father stands in the kitchen with his phone in his hand. He's dressed in a black suit and signature gray tie. For being nearly sixty years old, he could pass for being in his forties.

Tones of silver highlight his dark-brown hair at his temples and pepper the facial hair lining his jaw.

"Hi, Daddy," I murmur, circling the island to hug him.

"Hi, sweetheart," he greets me, wrapping his arm around me and pecking a kiss on my cheek.

"Why have you been blowing off my calls this week? I've been trying to get ahold of you, but they keep going straight to voice-mail."

I drag my lip through my teeth and cross my arms over my chest. I should've known if I kept this up, he'd come searching for me. He picked a bad day to do it too.

"It's been a busy week. A lot going on at work. You know how it is."

He nods, but his eyes narrow on me.

"You still considering my offer? I've been waiting for you to get back to me with your answer. We've built an empire, sweetie, and you don't seem to want any part of it."

He's right; I want nothing to do with Granite Industries.

This is his dream, not mine. I don't know how many times I have to tell him before it finally sinks in.

I sigh. "We've gone over this countless times, Dad."

"We have, Brielle, but you can't tell me this little writing job is enough for you. Why not have it be something you can do on the side? Like a hobby, then you can have the best of both worlds."

He said the same thing when he found out about my writing in high school. When one of my short stories got published by a local college, he skipped past the congratulations and telling me how proud he was of me, and focused more on questioning if this is what I wanted to do with my life.

"I'm not having this conversation with you."

Especially not when I know Madden can hear us. Not when my father has no clue what I truly do, and Madden is clueless about my family name. I hate how I've kept so much from them, but if I don't cut this off now, it could spin out of control and end disastrously.

"Annabelle told me you stopped by Granite in Manhattan?"

Shit.

My family owns four hotels in the tri-state area. He's tried everything to get me to come join them, even down to offering me a job on the board of directors, but I've declined.

"Yeah, I met up with a friend for dinner."

He chuckles. "That's not what she made it sound like. She thought it was a date with some rock star drummer. I tried telling her 'not my baby girl,' but she insisted it was you."

My eyes flick across my apartment to see if I can spot Madden upstairs from the reflection in the window. There's nothing.

Unless he listened, which doesn't sound like Madden, he's nowhere to be found.

"He's just a friend, Dad."

The lie tastes sour coming off my tongue, and it's even worse knowing Madden is listening.

"What happened to Mitchell? I thought things were going well for the two of you."

I shake my head and drop my arms, turning my back to him and stalk across the kitchen to turn on my coffee pot. At this rate, I'll need something a whole lot stronger, but we'll start here.

"We broke up months ago. We've gone over this. There's nothing left to tell."

"Certainly, there's more to it, though. You two were together for years. I saw his parents at Carbone, and they said he was looking at rings when you two split. Rings, Elle. You can't tell me you didn't love him, and he's perfect for you."

I open the cabinet door and pull out a coffee mug, softly setting it down on the counter, because the anger and annoyance zipping through me have me wanting to slam it down so hard it could crack the ceramic cup all over the counter.

"He's not perfect for me. You only think he is because he fits the profile of the man you want me to marry. Someone like *you.* Hell, you practically arranged our entire courtship. Can't you see we're nothing alike?"

I turn around and rest my hip on the edge of the counter. My eyes flit behind him to where Madden stands, bending down to pick up his shirt off the floor and quickly tug it over his head.

He managed to slip down here and get his pants on without either of us overhearing. My father nods, flicking his eyes away from me. I use the opportunity to shoot a warning look at Madden.

What does he do? He has the nerve to grin, like this is the funniest fuckin' thing in the world to have happened.

He's probably enjoying the embarrassment all over again. As if our first meeting wasn't mortifying enough.

"Tell him," Madden mouths, nodding toward my dad.

"No," I reply, dropping my face when my father looks up at me.

"I still think you should give him a chance," my dad says, shoving his phone into his pocket.

Madden clears his throat, and my father stiffens, my eyes going wide. This isn't at all how I expected this to go.

"Hello, sir," Madden says, holding his hand out to my father.

Even wearing yesterday's clothes, his shirt being wrinkled and his hair disheveled, he looks as confident as he did the day we first met.

My father looks at Madden and then over at me, his face stoic and unreadable. I do my best to maintain my composure, my face softening, and I lift my mouth into a smile.

"Hello," he drags out. There's a question there, but he skips past it. "My name is Clint Granite. Forgive me, who are you?"

Madden's eyes flick from him over to me, no doubt picking up on the change in my last name, before returning to my father.

"Madden, Madden Cole, sir."

He shakes his hand, and my father turns to me.

"You'll have to forgive me. Brielle hadn't told me about you or that she had a guest."

"Oh, uh, well, actually, she did, sir. I'm Brielle's *friend*," Madden emphasizes. "The friend she met with the other night at Granite for dinner."

"The rock star." He nods, his eyes trailing over Madden as if inspecting him to see if he measures up to his expectations. "Right, right."

"Madden and I were introduced through a friend a few weeks back," I lie. I can feel his eyes on me.

Madden opened this can of worms by cutting in and introducing himself. He'll have to go along with it until I have a chance to explain.

"He's in town on business, and we met up for dinner. Isn't that right, Madden?"

He nods. "Correct, sir."

"Speaking of being in town visiting, Madden will be flying out in a few hours to head back home, and I promised to give him a ride. I'm sorry to cut you off, Daddy, but we have to get going. Can I call you later when I get home?"

"Sure." He nods, stepping away from the two of us. "How about you stop by tomorrow afternoon? Your mother was just saying how much she misses you. I'm sure she'd love to have you home for lunch. Your brothers will be by too. It'll be nice to have all of us together again."

I force a smile and nod. "Sounds wonderful."

His face warms for the first time since he got here, and he hugs me, kissing me on the side of my head.

"It was nice to meet you, sir," Madden says as he passes by.

He nods, flicking his gaze over to Madden like he somehow forgot he was there.

"Yes, thank you."

He turns and holds his hand up in a wave before disappearing down the hall. Madden turns his attention back to me, but we both remain silent until we hear the familiar sound of the elevator ding and the door shut.

As soon as he's gone, I squeeze my eyes shut and sigh. The tension in the air shifts. I don't even know how to begin to explain this to Madden, so I turn to where I left my coffee cup waiting on the counter.

I pull out the carafe and pour myself a cup. Normally, I would add creamer and sugar to sweeten it up, but not today. I don't even bother waiting before taking a drink and wince when it burns my tongue.

"The guys and I started playing together when we were about twelve years old. It was not long after my parents bought me drums for Christmas. It was supposed to be a hobby. At the time, I think my father thought it would help me take out a little aggression, maybe tire me out. I was a bit wound up back then."

I set the mug down on the counter and turn to face him, leaning against the counter to listen.

"Tysin had been working for months, doing odd jobs around the neighborhood like mowing, landscaping, that sort of thing. He saved for a few months to earn enough money to buy his guitar. We both started playing together and came up with the idea to start the band. Brix was always the one taking charge, at least when it came to our music, although he doesn't have a responsible bone in his body, so everything else fell onto me.

"The more we practiced, the more we started to take it seriously. We knew we wanted to find a way to take A Rebels Havoc all the way. The sky wasn't even a limit for us. My father was okay with us playing in the garage for a while until he got sick of listening to us and kicked us out one day. We played at Brix's house for a while before, eventually, Tysin moved out and was living on his own, so we started practicing there. By that point, things started to pick up. We played some shows around Carolina Beach and other local towns. Whiskey Barrel was the first place to add us to their regular lineup. We'd play there two to three weekends a month.

"When he told me to get my shit out of his garage, though, it started a huge fight. I think he wanted me to see how my dream of being a drummer, of taking the band to the next level, was a pipe dream. Those were the words he used. No one believed in us."

He leans against the island across from me.

"No one but us and my sister."

"I know the feeling," I murmur, setting my cup down, and take a step toward him. "I'm glad you didn't give up, though. Otherwise, you wouldn't be here."

He lifts my chin and kisses me. Meanwhile, my mind races with how I open up and give him the answers he no doubt wants.

"I haven't told my father about my job," I say quickly before I overthink it.

Madden's brows deepen in question.

"As far as he knows, I'm doing freelance writing and still living off my savings. He doesn't know about my job writing for *Limelight*."

"He doesn't?"

I shake my head.

"I'm sure there will come a day when I tell him. It's partially why I write under the name Brielle Silvers. I wanted some separation between my personal life and my career."

Madden shared in his interview how their rise to fame, being in the public eye, and the media have made it hard for him, so I know he understands when I say I wanted to keep my job and life separate from each other.

"I'm sure you picked up on my name when my father introduced himself and put two and two together, but my family owns Granite hotels."

My father and brothers have been working on an expansion project too. In a few years, it's projected to be worth over a billion dollars.

I run my hand up Madden's forearms, staring at his chest not ready to meet his eyes, afraid of what I'll find looking back at me.

"I think it says a lot about you," Madden says, breaking the silence. "You could've taken the quote-unquote easy way out, right? You could've followed the path they laid out with the career and married the man they chose for you, but you didn't. You stuck to who you are and what you want, and you're creating your own way."

I tilt my head back to meet Madden's gaze and smile. He gets it.

"I have to tell you, baby, it's sexy as hell."

He lifts me in his arms, turning to set me on the edge of the counter. I grip his shoulders, and he buries his face into my neck. He inhales deeply, his fingers digging into my hips.

"I'm not ready to let you go yet," he murmurs.

"Who said you have to?"

It made it more difficult not knowing when I'd see him again. We both have busy jobs, and there's no telling when we'll have time to get together.

His lips seared a line along my neck until he captured mine. It's slow and sensual, and I reach my hand out to grip the front of his shirt to hold onto him, not wanting to let him go.

When he pulls back, he leans his forehead against mine and whispers, "I'm glad you went against your parents and carved your own way. If you hadn't, I never would've met you." He sighs. "I would've never had the chance to kiss you like this either," he breathes out, just before he crashes his mouth on mine again.

CHAPTER THIRTEEN

BRIELLE

I never ended up going to my parents' for dinner yesterday. I sent a text to my mom shortly after I woke up saying something came up and I'd get ahold of her later in the week.

Shortly after, a barrage of phone calls from my father ensued, to the point where I turned my phone on silent and buried my face in a book for the afternoon. I took a break to pick up dry cleaning and swing by the store before noticing a few messages from Madden.

He texted me earlier in the day, letting me know he had plans when he got home. I didn't expect to hear from him until he called me as he crawled into bed. We talked for a little while before we both agreed to get some sleep. He was exhausted from his trip, and neither of us got much sleep the night he stayed with me.

I needed the sleep too, or I'm positive it would've ended up being another morning of me sprinting through the lobby at work. It's not a moment I want to relive ever again.

I'm sitting at my desk, scrolling through emails, when one comes through from Davis with a message saying, "Thought you'd want to see this."

I click on the link, and it pulls up an article from Hollywood Tea.

MADDEN COLE IS SPOTTED HAND IN HAND WITH MYSTERY WOMAN

It looks like Madden Cole has moved on once again. We've all heard the rumors and know it's true. He's no stranger to the dating game.

On Saturday, Hollywood Tea caught the drummer walking into Granite hotel alongside a mystery woman.

This isn't the first time in recent months the A Rebels Havoc band member has been spotted out with unknown women, only this time he seems to be cozied up with a blond bombshell.

Some believe he could be taking it to the next level with this one, though, since he's not normally one to be spotted out in public showing PDA toward rumored flings.

Sources say Madden and his "hotel rendezvous" are only friends and are not romantically involved, but if that's true, what's the story behind the hidden kiss?

Who knows if the duo are friends or in the beginning stages of something more? What do you think? Does our last remaining single rebel have a new woman in his life, or do you believe they're just friends?

I read the article several times, massaging my fingers over my forehead. The photo appearing in the article is grainy and hard to see in the dark. My head was down during my attempt to slip past Cedric.

My stomach twists, knowing people saw us together. The last thing I need is to have my face plastered all over the media alongside Madden, especially when I'm still finishing the article.

I don't want my boss to find out we've been spending time together.

I roll my finger over the mouse, scrolling up and down the article, debating what to do. I've met a few people who work for Hollywood Tea over the years. All professional relationships, but I'm closest to Clive Teller, their editor-in-chief.

If anyone could help me stop anything before it hits the headlines, it would be him.

It's ridiculous, though, because what's there to reach out about? No one knows who it is or who I am.

Two knocks hit the doorframe of my office, and I spin in my chair to find Davis standing behind me.

"Did you see what I sent you?" He smiles big, showing his teeth and fluttering his lashes.

"Yeah…" I sigh, sliding down in my chair. "Come in, though, and shut the door, will ya?"

He looks around to make sure no one's coming before he does.

"You never told me you were hooking up with Madden Cole."

"I'm not hooking up with Madden Cole."

He curls his mouth into a smile and barks out a laugh. "You're a terrible liar."

My face warms, and I know without looking in the mirror I'm bright red from embarrassment.

"Do you want to try again to see if you can do better the second time around?"

Why do I feel like talking to him is like trying to talk to Serena? Speaking of which, she's going to be calling me soon, and I can only imagine what she'll have to say.

"We're not hooking up."

I don't see it as hooking up, which to me is the truth. Feelings are involved. Hooking up is like friends with benefits, only without the friends. It's clinical. A means of scratching an itch.

I'd like to think, especially after my conversations with Madden, there's more to what is going on between us than simply hooking up.

"Well, we won't get all technical with our labels, but something is going on between the two of you. I could feel the sexual tension between you the first day you two met."

"Yeah, right." I scoff, rolling my eyes though secretly hoping he'll keep talking.

"You need to get your eyes checked then, ma'am, because that man looked like he wanted to rip your clothes off and devour every inch of you."

I slap my hand over my mouth to conceal my smile.

My phone rings on my desk, and the caller ID says it's a North Carolina area code. My eyes dart over to Davis.

"I need to take this," I mutter.

He nods, moving to stand. He flicks his eyes over to the phone and back to me, grinning like the Cheshire cat.

"Tell Madden I said hello." He holds his hand up, fluttering his fingers at me in a wave, and disappears out the door.

"Brielle Silvers, Limelight Magazine," I answer.

"Hello, Ms. Silvers," Madden's deep voice grumbles through the line. I squeeze my eyes closed and sigh.

It's like the first time we met. I knew if he ever tried to turn it around on me, I'd melt into a puddle at his feet from just the sound of his voice.

"What are you doin'?" he asks.

"Nothin', just talking about you."

"Oh, you were, were you? Was it juicy, and with whom?"

"Davis." I smirk, imagining Madden knowing Davis has been gushing over him all over again.

"What were you two talking about?"

"Did you happen to see the Hollywood Tea article posted earlier this morning?"

I hear rustling on the other end of the line, and his tone changes when he says, "No, I didn't."

I wince, picking up on the panic in his tone.

"Not again," he grumbles under his breath.

"It's nothing bad," I rush to clarify. "But someone snapped a picture of the two of us together walking into Granite. It's a terrible photo. You can hardly make out our faces, but it's clearly you. They couldn't identify me, though."

"Well, that's good."

My brows knit together, my stomach dropping. I know what he meant by it, but it still doesn't make me feel any better about the note of happiness he way he said it.

"Yeah," I say, curtly.

"Wait, Brielle, that's not how I meant it," he adds. "I just didn't think you'd want our relationship announced this way, not when we haven't talked about what's going on between us or what we are. Especially when you've been worried about it being an issue with your job."

"I know what you meant. We're on the same page."

"Mm-hmm," he says. I guess we're both feeling the same about it then.

"If that's not why you're calling me, then what's going on? Is everything okay?"

"There were a couple of reasons, actually. We have our album release party this Saturday. It's here in Carolina Beach. I know it's last minute, and it may be hard for you to get the time off on short notice, but I was hoping you would join me. As my date," he says. "My *real* date."

"A real date, huh? This seems like it's getting serious."

"Mm-hmm," he hums again. "Very serious."

I smirk. "Two dates in such a short period. What will people say when they see us together now?"

"Who cares? We both know they'll always find something to talk about, and I just don't give a shit about some things anymore."

"I know." I sigh. I never thought it would be my job making this difficult between us. "We can still go as *friends*, right?"

"There's that friend line again," he grunts. "I'm starting to hate it."

"It's only while we're at the drop party. Then after, when we get back to your place, we can go back to us."

"Us," he says. "I like the sound of that. What you mean is when I go back to having you all to myself and enjoying every inch."

My face warms, and I squeeze my eyes shut, imagining him spreading my legs open while he runs his finger through my folds before he licks my pussy.

I don't even realize the change in my breathing or the way I clench my thighs together in a desperate plea for friction. Something, anything to ease the desire.

"Is your office door shut, Brielle?"

I exhale a deep breath through my nostrils and turn back to the door, double-checking that Davis closed it behind him when he left.

"Yes," I mutter.

"Mmm, good. Go ahead and flip the lock."

I roll my chair back and twist the lock on the door. It dawns on me that if someone were to come looking for me, they may try to open my door and realize something is going on.

"I don't need anyone walking in on us."

Us. There's that word again.

"What are you wearing?"

I glance down my body to the tweed pencil skirt and the black ruffle top, getting a peek of my white lace bra underneath.

"A skirt and a top."

"Perfect," he hums. "Pull up your skirt, Brielle. Up to your waist so you can reach my pussy."

"Madden," I mutter breathlessly, craning my neck to the side to hold the phone to my ear while I tug the material around my waist.

"Okay, I did."

"Good girl," he says, and I roll my eyes closed at the sound. "I think it's time I show you how good of a *friend* I can be."

"Madden," I plead. "Tell me what you want me to do, but hurry. I need you so bad right now, and I don't want to get caught."

"Are you wet, baby? Slide your fingers into your panties and tell me how wet my pussy is for me."

I push my underwear to the side and slip my fingers into my matching white lace underwear. My heart sputters when I do, continuing my path to enter myself, and I moan.

"Fuck, baby, you even sound turned on. It's fuckin' sexy. Tell me, I need to hear how wet you are for me."

"So wet, so turned on."

"We'll make this quick because I'm hard as a rock too."

The visual of Madden's large hand fisting his dick is clear in my mind. Even thinking of the night we spent at my place sends a shiver through me.

His hands, those fingers, set a perfect rhythm while he got me off.

"Spread your legs open for me and lift your heels onto your desk, and I want you to slide your fingers inside you. Fuck your pussy for me, baby."

I do as he says, slipping my shoes off and leaning back into my seat with my feet on the edge of my desk. I slip my finger back inside me, adding a second one, and release a breathy sigh.

"That feel good?"

"So good, I'm picturing they're your fingers."

"Brush your thumb over your clit for me."

I twist my wrist and strain my ears when I hear the slick, jerking sound.

"Fuckkk," he moans. I picture him spitting on his hand and increasing the tempo.

The sound of his throaty groans mixed with each flick of my finger over my clit has my vision going blurry, stars dancing in my eyes.

"I'm close," I mutter, each word coming out strangled and forced.

"Let me hear you, baby. Fuck your fingers and let me taste them."

His crass words in my ear urging me on send a wave of euphoria over me. My body tenses as I start to tremble, fighting to keep my moans low out of fear that someone could hear me.

"Oh fuck, baby, oh fuck." Madden curses, and I sag in relief against my chair.

Look at what this man has done to me. I've never been like this, so brazen and wild, with anyone else.

I'm so fucking weak when it comes to him. I'll do anything when his dirty words are only for me.

We stay quiet for a few minutes.

"You never told me what the other thing is you wanted to talk to me about."

"Oh, right." He pauses. His voice changes as if he's hesitant to talk about it now. Maybe out of fear of it changing the mood. "We have an event tonight. I meant to tell you about it when we were together last weekend."

"You mean the Grammy's?" I smirk.

"That's the one." He chuckles. "I know you'll probably see pictures online or even watch it on TV, and I wanted you to hear it from me, but I have a date I'll be taking with me."

"Oh." The line falls silent.

"I know what you're probably thinking—"

I cut him off. "What am I thinking, Madden?"

He sighs, and I sit up in my chair, massaging my fingers into my forehead.

What am I supposed to think? My biggest fear is letting myself get tangled up with him, only to turn into another one of his meaningless flings. He's gotten what he wanted from me. Do I wait for him to toss me to the side now?

"It's not what you're thinking, I can tell you that much. I've been friends with Tonya for years. Not the type of *friend* you are, either."

"Tonya Lively?" I ask.

"Yeah," he mumbles. "She's joined me at other events in the past. It's good exposure for her, and I hate being the only one to show up to these things alone."

Of course, I know who she is. She's been photographed with Madden before. Even though he's reassured me it's not what I think, I still can't help but wonder now what their history is.

"I wish you were going with me instead."

"Yeah..." I whisper. "Me too."

CHAPTER FOURTEEN

MADDEN

"You have anything you want to tell me?" Kyla asks after I hang up with Brielle and saunter out of my bedroom. I adjust my tie before I button my suit jacket, running my hand over the front.

I dart my eyes from side to side, questioning if she's talking to me. I feel like I got caught with my hand in the cookie jar.

"Um... I don't think so?"

"Did you see the newest headline of Hollywood Tea?"

I wince, recalling that detail from our call. I've been in a daze with how we ended things. I almost forgot about the fact my face and name once again found their way back to their headlines.

"I did," I grit out. "Before you say anything, though..."

Kyla holds up her hand to stop me.

"Madden, you don't have to justify yourself to me."

She's damn right I don't, and I won't either.

"I am curious, though. What's going on between you two?"

"Honestly, I don't know right now. We've been talking since she was in town for the interview. It's nothing serious, though."

She narrows her gaze at me, and I shrug.

"Is that why you're taking Tonya to the event tonight?"

I swallow hard, flaring my nostrils. "You and I both know nothing's going on with Tonya."

She nods. "I just don't know why you wouldn't have invited her instead."

We made arrangements for Tonya to join me before Brielle was ever in the picture. I would've canceled with her, though, if I thought Brielle would come.

"She is worried that us being seen together could hurt her job. She just started with Limelight when she landed our interview."

I don't dare mention how her family is loaded, and she's worried about what her father thinks of me. I don't care what he thinks, and I'm not going to let her stress over it either.

"Plus, it's still too early to say. We're not seeing each other exclusively, and she lives in New York. All we did was go out for dinner."

Kyla smacks her hand down on the hotel bar, her eyes bright. She loves when anyone dishes some tea, even more when it's not her and Tysin making the headlines.

"You did?"

I nod and chuckle. "Yeah, I guess after how we first met and the kiss we shared outside of Whiskey Barrel, I didn't want her to get the wrong idea and think I was just trying to get her into bed."

"I thought you didn't kiss her that night?" Kyla smirks, and I realize I've just admitted to it despite saying nothing happened.

She holds her hand out, urging me to continue.

"When we were in the city for our press tour, I told her I wanted to see her. I took her on a date that night. We ended up going to the restaurant at the hotel. They shut down for us, and we were able to have some time to ourselves."

She presses her hands together and sighs. "Who knew you could be so romantic?"

I smirk. I'm not going to tell her how dinner included an intermission of her grinding on my lap while I tried not to fuck her.

She doesn't need to know how I ravaged Brielle on every surface of her apartment on the second night we spent together or how we both got off to her fingering herself for me while she was at work either.

So much for her being scared about us getting caught by her boss.

"A real-life Prince Charming," I bark out.

Kyla rolls her eyes and resumes shuffling through papers.

"Have you checked the charts again? You guys are still holding that number one spot."

I grin. I've tried to chill out but have been checking since our album went live. It still manages to blow my mind. Somehow, we've topped all the charts in less than twenty-four hours from the album dropping and held that spot for the past week.

"Still number one, baby," Brix bellows, slapping his hand down on the counter. Tysin is following him.

Trey is still in his suite getting ready or on a video call with Layken. He's anxious being away from her. She's due any day now. I think he's worried the moment he steps away, she'll go into labor.

"Crazy, man," I say, clapping their hands and pulling them in for a hug.

"Madden, Tonya should be here any minute. I'll have Abel head to the lobby to meet her. Brix, will you let Trey know we're about ready to head out? We need to be there at five o'clock to make sure we hit the red carpet on time."

I don't know what we'd do without Kyla keeping us in line.

Tonya is waiting for us when we make it out the door. She's wearing a long silver dress, her blond hair curled over one shoulder.

She smiles when she sees me and kisses me on the cheek before Kyla ushers us into the SUV.

I hate doing red carpets about as much as I hate talking with the press. A million photographers snap our photos, and interviewers throw hundreds of questions our way. Thankfully, Brix, Tysin, and even Trey seem to take the brunt of them until one interviewer turns to me.

"Madden, you're here with Tonya Lively tonight. You both look stunning together. So tell us, is this the mystery woman we saw photographed with you outside Granite hotel recently?"

My body stiffens, and I flick my gaze over to Tonya.

The guys chuckle behind me. I've managed to steer clear of these sorts of comments in the past. I don't doubt they love having them fired at me for a change.

"No, it's a friend of mine who I was visiting in the area." I smile, hoping they'll drop it.

"This isn't the first time you've brought Tonya with you to an event. Any chance we can get a little tease as to what special woman you've been spending your time with as of late?"

"Not at this time." I grit my teeth, clenching my hand resting on Tonya's hip into a fist.

Something about being here with her, when I wish I could be with Brielle instead, makes my hand feel out of place. Like I shouldn't be touching Tonya right now.

I fight against the urge to drop my arm to my side and step away, making it clear where we stand. I don't doubt Brielle will see these photos and read the interview, and that thought alone makes me want to do something I know I shouldn't.

"Tonya and I have been friends for a while now. We have a good time when we're together, but we're only friends. The woman you saw me with in New York is someone I care a lot about. It's still new, and we're taking it slow, and I hope in the future I can tell you more about her."

Tonya pats her hand against my chest, and we step away, effectively ending the conversation.

"Why didn't you warn me you were seeing someone?" she whispers under her breath.

"I didn't think it would matter. This is business for us, right?"

"Right, but like you said, we've been friends for a while now. A heads-up would've been nice."

"It was plastered on the front page of Hollywood Tea. I would've thought you knew along with the rest of the world."

She chuckles. "I don't pay attention to the garbage they post. You should know better by now."

"Then don't worry about what anyone thinks. The woman they saw me with knows we're here together tonight. She understands this is business for me."

I swallow hard. At least I hope she does. Maybe I'm wrong, though.

Maybe you distracted her by making her come and ignored how she felt because all you cared about was one thing.

Fuck. I feel like a prick.

I need to get my shit together if I have any hope of proving to her what we have means more to me than some meaningless fling, like she overheard when we first met.

I'm still finding it hard to lower the wall around me even though I want to trust her and not believe she'll use me like everyone else I've met in this industry.

I respect Tonya because she's always been up front and honest. We talked in the beginning about her coming to these gigs after she first joined me for an event. This was about putting her name and face out there, and she managed to land some high-fashion modeling campaigns.

It's an equal give and take. I didn't have to worry about impressing her, and it didn't come with the pressure of wanting more.

We both had fun together.

The rest of the award show went off without a hitch. We played our bestselling song, "Left in Ruins," currently sitting at number one on the Billboard Hot 100. It felt good to get on stage and play our newer music.

The crowd and the energy from the production behind the televised live show was electric. It's a rush, one minute coming out on stage. Adrenaline pumps through me from the awards and other performances, only for it to be over after one song.

It hypes me up for when we'll head out on the road this summer for our sold-out *Come Hell or Havoc* tour.

We won Best Rock Song for "Kiss Me Crazy," one of our fan favorites, and Best Rock Album for our debut, *Wreak Some Havoc*.

It's like the icing on the fuckin' cake showing all our hard work over the years has finally paid off.

After the event, we're back in the SUV again, heading off to an after-party.

In the past, I was one of the first to head out and live it up on nights like this, picking up women and throwing them back into the early morning hours.

We're in Sin City, for fuck's sake.

Now, things are completely different. I slip my phone out to see if Brielle has sent me a text, but there's nothing. My stomach twists and I sag against the wall.

"You good?" Kyla asks, glancing from me down to my phone.

I shove it back in my pocket and nod. "All good."

"Let me guess, you haven't heard from her?"

I shrug. "It's late," I say, realizing it's after midnight in New York at this point. "She's probably in bed now."

She works in the morning. We've both made it clear our jobs are the most important part of our lives, and they will always come first.

She's still new at *Limelight* and busting her ass to prove herself. Still, it doesn't change the fact I wish it was her on my arm tonight, or hell, she sent me a text to congratulate me on my awards.

I check the time on my phone when we make it back to our hotel. I have a few beers in me and took a few celebratory shots too. I'm itching to call Brielle just to hear her voice, even if it's only for a second.

I hadn't noticed the email notification from a few hours ago. When I see Brielle's name, my heart drops, and I click on the email.

From: Brielle Silvers <bsilvers@limelightmag.com>
Date: April 3rd, 2022
To: Madden Cole <maddrummer@email.com>
Subject: Submission

xo

Attached: A Rebels Havoc Limelight Interview

Brielle Silvers, Limelight Magazine

I click on the link. I swear, seeing the interview in my inbox has me instantly sobering up.

My eyes skim over the article. She starts talking about what it was like to meet us and sit down for the interview before diving in with her questions. She discusses everything from how the band was formed to the battle between Tysin and Trey when Trey first joined the group.

We can laugh about it now, but their ongoing feud was a pain in the ass when we first went out on tour.

She talks in length about witnessing our friendships along with them talking about their relationships too. While she goes into detail about our conversations, she did what she promised she would from the beginning, and that's focus on telling our story.

She's opening my eyes to not everyone you meet being out to tear you down.

I'm relieved one of those people is her.

CHAPTER FIFTEEN

BRIELLE

"So what, you're gonna sit here all night and mope over a bottle of wine while you try to catch him walking the red carpet with his date? Good grief, woman, pull yourself together." Serena scowls at me, crossing her arms.

She picked up on my less-than-stellar mood when she called earlier. After coming down from the high of my office orgasm, I faced the reality that Madden would be photographed with his arm candy, which would once again create a fury of rumors.

I hated the thought one of those rumors would be him once again being spotted with a different woman.

I hated even more that it was her going with him and not me.

"No..." I bob my head, rolling my eyes. "I'm actually going to sit here on my couch with my laptop and work up the courage to send him the article I've been agonizing over all week."

She stomps across the room to the other side of my sectional couch and collapses next to me, kicking her feet up with her.

"If that's what has you in knots, then there's nothing for me to do. You knocked it out of the park."

"You haven't even read it." I chuckle.

"I don't need to, and that's the point. You kill everything you set out to do. You seem to forget I've been next to you for most of our lives. I've read all of your short stories and most of your creative projects, along with many of the articles you've written before your job at *Limelight*. This one is no different. You're an excellent writer, and I promise you've killed it. Now hit send, and let's finish off this bottle of wine."

I lean back against the sofa, practically burying my head between the two cushions, and stare at the screen. The TV plays on low in the background, but I haven't been paying much attention to it, despite waiting for the mention of A Rebels Havoc.

Madden told me earlier today they will be on stage performing, so unless I happen to catch him in the crowd or they show him walking the red carpet beforehand, I'm only watching for their awards and performance.

I run my finger over my lip, staring beneath my brow up at the TV. They transition to a commercial break but first show more of the celebrities arriving at the event.

"Oh shit, there he is." Serena shoots to her feet and points at the screen.

I narrow my eyes at his date and scowl when I see his arm around her waist.

She's beautiful, wearing a dress so tight there's no way she could wear underwear beneath that thing and get away with not seeing it.

Her cheekbones look chiseled from the gods. She's sunkissed and fit, and I'm over here green with envy.

"Well, at least we got it over with, right?" She crosses her arms, turning back to me.

I exhale a huff, focusing on my laptop. I furiously type out the email and attach the article, and without thinking, I quickly hit send before slamming my computer shut.

"Where are you going?" Serena scurries behind me when I push myself to stand, taking off for the kitchen.

"Wine. I need more wine."

"Are you sure that's a good idea?"

I turn toward her, draining all my emotion from my face. She nods enthusiastically.

"On second thought, you're right. See, you're the one with the brains. You have all the best ideas."

Turning back to the wine fridge, I smirk and pull out another bottle, popping the top. Never mind the fact we still have at least a glass left in the other bottle sitting in the living room. I'm certain we already need another.

I don't remember what time I crawled into bed, but sure enough, the wine did its job on drowning out all my worries and cares.

It's just after three in the morning when I hear the faint sound of my phone ringing from where it's buried under my pillow. I blindly pat my hand around, searching for it, and hit the button to answer with a muffled, "Hello."

"I'm sorry for waking you." Madden's deep voice hits me like a shot of adrenaline, forcing my eyes open wide.

"It's okay," I mumble. "Congratulations on your awards and your performance. I watched it, and you guys killed it."

He sighs. "Thanks."

I push my covers down my chest and brush my hair away from my face.

"The only thing missing was you."

My body relaxes, and I nod, as if he can see me. "I wish I was there." My voice cracks. "I'll see you soon, though. I got the time off work, so it looks like you got a *friend* for the drop party."

He chuckles. "I'll have the most beautiful date there."

I'm impressed I managed to set my alarm and even made it to work on time the next morning.

For the rest of the week, I'm going through the motions. Madden and the guys have more press while they're on the West Coast before they fly back to Carolina Beach.

We've kept in touch, talking daily every chance we get. I'd be lying if I said I wasn't looking forward to seeing him.

If anything, this has only solidified that whatever is going on between us means a lot more to me than some meaningless fling.

I think what terrifies me most is that it's not to him.

My flight arrives in Wilmington on Friday evening. I told Madden not to worry about picking me up when he mentioned having practice with the guys. So when the sliding glass doors open outside the airport and I see him standing next to his car, I can't help but grin.

I glance around me, my eyes shooting from side to side before I take off running toward him.

"Gettin' a little risky, don't you think? Going out without the big guys hired to protect you." I smirk.

He curls his lip and shakes his head, pulling me toward him. His large arm swoops around me, holding me snug against his body when he leans in and grumbles in my ear.

"I can protect myself just fine, thank you."

I tilt my head back, running my finger over his chest. "So big and strong. I think you're right."

He releases me and steps back, shaking his head. "Get in the car."

I giggle when he reaches for the door handle, holding the door for me while I climb in.

When he takes the seat next to me, he leans in close, his warm breath heating my neck up to my ear.

"Wait until we get back to my place," he taunts. "I'll show you just how strong I am."

My breath hitches, and I turn toward him, my eyes tracing over his sharp jaw down to where his muscles flex in his forearm when he grips the steering wheel.

"Care to elaborate?" I ask.

He grins and shakes his head. "You'll have to wait."

I start to think back to when he was in NYC and stayed at my place. The way he carried me to my room and tossed me onto my bed like I weighed nothing.

The thought spurs something inside me, and I lean against his arm, running my finger over his chest and down his stomach to the bulge growing in his jeans.

"I think I've waited long enough, don't you?"

"Brielle," he warns.

"Madden…" I hum, peppering kisses along his cheek to his ear.

He leans his head into me, and I grin when I notice the slight shiver when I flick my tongue over his earlobe, earning me a low growl.

He floors it, his car zipping in and out of traffic, keeping his eyes trained on the road while I continue my slow torture. Each brush of my hand over his body pushes him an inch farther.

When he pulls up outside the gate leading to his property, he throws me off guard when he slams on the brakes and shifts the car into park the moment the gate closes behind us.

"Get over here," he mutters. Reaching for the lever next to his seat, he pushes it all the way back.

His sports car has limited room, but the move managed to create more space for me.

He reaches for the button of his jeans, swiftly unzipping them, and my mouth instantly goes dry. Without thinking, my tongue darts out and swipes my lower lip, and he growls.

I flick my gaze back up to his, and he nods toward me.

"Pull up your dress," he orders, and I snap my mouth shut. He mumbles something that sounds like, "These fuckin' dresses."

I quickly look around, waiting for the moment when someone pops out and starts snapping photos of us. Except not a single person is in sight.

"I think we've waited long enough, Brielle. Isn't that what you said? Get your sweet ass over here."

I kick off my shoes and turn over to kneel in my seat. He grins when he watches me hike up my dress, gathering the material around my waist. I shimmy my panties down my legs, and he follows suit, pushing his pants over his hips.

The sight of him with his hand wrapped around his dick is not one I'll soon forget.

He leans back, curling his arm behind his head, and nods again for me to join him. I hurry to climb over the center console and straddle his lap. When he positions himself at my entrance, rubbing the tip through my folds, I suck in a sharp breath and slowly lower myself onto him.

"Goddamn," he mutters, tilting his head back and moaning.

I grind my hips when he's inside me and squeeze my eyes shut at how deliciously full he makes me feel.

He reaches between us, brushing his thumb over my clit, and I buck my hips, slamming down on him again in one quick thrust.

"Let me see you fuck me, baby. Ride me hard."

He pushes himself up, resting his elbow on the seat, and he pulls the strap of my dress down along with my bra, enough to expose one of my breasts.

I do the same to the other side, letting my tits bounce free, and he leans forward to suck the beaded flesh into his mouth.

I fling my arms around his neck, holding him through every rise and fall into his lap, fucking him hard and fast. Each move hits the spot right where I want him.

He grins when he leans back, gazing up at me.

"You ever think you'd be riding my dick like this when you first showed up here a few weeks ago?"

"N-N-No," I sputter, throwing my head back.

He brushes his thumb over my tender nipples, and I release a deep, throaty moan.

"I didn't think it would ever happen either, but fuck, baby, it doesn't mean I didn't imagine what it would be like if I did."

I stare down at him through hooded eyes. "You did?"

He nods, thrusting his hips up to meet me in time, and I cup my breasts in my hands.

"Hell, I thought about it the moment I walked out and saw how turned on you were from listening. You were caught red-handed."

My cheeks flame, and I squeeze my eyes shut.

"I wish it were you," he mutters. "It should've always been you. I swear this pussy was made for me. Now all I want is you."

"Madden," I breathe harshly.

"What are you doing to me?"

If only he knew. He has no idea how I was going out of my mind all week, picturing him with Tonya. He's telling me everything I've wanted to hear.

I lean forward, gripping my hands against the back of the seat, and he thrusts his hips into me.

He presses his forehead to mine, our heated breaths and moans entwined together. He grips my chin and kisses me hard. I'm so lost in him, leaving every one of my defenses weakened.

"Does that feel good, baby?" he asks.

I nod, holding his face in my hands, and kiss him again.

He tangles his fingers into my hair, tugging on the long strands, and I groan.

"Let me feel your pussy tighten around me. Come for me."

I sit up again, changing positions. This time when he thrusts into me, his expert fingers find my clit, and the desire glosses his hooded eyes while he watches me.

When we're close, our breaths and words come out strangled and broken.

I collapse against his chest, and he buries his face into my neck, kissing me while we float back down to earth.

"My good girl has gone bad," he growls.

"Only for you."

CHAPTER SIXTEEN

BRIELLE

Madden stands at the foot of the stairs waiting when I finish getting ready. He doesn't notice me at first, with his eyes focused on his phone. When he hears my heels clicking on the hardwood floor, his gaze darts to meet mine, and his face lights up when he sees me.

"Jesus Christ," he mutters. "On second thought, we can skip the party instead. It's not that important. I'm sure the guys have it covered without me."

I snicker. "It's your album drop party. Plus, aren't you supposed to perform tonight too?" I smirk, taking the final stair, and he quickly snatches me into his arms.

"I doubt they'd even realize I'm gone," he points out, running his nose along my cheek.

"You're right. Who needs the drummer anyway?"

His face falls, tightening his arm around my waist.

"I know someone who should," he suggests. "I could make her need me all night long if she keeps it up."

"Whoever she is, she's a lucky girl."

"Damn right, she is."

I push off him and roll my eyes. "Smug bastard."

He barks out a laugh and reaches for my hand, lacing our fingers together.

His eyes continue to roam over my face, down to the blue cocktail dress I picked out when shopping at Nordstrom earlier this week. It plunges low in the front, and even though I'm nervous about how revealing it is, it's worth every second to see the look on Madden's face.

"Fine, we'll go, but when we get home, I'll remind you how badly I needed to get you out of this dress. It'll be torturing me all damn night."

"You deserve to be teased for a change," I retort, pushing off him to walk out the door.

He growls when I pass by him, and he gets a glimpse of the back of my dress. It's held together with a few strings of jewels, dipping low and not leaving much to the imagination.

It's one of the sexiest dresses I've ever worn by far, and I may have picked it exactly for that reason.

Madden leads me to his car outside. It's a short drive to Whiskey Barrel, and the crowd is already forming, with cars overflowing out of the parking lot.

He pulls into the spots reserved for the band in the back and puts the car in park, leaning over across the center console to kiss me.

"We could probably have a quickie out here. I doubt anyone would even notice."

I smirk and shake my head. "Not gonna happen. This dress is hanging on by a thread. The last thing I need is to ruin it before I make it inside."

"You're right." He nods. "We'll plan for after instead."

He winks, reaching for the door handle.

I don't know what I expected, but I hardly recognize the place when we walk inside.

The lights are dim with neon rope lights strung overhead. They've added additional high-top tables throughout, leaving space for people to gather near the stage.

Some of their earlier music plays through the speakers. Madden spots the guys huddled in a group across the bar, standing with Kyla, Ivy, and Layken.

He glances down at me, linking our fingers together, and lifts our hands to his lips.

"I wanted to get this out of my system while I have the chance." His gaze softens, and he brushes his thumb over the back of my hand before releasing it.

My chest aches, wishing it didn't have to be this way. I try not to let myself calculate how long we reasonably have before we can dip out. I want to enjoy and celebrate their big night even though I'm dying for him to make good on his word.

Madden claps Brix on the back, and he turns toward us along with Tysin.

"Glad you finally showed up." Brix bumps him on the shoulder.

Tysin lifts his beer and nods toward us.

"Brielle, good to see you again." Brix smiles. "I want to thank you for the article too." They both nod.

"Yeah, thank you. It turned out great," Tysin adds.

It's hard not to think about the last time I was here and overheard their conversation with Madden when they didn't realize I was nearby.

"Absolutely, I enjoyed sitting down with you guys and writing it. Good to see you both again, too." I slip my hand around Madden's arm, leaning into him. "Congratulations to you on another kick-ass album."

Their faces seem to relax some then, and they thank me. The words I've been waiting to say are on the tip of my tongue. Even though I'd be less nervous with a drink in me, I want to get it out so I can stop stressing over it.

"I know you weren't exactly thrilled when you heard about Madden and me getting close," I blurt out, and Madden stiffens next to me. "I'll admit, I don't think either of us thought anything would come of it after our first introduction."

Madden pulls me into his side, leaning into my ear to say, "What happened to us not talking about it anymore?"

His reaction earns a smile from Brix and Tysin.

"I can assure you, though, that I'm not here to get on his good side only to hurt him later, or any of you for that matter."

Brix studies me intently, and Tysin takes another long pull of his beer.

"What I'm trying to say is, he doesn't have to suck up to me and he's certainly not sleeping with the enemy either. I'd like to leave our first impressions in the past. Can we agree on that?"

Madden interjects. "They'll have to whether they like it or not."

"I'm still surprised he didn't hurt me after he caught me with Kyla. I don't need to add another reason to his list." Tysin reaches his hand out to Madden, who's staring at him deadpanned.

"Don't forget it either." He cracks a smile, clapping each of them on the shoulder, and pulls them in for a hug before turning to me.

"All we care about is you do right by him. It's about time he found someone who makes him happy."

Madden puts his arm around me, pulling me into his side. Kyla and Ivy appear behind them, along with a server carrying a tray of shots.

"You're here," Kyla sings, glancing between the two of us, before she pulls me into her arms for a hug. Ivy is right behind her.

"Has anyone told you that your legs look killer in that fuckin' dress?" Ivy asks.

Madden grumbles under his breath next to us, something that sounded like, "Don't fuckin' remind me." We both snicker, but he stands there stoically, watching the exchange.

I've only talked to Kyla and Ivy a few times since the interview when I've been on a video call with Madden and they were nearby. Ivy and I bonded briefly over our shared history, with her career writing for *Mayhem Magazine*.

Kyla and Ivy take two shots from the tray, handing them over to Brix and Tysin.

"We got shots for you, too." Ivy lifts her hand to signal to the server for two more.

Lord knows I need a little something to help me loosen up a bit.

Layken sits at one of the high-top tables, leaning against the wall, holding what looks like a shot glass of lemonade. Trey's too captivated by his fiancée, burying his face in her neck.

We each take a shot glass, and Brix raises his hand in a toast before we throw them back.

A few other bands are here to show support for A Rebels Havoc. One of them is High Octane, who they've played with before.

"You think it's alright for two friends to dance?" Madden asks, slipping his arms around my waist, his warm breath sending a chill down my spine when he leans in close to my ear.

"I don't see a problem with it, if you don't."

He grins, barely giving me a chance to finish the sentence before he pulls me against his chest.

The music isn't exactly slow enough to dance to, but it doesn't stop us. He turns me in his arms, and I curl mine around his neck, pulling him closer to me. We sway our hips to our own beat.

He discreetly brushes his lips over the shell of my ear and hisses when I subtly skate my hand over the front of his pants.

"You have no idea what you're gettin' yourself into," he warns, his eyes darkening on mine.

I drag my lip between my teeth. "What'd I do?"

"Yo, we're up." Tysin interrupts, bumping against his arm.

They disappear into the crowd, heading toward the stage. Madden grits his teeth and turns back to me.

"Guess that means you're coming too." He smirks, reaching for my hand to lead me through the hordes of people.

We get stageside where I snapped pictures the last time I was here. The view gives me a direct line of sight of Madden sitting behind his drums.

"Don't worry." He leans in close to my head. "I'll be finishing what you started after."

He slips his hand down, gripping my ass through my dress, and lets out a low growl in my ear.

Right after High Octane wraps up, they take the stage, and the crowd goes wild. I recognize a few people; a few celebrities I've read about or listened to over the years.

It's hard to believe I'm here among them.

"Are you ready to fuckin' rock?" Brix bellows, pressing his foot against the speaker. He leans over to touch the hands of people in the front of the crowd.

Madden holds his drumsticks in the air, spinning them around his fingers. The cords in his arms and the sight of his expert fingers moving them so effortlessly is a turn-on all on its own.

The overhead spotlight roams above our heads before it lights up the stage. Madden kicks them off on the drums. I clap my hands, cupping them over my mouth to chant, "Rebels," along with the crowd.

Tysin and Trey join in on the guitar, and when Brix's voice follows, I swear it sends a shiver down my spine.

Somehow, they manage to keep getting better and better with each album. As I watch them tonight, I'm blown away by their talent.

My eyes are locked on Madden, taking in the look on his face as he nods his head and his leg bounces on the drum pedal. The cords of his muscles, slick with sweat, beg for me to trail my tongue over every delicious inch of him.

This is what they mean when women talk about arm porn.

When he steps off the stage after their set, perspiration dripping down his face, I don't retreat when he hauls me into his arms.

I run my hand over his chest, dragging my nails over the material. His eyes study me, his warm breath feathering over my lips. I lift my chin, tempting him, waiting for him to kiss me, but he steps back.

I press my lips firmly together and narrow my eyes.

"What's wrong, baby?" He tilts his head to the side. "You want me to kiss you, Brielle?"

His fingers brush along my spine, and my body trembles.

"I want you to do more than kiss me, but I'll settle for a kiss."

He smirks, leaning in closer until only a whisper separates the two of us.

"Say it," he taunts. "Tell me to kiss you."

I press my cheek against his and trail my mouth along the shell of his ear.

"I want more than a kiss, Madden."

Without waiting, Madden grabs my wrist and drags me with him down the hall leading to the back room we came through when we first arrived.

The lights are dim, and a table sits along the wall with two chairs on the opposite side with a door leading to the parking lot out back.

The empty room leaves us alone, away from curious glances. He turns toward me, his eyes bright with excitement when he lifts me into his arms and carries me across the room to the table.

I let out a low hiss, muttering for him to be careful.

"This dress is gonna be the death of me if I don't touch you."

He steps between my legs, forcing them apart, and holds my face in his hands, his lips crashing on mine.

I tighten my hold around his wrist, holding on for the ride. At some point, one of the guys steps into the room. I can't make out who. All I hear is them grumble, "Jesus Christ."

Madden lifts his hand. I imagine to flip them off, but his mouth never stops devouring me.

He grips my hips. I circle my legs around his waist, and he grinds against my center.

He breaks the kiss, his chest heaving while he stares at me through hooded eyes.

"Are you sure you don't want to go out to the car?"

I smirk. "We're missing out on all the fun, and you want to take off already?"

"You think I wouldn't have more fun ripping this fuckin' dress off you?"

We don't even notice we're no longer alone until the door slams shut, followed by a loud gasp. We both snap our gaze in the direction to see who it is.

It's like a bucket of ice water poured over our heads, bringing us crashing back to reality.

Hanna.

CHAPTER SEVENTEEN

MADDEN

"So it's true. You really are dating her?"

I recognize the voice, and the blood in my veins turns to ice.

Hanna.

What is she doing here? She shouldn't have even been allowed inside.

I slowly turn to see her standing in the corner with her arms crossed over her chest. She narrows her gaze at me, her lips pressed together, her body trembling as she fights off the tears she's holding back.

"Hanna, I thought we were on the same page. What we had was fun, but nothing more is going on between us."

"Don't say that, Madden," she cries. "Don't act like you don't care about me and what we shared means nothing to you."

Raking my hand through my hair, I squeeze my eyes shut. The week after Brielle was here for the interview, she showed up at my house wanting to "hang out." She knew our band practice schedule and was hoping to go for another round.

I cut things off with her then, or at least I tried. She reached out a couple more times, repeatedly texting about hanging out. This time, I was stern and told her to leave me alone.

I didn't want to hurt her and needed her to accept this wasn't anything serious for me. I thought we were on the same page about it too. We talked about it several times before Brielle was ever in the picture.

Until she saw me with Brielle at Whiskey Barrel, she never gave me any clue she wanted more with me. We rarely saw each other and only exchanged a few messages when we were planning to meet.

"Hanna, we went over this already. I had no idea you thought anything was happening between us. I'm sorry if I'm hurting you, but I don't share those same feelings. I'm moving on, and who I'm with or what I do now is not your business. It never was."

She clenches her jaw, her nostrils flaring. She shakes her head, but her eyes stay wide, trained on me.

"You're making a mistake."

"I'm sorry, but I don't think I am," I retort.

"You're going to regret this, Madden. I promise you'll regret hurting me."

"What's that supposed to mean?"

"If I can't have you, I'll make sure no one else will either."

She spins on her heel and disappears out the door before I even have a chance to order her to tell me what the fuck she means.

"Jesus. Madden, are you okay?" Brielle's soft hands slip around my waist, and I turn to find her concerned eyes on me.

I tuck a strand of hair behind her ear, and her eyes flutter, leaning into my palm.

"I am now," I whisper.

It's late, and the crowd has started to thin out. As much as I've loved having our first album drop party, something we never got when we released *Wreak Some Havoc*, I'm ready to take off and get her back to my place.

"What do you say we get outta here away from all these damn people?"

"I like the sound of that," she hums, rubbing her lips together.

Trey has Layken sitting on his lap, and Brix stands behind Ivy with his hands wrapped around her waist, whispering something in her ear. Tysin and Kyla are nowhere to be found, and I don't want to think about what the fuck they're doing.

"You two heading out?" Brix asks, his eyes flicking from me to where my hand grips Brielle's waist.

"If that's cool with you."

Brix and Trey both nod. "I'm actually thinking about doing the same," Trey adds.

Trey runs his hand over Layken's stomach. She presses her palm to Trey's face and leans in to kiss him.

I'm jealous as hell of what he's found with Layken. Everything they've been through together—hell, all the shit the guys have been through with their relationships—has only shown me why I shouldn't hold back from what I have with Brielle.

I won't let threats like the one Hanna made, the media, or even Brielle's father or her job stand in our way.

We say our goodbyes, and I spot Tysin with Kyla near the door when we make our escape. I thank Kyla for making tonight amazing for us. Without her, we probably wouldn't even be having the release party.

When we pull into my garage a few minutes later, I slip my fingers between Brielle's and lift them to my mouth to kiss the back of her hand when I lead her into the house.

"Thank you for being here and coming with me tonight," I murmur. "It seems surreal having you here, but I'm glad I have you to myself for the weekend."

"I am too." She drags her lip between her teeth, and I resist the urge to kiss her.

I'd rather get her inside where I have better access to her in that sexy-as-hell dress she's wearing.

"Do you have any idea how hard it's been keeping my hands off you tonight?"

"I think I have an idea."

She runs her hand over the front of my jeans, and I suck in a sharp breath.

"Brielle," I grit, a tone of warning in my voice.

"Yes?"

"Come with me."

She raises her brow, and I follow it up with, "Now."

She giggles behind me, wrapping her arm around mine as we climb the staircase leading up to my bedroom. The bag she brought with her, holding her wallet and camera, hangs from her shoulder when we step into my bedroom.

I kneel on the floor, unhooking the strap of her shoes and helping her step out of them.

She sighs, wiggling her toes on the carpet while I do the same to the other foot.

"I got some good photos of you guys playing during your performance tonight."

"Oh yeah?"

She nods, unzipping the bag to pull out her camera. She turns it on and pushes some buttons to scroll through the pictures.

I push myself to stand, looking over her shoulder at the ones she snapped of us.

"Those turned out amazing."

She has an incredible talent. Without any edits or retouching, they look like something you'd see straight out of a magazine. She continuously impresses me.

"I'll print them when I'm back home and give them to you the next time I see you."

My chest warms at the mention of the next time we'll be together. I hope this means she sees more between us too.

"I guess that's good you're already thinking about the next time."

She turns, looking up at me, and nods. "Aren't you?"

"Oh, I am, but I'm also thinking about all the ways I could have you tonight while you're here too."

I take the camera from her and set it on the bed. I grip her chin between my fingers and lift her mouth to mine. She moans, her lips vibrating against mine when I deepen it.

My dick strains against my zipper, where it has been all night since she came out wearing that sinful-as-hell dress.

The bright blue matches the color of her ocean-blue eyes, and something about the sight when she stares up at me makes me think about how badly I want to see her look up beneath those long lashes when she's on her knees for me.

I slide my hands over her cheeks to push her hair back, tugging gently on the strands, and her moan turns into more of a low throaty groan.

She pulls back, fluttering her lashes, and whispers my name.

"Get on your knees for me, Brielle."

Her breath hitches, and she nods slowly. I drop my hands to my side, watching her kneel for me, and dear God, seeing her like this weakens my knees.

Submissive. Compliant.

Mine.

I reach for the button on my pants, dragging the zipper down slowly, and her eyes burn into my hands as she studies me.

My dick is hard. When I tighten my fist, pumping it once, then twice, she quickly darts her tongue over her lips like she's priming them for when I slip into her warm mouth.

"Brielle," I command, and she lifts her eyes to meet mine. "I want to fuck your sweet mouth just like I will your pussy."

Her breath grows heavy, and she nods.

"I want to watch tears form in your eyes and stream down your beautiful face."

She darts her hands out to grip my thighs. I can't help but groan when she complies by swiping her tongue over the tip. She hums in appreciation, dropping her mouth open and waiting.

She's tempting me, and I love it.

"Look at me," I order, and she obeys as I slide my dick into her mouth.

I roll my eyes closed, pushing my hips forward to thrust deep.

"Oh fuckkkk," I mutter, forcing my eyes open to watch her.

I slide my fingers into her hair, pushing the strands away from her face, and she moans again.

When she reaches her hand up to touch my balls, I lock my knees to keep them from buckling beneath me.

"You like fuckin' teasing me, don't you, Brielle?"

Her eyes glisten as she watches me, saying without words exactly what I know to be true. Even when she was trying to fight it, keeping me at arm's length, we both know she wanted this.

"Do you like having your lips wrapped around my dick, baby?" I ask, grabbing the camera from the end of the bed.

Her eyes flutter, and I thrust forward. She gags, and I murmur for her to relax her throat.

She breathes through her nose, taking me deeper. She struggles through each stroke, tears forming in her eyes.

I turn on the camera and aim the frame at her. Fuck, I swear nothing is more perfect than the sight of her on her knees for me.

"You look so fuckin' beautiful with my dick in your mouth."

Tears stream down her face as I piston my hips back into her and moan her name. When she reaches her hand up to cup my balls again, it takes everything in me not to stop where we're at and order her onto the bed.

With one hand in her hair and the other focusing the camera on her face, I thrust deep into her mouth.

The sound of her gagging, her eyes staring up at me, and the clicks of the camera snapping photos of her while she takes me hard and fast push me to the edge.

All I keep thinking about is her leaving me to go home to New York, taking the camera back with her, and she's left with photos of us tonight.

I imagine her lying alone in her bed, staring at the pictures while she brushes her finger over her clit, getting off at the thought of us together.

I put the camera back on the bed and chase my release, my hips moving faster.

"Take me, baby," I mutter. "Oh God, you feel so good."

She digs her fingers into my thighs, and I push her hair away from her face as spit slides down her cheek, mixing with her tears.

"I'm gonna come, baby. Fuck me, you feel so good."

When I move to pull out, she tightens her grip on my thighs to stop me.

"You want me to come in that sweet mouth?"

She moans around me, and the words are no more out of my mouth before I do. She tightens her fist around the base of my dick, flicking her tongue against the tip, enjoying every last drop.

"What have I done to you?"

I stare down at her, and she tilts her head back and grins.

"Ruined me for all others."

CHAPTER EIGHTEEN

MADDEN

When I found out Brielle could make it for the album release party, I wanted to find time to do something special for her.

On our first date at Granite, I told her about life growing up in Carolina Beach and how I wanted to raise a family here too. She still has it in her mind we're from two different worlds. It was her attempt to, once again, write off any chance we could be together.

I wanted to give her a taste of what life here could be like.

"You ready, baby?" I ask, leaning against the doorframe next to the bathroom. She hasn't come out since she finished showering. It's hard to hear what she's doing in there with the soft sound of music playing.

I told her to pack something casual, so when she pushed me out the door with her towel on, scolding me for thinking I could sneak a peek while she got dressed, I had no idea what to expect.

"Yeahhh..." The words echo around the bathroom.

I take a seat on the end of the bed, waiting for her to come out.

It takes a few minutes before the door handle turns and opens. My eyes widen at the sight of her in a black tank top and distressed denim jeans dipping low on her hips with her strappy high heels.

"You said casual, and this is about as casual as I get." She smirks.

I reach for her hand, tugging her into my arms, and I'm hit with the floral smell of her perfume mixed with her shampoo. I close my eyes, pressing my mouth against her temple, fighting like hell against the emotions having her here evoke in me.

I'm not ready for her to leave tomorrow, and I'm struggling to come up with reasons to convince her to stay.

"Where are we going?" she asks, leaning back to study my face.

I tuck a strand of hair behind her ear and lift her mouth to mine.

"You'll see," I whisper, linking our hands together and leading her out of the bedroom.

She forgets her purse, and I convince her to leave it here, reassuring her she'll only need to bring her ID and phone. I'm expecting she'll want to snap a few photos when she sees where we're going.

When we step outside and she spots my motorcycle parked out front, her mouth drops open, and she stares wide-eyed at me.

"This is what we're taking to dinner?"

I grin, watching the slow smile stretch across her face.

"I've never ridden on a motorcycle before," she admits.

Now it's my chance to stare at her in shock. "You serious?"

She smirks and nods. "You seem to forget that my family isn't exactly the type to go riding, and the only man I've ever dated went to law school at Columbia. His idea of dressing casual is dress pants and a polo, and that's pushing it."

I bark out a laugh and tug her into my arms.

"Well, then, what the hell are you doin' with me?"

She answers by grabbing the back of my neck and yanking me down, crashing my lips on hers. I moan, gripping her hips, her body molding against mine.

"More like what the hell was I ever doing with him?" she whispers when she leans away.

I crack a grin. "Mmm, that's what I thought."

I eye her as she struts down the stairs, circling the motorcycle to check it out. She studies me when I hold up the helmet, smiling as she lets me do the honors of strapping it on.

When I swing my leg over the bike and hit the kickstand, nodding for her to join me, she cups my face in her hands.

I've seen the look in her eyes she's giving me.

"Brielle," I warn, holding my hand out to her to help her on, but not before she kisses me again.

She carefully steps on the footrest and climbs on behind me. When I start the motorcycle, she giggles and wraps her arms around my waist, her hands roaming up to my chest and back down.

She's not going to make this easy on me.

I grip her thigh, squeezing it, cautioning her to be careful. I don't need her wandering hands distracting me, even if I love every minute of it.

"Wow," Brielle mumbles when I cut the engine, pulling up outside of Breaking Waves. "I thought the view from my apartment was incredible, but all the high-rise buildings have me missing the best part."

The sun has started to set, turning the sky a mix of blue, yellow, and orange. The water glistens as waves crash along the shoreline and the scent of sea salt lingers in the air. The weather is warmer, but nothing like the heat of the summer.

It's a nostalgic feeling being here again after so long.

The crowd along the beach and the boardwalk has started to thin out.

"What is this place?" she asks, stepping off the back of the bike to gaze out onto the beach, then over to Breaking Waves.

"We used to come down here all the time when we were younger. We tried one summer to give surfing a strong go before realizing we weren't cut out for it and decided to stick to music instead."

She giggles, and I reach for her hand, guiding her to the patio along the back of the surf shop, down the stairs leading to the dock. Two boats are parked in the marina, but other than that, not a soul is in sight.

Brielle studies me when we get to the end of the dock, and I kneel, urging her to take a seat between my legs. She never lets go of my hand until she reclines against my chest, and I wrap my arms around her.

We sit there for a while, talking about trips she's taken with her friend Serena, including one up to the Hamptons. It was her first time ever driving a jet ski. We listen as the waves roll in and watch the boats moving past.

"It's crazy to think we'll be heading on tour again in a month," I mutter against her temple.

"Are you getting excited?"

I lean in, pressing my face against the side of her head, thinking about what it would be like to bring her with me on the road.

"I'm pumped. A lot has changed since our tour last year. I'm just excited to get on stage and play new music."

"I bought a ticket for your show in New York," she says, and I slip my arm around her, pulling her against my chest.

"You did?" I roll back, and she follows with me, bursting into a fit of giggles.

She turns, climbing up to straddle my lap. Her hair hangs over us, and she grins.

"I sure did." Her smile beams. "I guess I wanted to see what the fuss is all about."

"Is that right?" I circle my arm around her waist and turn her over, pinning her against the dock.

When I lean in close to her face, rubbing my facial hair over her cheek, she fights to get away before I mutter a low tsk in her ear.

"You think I'm gonna let you go anywhere? Not a chance." I grip her wrists, leaning over her and tempting her with a kiss.

She lifts her head, trying to meet me halfway, and huffs when I pull back.

"Oh, so you're gonna tease me now?" She narrows her eyes.

We both freeze when my phone starts ringing, blaring one of our songs. I reach into my pocket, not bothering to see who it is, and send the call to voicemail.

"Now, where were we?"

"You were getting ready to kiss me." She snickers.

I lean in until my ringing phone once again interrupts.

Very few people know my number and even fewer would be calling me right now.

I slip my phone out, this time checking the screen to see it's Abel. A knot twists in my stomach, knowing whatever it is, it can't be good.

"Yeah?" I answer, bypassing the greeting.

"About time you fuckin' answer."

"What's going on?"

"I need you to get back to your place as quick as you can."

"Why?" My stomach drops.

"There's been an incident." He pauses. "Someone tried breaking into your house."

I push myself off Brielle, and she follows me, concern on her face likely judging by my tone.

"All right, we'll leave right now. I should be there in five, maybe ten minutes."

I end the call and turn back to Brielle.

"I'm sorry to do this tonight of all nights. Abel said someone tried breaking into my place."

I rub my fingers over my forehead. Brielle doesn't hesitate, immediately climbing to her feet. She presses her palm against my chest.

"Whatever it is, it'll all be okay."

I slip my hand in hers and lead us back to the stairway we came down earlier to my motorcycle.

A police car is parked out front when we pull up. Abel stands stoically, his arms crossed with his brow furrowed while he talks intently with the officer.

"The security company alerted me when the alarm went off, and I got over here as quick as I could."

I jog up the stairs to meet them, Brielle following me.

"What the fuck happened?"

"We have it on surveillance someone attempting to break into the property through one of the large windows toward the back of your home. One of your patio chairs was used to bust through the window," the officer says.

Abel glances at the ground, a grim look on his face. There's more, but he's letting the officer finish before he interjects.

"Do you know who it is? If we can see them on the camera, certainly we should be able to get a good look at them, right?" I question.

Abel shakes his head.

"What do you mean no? I pay for one of the best security systems money can buy, and you're telling me we can't figure out who the fucker is?"

"It's a man, that much we know," Abel clarifies. "He's dressed in all black and is wearing a ski mask. We couldn't get a look at his face."

I drag my hands through my hair. "Un-fuckin'-believable!"

Brielle caresses my back, attempting to calm me down. When I drop my arms and turn toward her, the concern on her face eases the tension some.

I squeeze her fingers in mine, turning back to Abel.

"What else? There's something else you're not telling me, so spill it."

"Well, the window is broken, but it can be replaced. They got into the house, though, and into your studio."

"No." I shake my head. "You've gotta be fuckin' kidding me. Please tell me they didn't destroy anything."

"The drums are a loss, and the two guitars are destroyed. There's a massive hole in the wall, but other than that, everything else can be fixed."

Other than that... like they didn't come in and ruin the one room in the house I give a shit about.

I start to pace along the patio. Brielle steps in front of me and wraps her arms around my waist to soothe me.

"Hey, hey," she mutters, trying to get through to me.

My mind races, and my body is alive with adrenaline. I wish I knew who it was so I could find them.

I tighten my arms around her, burying my face into her neck.

"I'm sorry this happened tonight," I whisper into her ear.

She shakes her head. "No, don't do that. This isn't your fault. I would've wanted to be here with you through this anyway."

"I'll take care of filing the police report and will figure out covering the window, all right?" Abel reassures me. "I'll let you know if I need you for anything."

The equipment, the window, all the damages—it can all be replaced. It's going to cost thousands of dollars, but it's more so what it represents and the principle of it all.

Brielle slips her hand in mine and nods toward the door. "C'mon, let's get inside."

She leads me into the kitchen, where she insists on finding something to cook for dinner for the two of us.

I cross my arms over my chest and lean against the counter, watching her browse through the cupboards and fridge to see what we have to work with.

"Do you have any idea who it could be?" she whispers.

"Not a single clue."

I'm so frustrated. I don't have the energy to go see the damage. I'll do it eventually, but just knowing they went into our studio where we practice and keep all our band equipment pisses me off.

I'm trying not to let my temper get the best of me with Brielle here, but this would be the time I'd sit behind my drums and let out some steam.

Thankfully, I have another set in my music room. It's a smaller space, away from our recording studio. This feels personal, though, knowing they damaged not only my drums but Tysin's and Trey's guitars too.

Brielle crosses the kitchen and loosens my arms, stepping between my legs, and I lean into her body, soaking in the warmth of her skin against mine.

She smells like flowers and the scent of sea salt lingers in her hair.

I kiss her neck and trail my lips up to her ear. "I'm glad you're here with me right now because I think I would've handled this differently if you hadn't been."

She leans back. "Handle it how?"

I shake my head. "I don't know. Sometimes I want to shut down when shit gets to me, but with you here, I don't want to be that way. I'm trying not to push you away."

She folds her hand against my cheek, pulling me down to kiss her.

"Promise me you won't when I leave tomorrow either," she whispers.

"I promise," I murmur, kissing her again. "The last thing I want is to push you away."

CHAPTER NINETEEN

BRIELLE

"I hate that you're leaving like this..." Madden's voice trails off.

He leans forward, tilting his forehead to mine. His large hands are pressed against the small of my back.

We were both on edge last night, making it hard for us to fall asleep, but when I'm standing here with him, and his arms are around me, I feel safe.

I hated I was leaving like this too.

"Tell me I won't have to wait long until I get to see you again," he whispers against my mouth.

I nod. It's the elephant in the room.

Yesterday was our second date. After we spent this weekend together, the topic of where we go from here has weighed heavily on my mind.

I have a whole life back in New York. A new job I love and my friends and family. Madden has his life here in Carolina Beach with the guys. When he's not here, he's traveling from city to city playing music.

We are from two different worlds, and as much as I love being here with him, I'm finding it hard to figure out how we fit together.

What terrifies me, even more, is the feelings growing between us are unlike anything I've felt before. They don't even compare to what I had with Mitchell.

"I guess that means I'll see you soon?" I say, the statement coming out more like a question.

I pull back to flick my eyes up to his, and he nods, gripping my chin and kissing me hard. The move is possessive and all-consuming. I hold his forearms to prevent my knees going weak from the heady combination of his lips on mine and the light scent of his aftershave left over from last night.

It took everything in me to break the kiss and reach for my suitcase to walk away. I think on some level, a part of me worries this would be it for us.

The article is out into the world, and nothing ties him to me.

He has nothing left to be worried about now.

I turn back to him one last time. He's leaning against the side of his car, watching me. His face is hard and emotionless until he notices me looking back, and it softens. I lift my fingers to my mouth and blow him one last kiss goodbye.

The flight back to New York went by quickly. I slept for most of it. I needed it a lot more than I thought I would.

Note to self: don't book your returning flight home early in the morning and expect to return to work as soon as you land. I had enough time to make a stop home before I turned around to head into the office.

Thankfully, most of my day was open, all I planned to do was get through my emails from the weekend and start preparing for my next article. I almost hoped it would be busy to keep my mind off wishing I were back in Carolina Beach.

Madden might not have come out and said it, but he spent as much time as he could introducing me to his life. The longer I spend there, the more I understand why he never wants to leave.

My phone rings when I step into my apartment. It's Serena, and when I answer, she bypasses the greeting, jumping right into things.

"I'm so happy you're finally home. I have so much to tell you," she squeals.

She was talking all last week about a date she had this weekend, and I know she's been biting her nails to hear about how my trip went too.

"How did the date go?"

I pop the top of the wine bottle I opened last week and pour myself a glass.

"Amazing. Not only does he have a set of perfectly skilled fingers that know how to hit all the right places"—she giggles—"but he took me out to dinner and was a perfect gentleman the whole time."

"Then how do you know about his skilled fingers?"

"Well, I may have had one too many glasses of wine with dinner and told him I wanted to go home with him."

I toss back my head to laugh. "If there's one thing you are, it's forward."

"Probably not the best way to find a husband, but I think it worked. We'll see when he takes me for date number two tomorrow night."

The line beeps, and I check to see my father calling in. I wince, knowing I can't keep putting this conversation off.

He's called me several times over the past few days. The first time I told him I was busy and would have to get back to him. The other two calls were bad timing.

I already know where the conversation is going to go, and the last thing I wanted was to have it while I was in Carolina Beach.

"Helloooo?" Serena sings. "Are you still there?"

I snap out of it. "Sorry, I'm gonna have to call you back."

"What? You didn't even tell me about your trip. I need to hear all the juicy details about you with your man."

I run my fingers over my forehead, massaging the skin.

"It's my father. He's been trying to get ahold of me."

"Ooh."

I don't have to explain it further. She gets it.

"Well, call me right back. I need to hear about the rock god and his skilled fingers too."

I slap my hand over my mouth to contain my laughter and end the call, reassuring her she'll hear from me after I eat dinner.

By the time we hang up, my father was sent to my voicemail. A notification pops up, but I ignore it, and instead redial to call him back.

"I was starting to think I was going to have to show up at your place again."

I roll my eyes. "Let's not make a habit out of that, okay?"

"Well, it's great to hear from you too, sweetheart. I've missed you."

"I'm sorry, I was out of town visiting a friend, and it wasn't a good time when you called before."

I lift my glass of wine to my mouth, sauntering into my living room and climbing onto the couch. The sunset turns the sky into a swirled mixture of pinks, oranges, and yellows in the distance beyond all the tall buildings.

"A friend? Is this the same friend I met who was also photographed with some blondie at the Grammy's last week?"

So he has been keeping tabs on him? What the hell?

"That's the one." I wince.

"What's going on between the two of you? Are you seeing each
other, and if so, why didn't you go with him and not her?"

I can practically feel my forehead pulsating with the headache
coming on. I'm not ready to answer all these questions when I
don't even know some of the answers myself.

"Like I said, Daddy, we're just friends."

He sighs. I picture him sitting behind his large oak desk in his
office, rocking back while he taps his finger, mentally shuffling
through all the questions he's been meaning to ask me.

"Is this why you called me, to ask me about my relationships,
or is there something you wanted to talk about?"

The line goes silent, and I wonder for a moment if he hung up.

"I'm just trying to catch up with my daughter. We've missed
you coming around on Sundays for dinner, you know. Is it so bad
stopping by to see us, even for a couple of hours?"

Guilt coils in my stomach, but I shake myself out of those
thoughts. How am I going to take the blame for not coming
around when growing up, I was left alone all the time while he
busted his ass working?

Why is it bad for me to have my own life when he's been busy
building his for so long?

"I've just been busy." I sigh. "You know how it is, don't you?
You've raised me to be this strong, independent woman. It
shouldn't come as a surprise when I'm off focusing on my career
and my relationships too."

He clears his throat. I start to wonder if I shouldn't have said
anything at all, but it's the truth.

"Is it because I've been pressuring you to come work for us at Granite? Am I pushing you away?"

It's not often I see or hear this side of my father, but the crack in his voice tells me this is a question he's been holding, as if fearing the truth.

I haven't been forthcoming about what I'm doing for work, but this is one area where I refuse to hold back from him.

"Yes."

He exhales a heavy breath, and I hear the familiar creaking sound of his chair as he moves to stand. I don't doubt it's to start pacing back and forth across his office.

"How would you feel if your dad looked down his nose at you for following your passion? What would you have done if he tried to convince you not to start Granite Industries?"

"He did."

"Well, and... I think it's safe to say you didn't listen to him, did you? It didn't stop you from following your own passions and dreams."

He sighs. "I'm just trying to take care of you. I've built this company from the ground up, and I want to know when I step away, I'm leaving it in smart, capable hands."

"You have Broderick and Brecken."

"I always envisioned it being the three of you. You're like your mother, the compassionate and sensible one. You always look at things from every angle and consider every possible thing that could go wrong."

I want to tell him that it's years of overthinking myself sick that have helped with this skill, but I don't bother going down that road.

"I understand, but it's your dream. It's what you've wanted. I'm sorry, but it's not mine."

The silence that follows speaks loudly. I take another large drink of my wine, finishing off my glass.

"So writing, huh? That's your dream? What you want to do?"

"You know, sometimes I still feel like I'm figuring it out, but I'm happy where I am and with what I'm doing." This is my chance to tell him. "I started a job at *Limelight* magazine a month ago, and I'm letting life take me wherever it goes. It's giving me a chance to tap back into photography again too."

Growing up, I was in the class newspaper and helped with the school yearbook. Those were my first tastes of writing outside of short stories and poetry I had written, anything that would give me a creative outlet.

"You know, I don't tell you this enough, but I'm proud of you for going after what you want and not giving in."

"Dad..." My voice trails off.

"I know, I know, and I'm not just saying it now. I should've told you this a long time ago. I'm proud of you, and I'm sorry I didn't tell you enough."

"You're telling me now, and that's all that matters."

We get to talking about my job, and I share how my first assignment went interviewing A Rebels Havoc. I don't notice how much time has passed, but eventually, I get up to start cooking myself dinner. I'm relieved some of the nervous energy I've been holding about this call seems to have released before we hang up.

He asks me to stop by to visit soon, and I make a promise to come out for family dinner one of the upcoming weekends. I still don't know when I'll see Madden again, if I'll be flying out to him or if he'll be able to make it here.

I don't want to be away from him much longer either.

CHAPTER TWENTY

MADDEN

I've been on edge the past few days, and the only thing that's helped keep me sane are my drums.

I'm thankful I have another set or I'd probably be going out of my mind.

Squeezing my eyes closed, I let the energy reverberate through my body. Sweat drips from my brow, the audio plays back through my headphones, and I get lost in the music.

When the song ends, I reach for my water bottle and unscrew the cap, glancing up to find Abel standing across the room. He leans against the doorway, watching me, waiting for me to stop.

"What's up?"

He nods. "I don't want to interrupt you, but we have some shit going on again."

"What?" I ask, my body tensing.

"It's Hanna. I caught her outside about twenty minutes ago."

My brows knit together. "What do you mean you caught her?"

"She was on the back of the property, walking along the lower level. It looked like she was trying to peek inside the window. What she was looking for, though, I have no clue."

What the hell?

What could she possibly want? I thought after our conversation at the album release party, she'd get the hint to leave me alone.

You're going to regret this, Madden. I promise you'll regret hurting me.

"Did you ask her?"

He nods. "She didn't say anything and took off running back to her car. I couldn't tell for sure, the windows were too dark, but I think someone was inside with her."

"Are you serious?"

I set my sticks on my drums. Pushing myself to stand, I use my T-shirt sleeve to wipe the sweat dripping down my face.

"All right, thanks for letting me know. I'll talk to her."

"I think you should be careful, man. Somethin's not right with that girl."

My brows deepen in question, and he shrugs.

"I don't know. I can't describe it, but something about the look in her eye gave me a weird vibe. I don't think she's thinkin' straight, and I'd hate for you to get stuck in her crosshairs."

I nod. "Got it," I grit, stalking past him upstairs.

I'm on a mission, heading straight for the bathroom to shower. If Hanna still hasn't listened, it looks like I'm going to have to take matters into my own hands and go talk to her again.

We need to get to the bottom of this, and I wasn't going to let her come around snooping through my shit. Not after the window and our studio were damaged.

We still haven't figured out who it was or why they took it this far. What we were able to get from the video footage, it wasn't

Hanna. The figure was dressed in all black and was built like a male.

After I get cleaned up and dressed, I climb into my Acura and pull out of my garage, gunning it as I head down the long driveway. The gate opens as soon as I'm near, and I floor it when I hit the highway leading into Carolina Beach.

I love living on the outskirts of town. It is quiet, away from people, and it gives me the space and peace I enjoy.

The drive into town took a few minutes before I pull up outside Hanna's place.

She stands in the doorway when I park along the street in front of her quaint little house, as if she was expecting me all along. It's almost like this is what she wanted.

Well, I'm here now, so she can get to the bottom of what the hell is going on.

She tucks a strand of hair behind her ear and pushes the screen door open, jogging down the front steps. She's dressed in black denim shorts and a red tank top with sandals.

Tattoos cover her right leg, spanning from her ankle and disappearing beneath her shorts.

I roll down the window and nod for her to get in.

She bites down on the edge of her lip, fighting off a grin, and I roll my head from side to side, knowing I'm playing right into her hands. She's getting on my last nerve, and she's about to hear about it too.

When she climbs in next to me and shuts the door, I roll up the window.

Her eyes flick over to mine.

"You want to tell me what the fuck is goin' on?" I snap.

"What are you talking about?" Her brow furrows.

Is she kidding me? What else would I be talking about?

"Abel said he caught you on my property earlier. When he tried to talk to you, you took off. What the hell, Hanna?"

"I was looking for you. We need to talk, and you stopped responding to my messages."

I exhale a heavy breath, trying to remind myself to stay calm.

"I heard your little girlfriend left town."

"Hanna…" I warn.

She holds up her hand. "I'm just saying. If she's gone, what's wrong with us spending time together again?"

"What's wrong with it? I told you it's over. There is no us. That's the point."

She huffs, crossing her arms over her chest. "I'm sick of you saying that, Madden, when it's not true. You act like I have no right to be upset. One second, we're together, then the next, she comes into town, and you act like I don't exist anymore."

"How many times do I have to tell you, we were never together?"

She shakes her head. "You're wrong."

"I am?"

She nods her head, pursing her lips while she narrows her gaze on me.

"Besides, I have something else I've been needing to tell you."

The way her voice changes, the crack in her throat, has me on high alert.

"What then? Spit it out, so I can get the fuck out of here."

"I'm pregnant."

My mouth drops open. "I'm sorry, what?"

She nods. "I just found out last week. I've been trying to tell you, but every time I come around, *she* is around."

I shake my head. This can't be happening.

As much as I want to believe it's true, too much isn't adding up. I hate to think she'd use a baby as a ploy to convince me to be with her.

I've always thought Hanna was calculated. Every step she makes is methodical. We grew up together, went to the same high school, and ran with the same crowd.

She wasn't from the music industry and wasn't tarnished by fame. I thought that meant I could trust her, and maybe she wasn't after me for my money.

"Well, congratulations, Hanna, but forgive me when I say I won't believe it until I get a paternity test confirming it's mine."

"What?" she screeches, turning in her seat to look at me. Her jaw clenches, and she's practically shooting daggers my way.

I squeeze the steering wheel until my knuckles turn white and shake my head.

"It's not, and we both know it. I don't know what you're trying to do right now, but it won't work."

I shift the car into drive, revving the engine.

"What are you doing?"

"I'm leaving. You need to get out."

"You're making a mistake, Madden."

"You keep saying this, but the only mistakes I've made are coming here and messing around with you."

She quickly blinks her eyes, fighting off the forming tears.

"You don't mean it," she grits. "Take it back."

"Please get out." She reaches for the door handle before I stop her. "I'm going to say this to you one last time. Please leave me alone. I'll be in touch with my lawyers and we'll figure out arranging the paternity test."

The tears she was holding back give way, streaming down her face. I swallow past the ball of guilt forming in my throat, knowing if I give her any sign of sympathy, she'll twist it to mean something else.

I wait until she's back on the sidewalk before I gun it down the road.

I should've known better than to come here. What the hell was I thinking?

The entire way back to my house, all I can think about is how I'm going to break this to Brielle.

I should've ordered Hanna to show me some sort of proof. I can't explain it, other than the feeling in my gut, but I don't believe she's pregnant for a second.

There's no foolproof way of preventing pregnancy, but the few times we were together, I wore protection, and she told me she was on birth control.

My phone rings. It's connected to my car Bluetooth, cutting off my music. I jam the button on my steering wheel to answer the call.

"Hi," I say dejectedly.

I hadn't paid attention to my tone before, but now that I'm talking to Brielle, I'm keenly aware of the growl in my voice.

"What's wrong?" she asks, picking up on it right away.

I turn into my drive, and the gate slowly opens. It's not until I see it close behind me that I exhale a low sigh and shake my head.

"Nothing. Everything. I don't even know."

"Madden, what does that mean? What happened?"

I pull into the garage and cut the engine, leaning against the headrest and squeezing my eyes shut.

"I need you here," I say, the words hitting me in the chest.

She's quiet, likely picking up on the emotion.

Her voice lowers, and she whispers, "I wish I could be there. You know if I could be, I would."

I nod even though she can't see me.

"Yeah… I know."

We both sit in silence.

"This isn't about me being gone, is it? Is it the window? Or did something else happen?"

I shake my head. How am I supposed to tell her all this with her hundreds of miles away from me? If I do, she could disappear, and I'd never see her again.

She's already sent me the article. Her job with me is done. She could decide this is too much for her, cut her losses, and dip out without another word.

She doesn't owe me anything more. Lord knows, with all the drama, I've done enough.

"There's so much I need to tell you, but not like this. Soon, just not right now."

"Okay…" She trails off.

"Brielle," I croak.

"Yes?"

"I…" I trail off.

How do I say this to her? How do I possibly tell her how much she means to me and convince her not to leave me without telling her everything?

"Madden, whatever it is, we'll get through it. Okay? We'll figure it out. You and me. We'll get through anything."

I squeeze my eyes shut, rubbing my fingers over them. I'm trying to keep control of my emotions, but she can't possibly understand how much I need to hear this right now.

"You mean it?"

She sighs. "Of course, I mean it."

"I need you to come to me. I know it sounds selfish, and I'm sorry. I understand if you can't right away. I get you have work and other more important shit, but I just need you here."

"I don't know how soon I'll be able to leave. I'll talk to my boss tomorrow, and I'll let you know. I'll be on the first flight out as soon as I can."

The weight on my chest eases some, and those three words are on the tip of my tongue.

Now isn't the time, though. Not when we have so much to talk about. Not when we still haven't figured out what this is or what we are.

It doesn't matter, though. All that matters is I know I want to be with her.

I love her.

I'll wait, though, wait until she's here and in my arms. When she can see the look on my face and the love in my eyes. I'll tell her, and whatever comes our way, we'll face it head-on together.

"Thank you," I whisper. "I'll be here waiting for you."

CHAPTER TWENTY-ONE

BRIELLE

Two knocks hit the doorframe when I'm at work on Monday morning, and I turn to see Davis standing in the doorway.

"Morning," I grumble, holding my coffee cup to my lips and taking a sip.

"Good morning," he replies, but he lacks his normal, upbeat tone today, which tells me right away something is up.

I quirk my brow, waiting for him to spill whatever he's here to tell me.

"Did you happen to see the article I sent you this morning?"

I shake my head. I came in to over two hundred new emails in my inbox from over the weekend, and I've been mining my way through them.

"It must've gotten mixed in with the others. Why?"

He chews on his lip and nods toward my screen.

"You know, Davis, if you keep coming to my office with things like this, I'm going to start thinking something's wrong every time you show up."

He mumbles, "Sorry," and I set my coffee down, scrolling through my emails to look for the one from him.

I'm already on edge with the way my conversation went yesterday with Madden. Now, adding this to the fire, my anxiety has my heart rate skyrocketing.

The email is nothing but a link, and when I notice the URL directing me to a Hollywood Tea article, I know it can't be good.

MADDEN COLE REPORTEDLY BURSTS INTO A FIT OF RAGE AFTER FINDING OUT HE'S EXPECTING A CHILD WITH EX-FLING HANNA TAYLOR.

The article title stops me in my tracks, and the words, "What the hell," spill out of my mouth before I have a chance to stop them.

I wonder if this is why Madden was upset on the phone.

"Did you know?" Davis asks, and I shake my head, my eyes skimming over the article.

It goes on to explain Madden recently found out about the unexpected pregnancy after a conversation with Hanna. Their inside source shares when she told him, Madden didn't take it well, and in a fit of rage, he threw a chair, breaking.

"It can't be true." I press my hand against my heart, feeling my chest ache. "I think she's lying because this isn't what happened. It's not true."

My eyes flit across the page. The article goes on to say how the outburst left Hanna with injuries to her hand.

Hollywood Tea claims they've reached out to Madden's team, and so far, they have no comment on the incident.

Tears prick my eyes, and I turn to Davis, shaking my head.

"She has to be making it up. This can't be true."

"How do you know?" he questions, quirking his brow.

He already knows about our date from the article they posted about him visiting Granite with an unknown woman. That woman being me. Why hold back now?

"Well, I went to Carolina Beach last weekend to see him. They had their album release party for *Come Hell or Havoc*, and he invited me to stay with him. The next night, we went down to the beach to watch the sunset, and while we were gone, we got a call from security that someone had broken the window at the back of his house.

"I was with him the whole weekend, and I stayed with him when we went back to his house and met with Abel, his security guard, and the police officer. I heard them talk about the video surveillance showing it was a man who came onto his property and how they caught him doing it. She very well might be pregnant, but she's lying about him breaking the window in a fit of rage."

If this doesn't prove she was behind the break-in, I don't know what will.

This isn't the Madden I've gotten to know over the past few weeks. I can't help but feel like this is an attempt to drag his name through the mud. The barrier holding the tears back from spilling over gives way, and they start streaming down my face.

How could she do this to him?

What is her motive behind making up these lies?

I know she wants to be with him, but what's the point of stirring up drama and rumors? Is she trying to get back at him for choosing me that night at Whiskey Barrel?

He'll never be able to trust her now. Anyone who knows Madden knows how much trust and loyalty mean to him.

Going to the tabloids and spreading lies will only push him away more.

Maybe that's what she's trying to do. She doesn't care if she can't have him now. She just wants to hurt him by trying to drive a wedge between us.

I open my file cabinet and dig through my purse in search of my phone.

"Will you give me a few minutes, Davis? Please."

He nods. "Of course. Just know I'm here for you when you're ready to talk. Maybe we can sneak away for lunch. Or you can cut out of here early for the day and go grab us dinner with some wine. Lord knows you'll need it after today."

I nod. He's right; I will.

"I'm in." I force a smile. Davis nods and steps out, shutting the door behind him.

I click on Madden's name, and cross my fingers, praying he'll answer when the sound of his deep throaty voice hits my ears.

"Hi." He sighs.

"I heard," I mutter, not knowing what to say. "I just saw, and I wanted to call to see how you're doing."

"Honestly, I'm hangin' on by a thread."

I grit my teeth and shake my head. I hate thinking Hanna's doing this to get back at him for ending things with her.

"I'm sorry," I murmur. "I know it's not true. The part about you throwing the chair. You'd never do anything like that, not to her. Even if I hadn't been there when it happened, I would know it's not true."

"Yeah..." He trails off.

"I'm sorry I'm not there with you. I wish I could be."

"Soon, though, right?"

I nod, glancing down at the time on the bottom of my computer monitor.

"I still need to meet with my boss. She should be getting in the office any minute now, but I'm hoping to be able to leave as soon as possible."

He exhales a heavy breath. "Okay, sorry for pulling you away again. You just started your job, and you've been busting your ass. I just..."

"Want me there," I finish for him, and he whispers a low, "Yeah."

We end the call, and I agree to call on my lunch break.

As soon as the line disconnects, I push myself to stand and slip out into the hallway, noting Sawyer's office door is open.

She's sleeked her hair back in a high bun, and she's wearing a white dress with a red cardigan. She smiles when she spots me poking my head into her office.

"Brielle, good morning. C'mon in!" She waves me in, nodding for me to take a seat in the chair across from her.

"Good morning," I say, anxiety coiling in my stomach, and I force a smile.

How am I going to say this without telling her about my relationship with Madden? I'm not sure if I'm ready to yet.

"Forgive me for dropping in on you first thing this morning. I hope you don't mind. I've had some personal matters come up, and unfortunately, I need to see about the possibility of working remotely over the next week."

"I'm sorry." Her face falls, a look of sympathy shining through her features. "I hope everything is okay?"

I nod, attempting to reassure her. "It will be. It's just challenging right now when I'm needed somewhere else. I was hoping I could finish off the week working remotely. It would allow me to leave town while I could still work during the day."

"Of course. You're still working on the article for Isla Grace, right? That should be going off to editing early next week. If you need time away, though, I'm certain we can accommodate it too, so long as we get the article submitted in time."

I sigh. "Absolutely. I'll make sure I get it completed. It won't be any worry at all."

She smiles. "Go ahead and do what you need to do to finish up today, and you can take off. Please let me know if I can help you with anything."

I nearly sag in relief, thanking her and reassuring her I'll keep her updated.

Davis is in his office, scrolling on the internet, when I walk by and knock on his door. He glances up to look at me.

"Did you get a chance to talk to him?"

I nod, closing the door behind me.

"I just met with Sawyer, and she's letting me work remotely for the rest of the week. I'm going to fly out to Carolina Beach. Madden asked me to come to him as soon as I could."

His eyes widen. "Does that mean our lunch date is postponed?"

I nod. "For today, but as soon as I'm back, I'll make it up to you."

"That works for me. I have some juicy drama of my own I need to fill you in on anyway."

"I mean, I do have a little time if you want to just spill it now."

Davis smirks and shakes his head. "Nuh-uh, honey. I need something to hold over your head to drag you out with me, and you need to get to your man. It'll have to wait."

I open the door and lean against the frame. I'm about to leave when something stops me.

"Do you ever get burned out of this job when you see lies get spun and innocent people have their name dragged through the headlines?"

His brows deepen. "Of course, I do. Every job you find has bad eggs, though, right? That's why it's important we do this. To prove there are good ones, honorable ones, who aren't going to crumple at the demands of liars or with the enticement of money."

I smile. "You're one of the good ones, Davis."

"Right back at you, babe." He winks.

I head to my office and immediately pull up flights out of New York to North Carolina. The soonest one is this evening. I don't have much time if I have any hope of making it home to pack and getting to the airport on time. They have a few seats left on a direct flight from JFK to Wilmington.

Without thinking, I book the ticket and close my laptop, packing up my things into my bag. I skip taking the train and instead hail a cab outside of *Limelight* to take me to my place. The elevator dings when I reach my apartment, and the first thing I notice when stepping into my place is the dull silence surrounding me.

It's quiet and empty and almost feels cold and sterile.

Every inch of this place is neat and tidy, and that's almost the point. I've spent the past few years working so hard to prove to my father I can make it on my own, without him or his money, and I've accomplished a lot.

What is the point of it all, though?

All of this to prove to him that I'm capable of being an adult. Davis said it perfectly—I won't crumple to his demands or the enticement of money.

Money isn't everything, though. I've seen how it can bring out the ugly side of people. Hell, my father has grinded his entire life, spent every day married to his job.

Sure, he has a certificate of marriage, and in front of my mother and our families, he vowed to love her forever.

Doesn't change the fact that even though she's his wife, his priority has always been Granite Industries.

I take one last look around my apartment, overwhelmed by the emptiness in the quiet space. For the first time since moving here, I don't feel at home in my own place.

With that thought in mind, I climb the stairs to my bedroom and pull out my suitcase. In a few hours, I'm boarding a flight that will take me to the one place I've felt the most at home.

With Madden.

CHAPTER TWENTY-TWO

MADDEN

"Can you believe it?" Kyla bounces on her feet. "Can you believe Leanna is finally here?"

Ivy claps her hands. They haven't been able to contain their excitement since we got the call Layken was in labor.

"I can't wait to see them and hold her. I bet she's so adorable. I'm picturing her with Layken's freckled cheeks and Trey's eyes. Oh gosh, he's gonna be in for it when she gets older. If he thinks he's a sucker for Layken always getting her way, he's in trouble now." Ivy smirks.

"Total sucker," Kyla adds.

The guys all look at each other, rolling our eyes, even though they're right.

The thought alone has me thinking about when I have a child of my own. All the drama going on with Hanna has me shaking my head in frustration. This isn't how I ever thought it would happen.

"How've you been?" Brix asks, clapping me on the shoulder.

I shake my head and sigh. "As best as I can, I guess. I don't even know."

Abel, Kyla, and I all met with a lawyer this morning to discuss the article and paternity. They'll file an order of paternity petition. I hadn't thought it was her behind the break-in at my place, but considering the lies she spun mentioning the window being broken in a fit of rage, it's clear she had something to do with it.

All of this to try and get back at me? I don't get it.

The label had their PR team on the phone with Kyla all morning doing damage control.

I'm growing sick and tired of this shit.

Abel is working with the local authorities to see what leads they have on the break-in. Although we don't have proof, we know who's behind it all. He did manage to get a restraining order in place until we're able to clear my name.

"Don't worry, man. The truth will come out in time, and you know we'll all have your back until it does."

I nod, and he pulls me in for a hug.

Lord knows we've been through enough shit together. Nothing can or will separate us now. We always figure out a way through it, although I wish right now it hadn't come to this.

Trey steps out of the room and nods his head, waving us over.

"Can we all come in?" Ivy asks, looking around. It's clear she's concerned about whether it's okay for the group, not wanting to wait another minute.

"Yeah, sis." Trey chuckles and holds the door open for us.

Layken sits in bed, her hair pulled away from her face, holding what looks to be a little ball in her arms.

"Oh my goodness." Kyla steps in close to her bed, looking down at the two of them. Her eyes soften, flashing up to Trey, and she smiles.

Ivy moves behind her, following suit, and they both gush over how adorable Leanna is.

I'm thankful for the break away from reality for a while. It's the first time in a couple weeks I haven't been anxiously checking my phone, wondering what is being said about us in the media or on social pages.

Kyla had to threaten to take my phone away from me if I didn't stop. She worried about what it was doing to my mental health.

Truth be told, I think I'm growing more and more anxious, wondering what Brielle is thinking. We haven't spoken again since this morning when the latest article dropped. She told me she would talk to her boss about coming to visit, but who knows how soon she'll be able to make it here.

After Kyla and Ivy get their time holding Leanna, I'm able to swindle her out of their arms and take a seat in the rocking chair with her. They take off down to the gift shop, likely going to buy out everything they have for a little girl, leaving me alone with Trey and Layken.

"Sorry I haven't kept in touch much over the past few days. I heard about the news earlier, though," Trey mentions, taking a seat on the edge of the bed next to Layken. "Is it true? Are you going to be welcoming a little one of your own soon?"

I stare down at Leanna, the way her little lip moves to her button nose, and my chest aches. As much as I hate to say it, this isn't how I wanted it to happen, and I hope it's more of Hanna's lies.

"I don't even know what's true anymore." I shrug, bouncing my leg up and down to rock the chair.

"How is Brielle taking it?" Layken asks, tucking a strand of hair falling in front of her face behind her ear.

I shrug. "We haven't talked much about it yet, honestly."

Trey glances over at her and back to me. "Well, if anyone understands the strain this can put on a relationship, it's us. I think all you can do now is talk to each other, focus on the truth between you two, and do your best to shut out all the other noise."

Layken nods. "It's taken me a while to get used to this. Trey too. We both kind of went through it together, considering he hadn't quite experienced the downside of fame since joining the band. If the two of you are serious, and it seems like it is, focus on taking care of you and your relationship. These things will happen, but as long as you can talk to each other and work through them together, you'll be able to get through anything."

"For what it's worth, don't shut her out, either," Trey adds.

Layken playfully swats him on the arm. "Hey, you deserved it, though. Served you right, too. You needed some time to think. We both did."

Trey turns toward me and rolls his eyes, mouthing, "No, I didn't."

I smirk, catching Layken's eyes trained on him. She saw it and managed a roll of the eyes herself.

"I don't know what's going on between us yet since it's still new. We haven't been able to spend much time together with the interview, the album release and press tours, and then our party. It seems like one thing after another after another these days."

They both nod in understanding.

"I do know I want to be with her, though. I want to figure this out, and like you said, for us to get through this together."

"That's all that matters, man." Trey shrugs. "It'll all work itself out, though. I promise. I will admit, for a while, I was worried it wouldn't, but it did."

I end up leaving a little while later, giving Trey and Layken some time together with their daughter. They've had a lot going on lately themselves, and I don't doubt Trey wants time to be with his girls.

I don't bother checking my phone on the drive home. I've been too tempted to see what else is being said about me, and it's just best if I shut it all out right now.

I roll down my windows, turn up my music, and drown out everything. These are some of the simple times I miss. When I could climb into my car and go for a drive, not worrying about who's around and having security tagging along with me.

When I pull up outside my house, I'm still debating if I want to meet up with the guys at Whiskey Barrel later for drinks.

I could use the distraction, but I'm not sure it's the right place for me to be hanging with all the shit swirling around. Even though I have a restraining order against Hanna, I'm still concerned whether she'll even follow the orders.

She hasn't managed to listen once since I ended things with her. What makes me think she'll start now?

I toss my keys on the entryway table near the door, emptying my pocket along with my phone.

"I tried calling you to tell you I was coming, but you never answered or got back to me."

My eyes land on Brielle, standing at the foot of the stairs, smiling at me. For the first time since she left, I return a genuine smile.

The weight and tension in my body eases, and I stalk toward her, slipping my arms under her legs and lift her into my arms. She buries her nose into my neck and releases a soft sigh.

"Jesus, I can't tell you how good it feels to see you again."

"I know," she murmurs, trailing a path of kisses along my jaw up to my ear.

"I've missed you so much," I add.

She pulls back to stare down at me, her eyes flashing to my lips before she crashes her mouth on mine.

I moan, gripping the base of her neck to hold her against me.

There they are again. Those three words on the tip of my tongue.

She holds my face in her hands, and I slowly lower her to the floor.

"I'm sorry I wasn't answering. Trey and Layken had their daughter. I just got back from the hospital."

Her face softens, and she smiles. "That's okay. I don't mind surprising you. Abel was here when I got dropped off and let me in."

"He's been hanging around more. We're all on edge."

It doesn't help matters that I still have a fuckin' hole where my window was. We had to order special glass due to the size, and it won't be here until later in the week.

As much as I want to trust the courts will do their thing and the restraining order will keep her away, I'm not holding my breath. Abel's also looking into adding extra surveillance cameras to all our properties. It's just a reminder you can never be too safe.

I won't be able to breathe easy until I know it's all done.

"How are *you* doing?" she emphasizes, running her hands up my forearms to ease the tension she likely can see I'm carrying with me.

"Better now that you're here."

She smiles. "It was hard being away from you when I could tell in your voice how this shit weighs on you."

I nod. "I know it's your job, and it's what you enjoy doing, but I'll never understand why people like Hollywood Tea get off on spreading lies about people. The truth will come out eventually, but shit like this can destroy people's lives. Their careers. I just"—I shake my head—"I don't get it."

She flicks her eyes away and nods in understanding.

The look on her face says something's on her mind. She'd like to say more, but she doesn't.

"I'm sorry, I shouldn't put it on you. I know it's not you doing this. It's just, man, it's really starting to weigh me down. Ya know?"

"I know," she reassures me. "If anything, I'll do my best to help keep your mind off it while I'm here."

I lift her chin and kiss her again.

"I could use a distraction, and you happen to be my favorite one."

She grins. "Is that right?"

I bite my lip and eye her seductively.

"Don't be shy. Tell me what you have in mind," she urges.

"Mmm," I hum, slipping my fingers into the waistband of her pants and pulling her hips closer to me.

Her breath hitches, and I smile. "Or better yet, how about I show you?"

"Madden." She circles her arms around my neck again, and I lift her into my arms.

"Starting with this chair." I grin, carrying her into the sitting room where we had our interview the first day she was here.

"I remember you in your dress, your hair pinned back perfectly, and that cherry-red lipstick you were wearing. All I could think about was how badly I wanted to hike up that skirt and dirty you up."

I set her down in front of the chair, and she studies me.

"Take off your pants, Brielle. While you're at it, lose the shirt and everything underneath too."

Her cheeks turn a delicious shade of pink, and I grin, watching her fumble while she unbuttons her pants and pushes them, along with her panties, down her legs.

"Jesus," I hum, kneeling on the floor in front of her.

She pauses, her gaze burning into me while she watches me. I reach my hand between her legs, and she spreads them farther apart, giving me better access.

"Fuckk," I mutter. "You're wet for me already."

"Pictures." The word practically stumbles out of her mouth, and my brows shoot up.

"You want me to take your picture?" I stare at her.

She shakes her head. "No, I was saying I was looking at them before you got here."

I'll be damned. "My naughty girl. I'm gonna have fun dirtying you up for me."

She chews on her lip, and I nod for her to take a seat on the chair. She quickly pulls off her shirt and unhooks her bra, adding it to the pile before following my instruction.

Her eyes widen when I push myself to stand, stalking into the entryway to where her bags wait at the foot of the stairs. I noticed the camera she brought with her sitting on top.

I turn toward her, and she smiles when I wave it in my hands and wink.

My dick strains against my pants, and I reach for the button to ease some of the tension.

Her eyes flicking from where my dick presses against the front, up to meet mine, waiting for me to continue.

I press the button to turn the camera on and point the lens at her.

"Spread your legs over the arms of the chair," I order.

Her mouth drops open, looking from me and down to the camera.

"It's my turn, baby." I smirk.

I watch her recline back, spreading her legs open, and release a string of curse words when I get a glimpse of her wet pussy.

I kneel on the floor again, moving closer, and brush my finger over her clit down to swirl around her opening. Her eyes grow hooded, and she tilts her head back.

"Madden," she mutters, staring down at my finger, flicking her gaze between me and my hand.

When I lean in to follow the same path with my tongue, her loud throaty moan echoes around the room.

"Is this what you thought about when looking at those pictures? Were you picturing me with my head between your legs?"

Her chest heaves, struggling to take a deep breath, the need heightened.

"Or were you thinking about kneeling for me, letting me fuck your throat until you had tears in those pretty eyes?"

"You," she stutters. "Anything and everything with you."

I hum, leaning in again to swipe my tongue over her clit.

She drags her nails through my hair, holding me against her while I lick, flick, and suck her clit. Alternating through each one, I keep her guessing which is coming next.

When I pull back, I brush my finger over her clit again. Only this time, I aim the lens at her pussy. I trail my finger down to her opening, slowly pushing one digit inside her while clicking the button to snap pictures while I do.

She moans. "Oh fuck, Madden." She slips her hand between her legs, brushing her fingers over her clit, and I release a groan of my own, quickly snapping more photos.

When I curl my finger, pressing against the bundle of nerves, she thrusts her hips toward me and begs for more.

"Does that feel good, baby?"

She nods lazily, her cum coating my finger every time I slide in and out.

She reaches her other hand between us, gripping my wrist to hold me while the other brushes over her clit. She's close. I can feel it, hear it in her voice, and the way her chest rises and falls.

I've never wanted to claim someone until I tasted her.

CHAPTER TWENTY-THREE

BRIELLE

I've lost track of how long I've been working by the time I lift my head to look away from my laptop screen.

Stepping away from work for one day tends to come back to bite me with what feels like an endless stream of emails. I push the chair back from the dining table and meander into the kitchen in search of something to eat.

When I told Madden about my plan to work remotely for a while, he offered to set me up with an office in one of the rooms in his house. As much as I reveled in the idea of him making me feel more at home, I knew it was only temporary, and I didn't want to bother him by having him set up space for me when I could work from other places without an issue.

I finally pull off my headphones and pick up on the familiar sound of his drum set in the distance. He has a couple sets in his house. One down in his recording studio and another for when he wants to mess around.

I shut the refrigerator and stroll down the hallway toward his music room.

The walls are painted a dark gray with floor-to-ceiling curtains open to let the sunshine flow in. Madden has his headphones on and wears his black Dickies shorts I saw him in earlier.

He doesn't notice me standing in the corner. He's too lost in the music to see me.

The cords of his muscles strain with the force of the beat on his drums. When he finishes his song, he reaches for his T-shirt draped over his thigh and swipes it over his face.

His eyes flick over to me, finally catching me staring. His face is red, and his chest heaves in exertion. Damn, if it's not sexy as hell watching him play.

He moves one of the headphones off his ear, his eyebrow raised in concern. He has no idea I'm too busy trying to calm myself down from getting turned on by looking at him. His mind is in another place entirely.

I hate how on edge everything has made him. Where is the Madden I've gotten to know over the past few weeks?

"Everything all right?" he asks, and I nod.

"Everything is perfect." I smile, crossing the room toward him. "I wrapped up early for the day and was going to make something to eat. I thought I'd see if you were hungry too."

He relaxes when I circle the drum set to stand next to him. He turns to face me, and I cup his cheek, leaning down to kiss him.

His hands grip my hips, pulling me into him, and I take him off guard when I climb onto his lap, straddling him.

"Mmm," he hums. "I could go for something to eat."

I bite my lip to fight off my smile and curl my arms around his neck. He drops his drumsticks between us and pulls me closer until our chests press together.

I softly kiss him, and he moans, his tongue swiping along my lips, seeking entrance. When I open up to him, we both groan, and it takes everything in me not to beg him to carry me upstairs.

His hands slide to my hips and up my sides until he's cupping my breasts.

I need to feel him, for his hands to be all over my body.

I lean back and reach for the hem of my shirt, pulling it over my head and dropping it onto the floor.

He pulls my bra down until my breasts pop free and sucks my nipple into his mouth.

I drag my fingers into his hair and arch my back, the flick of his tongue alternating between sucks has my hips grinding against him, desperately seeking more.

"Tell me what you want," he mutters when he pulls away.

"You."

"Be specific." He smirks. I try to lean back farther, but there's no room.

He picks up his drumstick and brushes the tip over my nipple, causing it to bead before he flicks his tongue over it again.

"Madden," I mutter breathlessly.

He pulls away, flipping the drumsticks between his fingers and stares at me. He's trying to play coy, as if he's unaware of the effects he has on my body with one simple touch.

"Brielle," he counters.

He reaches for the button of my shorts. One of the perks of working from home is getting away with lounging in my denim shorts and a tank top. I kept my cardigan next to me at the table for the times when I had to jump on a video call, but for the most part, I've been able to dress casually.

I move to stand between him and his drums, letting him unzip my shorts and push them down my legs until they fall at my feet.

I climb back on his lap and wrap my arms around his neck, pulling him into me again.

"What about you?" I mumble.

"It can wait."

I shake my head, and he smirks, pushing me to lean back until my shoulders drape across the top of his drum.

My eyes flash to him in a panic. "You'll be fine. I'd never let anything happen to you."

The meaning behind those words with everything that's gone on recently makes me wonder if there's something I don't know.

I try to push those fears out of my mind. That's the point of me coming to see him anyway. For both of us to distract each other and be here together.

There's nowhere else I want to be.

He grips my breast in both of his hands, and I sigh. He's trying like hell to take it slow, but I don't miss the way his eyes keep flicking down to my center.

He slowly traces my nipple with his drumstick, and my stomach quivers when he continues his path. He lifts his thumb to his mouth, wetting it before reaching between us to circle over my clit.

I tilt my head back and release a throaty moan.

"Stop teasing me."

"I'm not teasing you," he growls. "You're just impatient."

"Yes, you are, and you're driving me crazy."

His eyes glimmer, and I can tell he's holding back the urge to laugh. When I reach under his hand to brush over my clit, he pushes me away and sternly mutters my name under his breath.

It's a warning, and damn if I'm not ready to push his buttons right back, like he does mine.

When I snap my hand back to my center again, he grabs my wrist, and his face drops.

"When you're with me, you and your pleasure are for me to give. Do you understand?"

"Madden."

"Do you understand?"

I yank my arm away from him with a huff, and he pulls me until I'm sitting up. He grips my hips, urging me to stand, and turns me around to face his drums. He traces a line up my spine before his voice comes out in a low rumble.

"Bend over," he orders.

I flick my eyes over my shoulder at him before he pushes on my back. He moves my hands to grip the stand next to the drums, giving me more leverage with something to hold.

It's not until he spreads my ass cheeks apart and I feel the warmth of his breath on my most intimate parts that I start to relax. Although it lasts only a second before I feel his finger brush over my clit and dip into my pussy.

I drop my head between my shoulders and moan, forcing myself back, seeking more of him. He digs his fingers into my ass and mutters for me not to move.

He growls, nipping and biting at my flesh.

"Tell me what you want," he grumbles.

"You know what I want," I say, but it comes out more of a whine.

He snickers, and I squeeze my eyes shut in frustration. When he pulls away from me entirely, my body sags in defeat.

"Tell me, Brielle," he retorts, brushing over my ass down to my pussy.

"I want you," I whisper, and it's true.

I've wanted to tell him how I feel. I've been waiting for the right time, but mostly I'm terrified of telling him.

It's true, though. All I want is him, and as much as it scares me to think about him moving on and finding love with someone else, I want him to know how I feel.

"I want you to think of me, begging you to fuck me every time you sit down and play your drums."

In one quick move, he pushes his fingers inside me, and I release a deep throaty moan. I hear the familiar sound of his belt unbuckling, and a small smile curves my lip, knowing I'm finally getting through to him.

There's a hitch in his breath, and I turn my head to find him staring down at where his fingers work me while his other hand grips his hard length. The desire on his face, the sight of his muscles flexing, and his body tense with need only turn me on further.

I rock against him, desperate for him to give me more.

"Brielle," he warns, his eyes flicking up to mine.

"I know what you want, Madden," I mutter, pushing myself up until I stand in front of him.

He doesn't even protest when I drop to my knees, reaching for the waistband of his denim jeans and attempting to jerk them down his legs.

He chuckles, staring down my body when he stands. He sucks in a sharp breath when I wrap my hand around the base of his dick and flick my tongue over the tip.

He drags his fingers into my hair.

"What the hell are you doing to me?" His eyes soften, using his other hand to brush his thumb over my cheek.

I lean into his palm. "I keep asking myself the same question about you."

When I suck the tip into my mouth, he tilts his head back, releasing his grip on me and drags his fingers through his short hair.

He's fighting a war within himself. Does he want to take what he wants from me, or does he want to let me please him?

He drops his hands to his sides, his head rolling down to watch me, and desire burns bright in his eyes. I stare at him from beneath my lashes, sucking him deep into my mouth until I can't take him any farther.

"Do you know how turned on I get looking at those beautiful eyes while you're on your knees with my dick in your mouth?"

I drag my nails up his legs, earning me a low hiss when I gently wrap my hand around his balls.

He gives in now, sliding his hands into my hair. He whispers for me to relax my throat, and I flick my eyes up to him, unable to ignore the desire to touch myself while he thrusts in deeper.

"Fuck, your mouth feels so good," he grunts, falling back onto his stool.

He grips my throat and lifts my chin to kiss me.

I don't wait for his invitation or bother telling him what I want. I quickly climb onto his lap, looping my arm around his neck while I position him at my entrance.

"Madden," I warn.

He tilts his head back, his hooded eyes finding mine.

"Every time you sit here, I want you to think about how good this feels." I roll my eyes closed as I slowly lower myself down his steel length.

He digs his fingers into my hips, his mouth latching onto my nipple, and I release a low moan. I rake my nails over his scalp, grinding and bouncing on his lap.

His hands roam over my body, tweaking my pert bud, stopping when he wraps his palm around my neck. I roll my eyes closed and moan.

"Brielle," he whispers, only the sound of skin slapping and our heavy pants surrounding us. "Look at me."

He brushes his thumb over my chin, and I press my forehead against his while we both chase our release.

"I'm close," I mutter.

I reach my hand down, brushing it over my clit. My body tenses and my vision starts to blur until I hear him whisper those three little words.

"I love you," he murmurs, and it's as if every thought and emotion surge through me.

"Madden," I groan, bucking my hips to increase the tempo.

He growls, his large hands gripping my ass, forcing me down on him.

I'm unable to hold it back anymore. My body trembles and my breath hitches as my release hits me.

I collapse against his chest with my arms and legs wrapped around his body.

He lifts me in his arms, carrying me out of the room and down the hall leading to the stairs up to his bedroom.

"Where are we going?" I whisper, my body limp against him. I don't have an ounce of energy left in me.

"To bed."

It isn't until he sets me down on the edge of his bed that I start to come down from the seductive haze.

"Hey," I say, stopping him when he attempts to step away. "What was that down there?"

He lifts my chin, his eyes staring deeply into mine before they flick down to my mouth. I quickly dart my tongue across my dry lips, resisting the urge to kiss him.

Not until he tells me what that was about downstairs.

Did he mean it when he said he loved me, or was it said in the heat of the moment?

"What?" he asks, distracting me by tracing his finger across my lip, following the same path.

I tilt my head, narrowing my eyes. "You know what I'm talking about."

"Oh, right. That part."

I nod, swallowing hard. I slide back from him, moving to climb up the bed before his large hand wraps around my leg and pulls me to him.

He shakes his head and shrugs. "I guess I just wanted you to know."

My chest seizes.

This man. This sweet, protective, and loyal man. How could I not fall in love with him?

He's nothing like Mitchell. I believe it with all my heart. Even if things end and we go our separate ways, I know he would never do anything to hurt me.

It's not who he is. He may be a grump or stubborn as nails sometimes, but he would never want to hurt the people he cares about.

I drag my hands up his forearms, holding him.

As nervous as it makes me to say this, nothing has ever felt more right either.

"I love you," I whisper.

He grips my chin, forcing my eyes to meet his.

"What'd you say?"

I exhale a deep breath. "I said, I love you," I confess, louder and more confident than before. "I love you, Madden, even if it terrifies me."

His lip curls into a grin, and I resist returning it with a smirk, instead shaking my head. I start to climb up the bed, and he follows me.

He pushes me onto my back, and I giggle. "What are you doing?" I ask.

"Showing you just how much."

CHAPTER TWENTY-FOUR

BRIELLE

I don't even register the first time I hear a bang when I step out of the shower. I drag the towel through my hair, listening closely to see if I can figure out the sound.

I quickly pull on my clothes. Madden left a few minutes before I got in the shower, leaving with Abel to go meet up with his lawyer about the paternity petition and restraining order.

I'm still trying to catch up on sleep. The days after I went home to New York were incredibly hard to get any rest at night. There were nights I'd lain awake and stared out the windows at the lights in the city, trying and failing to fall asleep.

Madden told me he'd be gone a little over an hour before he kissed my forehead.

I check the time on the clock when I hear another loud bang in the distance.

The noise causes my whole body to tense while I frantically search around the mattress for my phone before remembering I left it charging downstairs.

Dammit.

Madden had said yesterday that the replacement window needed to be specially ordered due to the size, and it wouldn't be in until later this week. Maybe the plans changed, though, and they're here early?

I quietly tiptoe across the room to where the door is left cracked open, straining my ears for any indication as to what the noise could've been.

I'm ready to shrug it off when I hear voices in the distance followed by a soft giggle. My body relaxes when I realize it sounds like Kyla. I reach for my cardigan I left on the chair next to the door and pull it on.

I make it to the top of the stairs when I hear muffled whispers followed by someone saying, "Hurry up. We don't have a lot of time."

I pause with my hand on the railing and glance over the side, checking to see if I can figure out who it is. It dawns on me then it's not Kyla at all, but I have a sneaky suspicion I know who it is.

I quickly check over my shoulder, wrestling with myself as to what to do.

My smart watch vibrates with an alarm, reminding me of a video call with Sawyer in thirty minutes. I fumble quickly, pressing buttons to make it stop.

If Abel went with Madden, how did Hanna get in here without setting off the security system?

"He has jewelry in his room. A watch and a gold chain, at least, I'm not sure what else. I'll go check upstairs. One of you finish loading up the guitar and drums. The other needs to go back into his office and figure out how we can get the safe out of here."

My mouth drops open before she rushes down the hallway into the entryway, carrying a large white box. She sets it down near the door, and I quietly step backward away from the staircase, frantically searching for somewhere to hide.

She's going to Madden's room, and I have no way of alerting anyone since my phone is in the kitchen.

There's a bathroom nearby, and I carefully open the door, trying to avoid any unnecessary sounds, and step inside, leaving it cracked so I'm able to hear where she is.

The steps creak as she rushes up them and passes by, heading down the hall toward Madden's room. I wait, what feels like forever, until she's gone, hoping to hurry and slip down the stairs.

As soon as I think the coast is clear, I pull the door open and hold my breath as I take the stairs. I'm not sure if the pounding is coming from somewhere in the house or the beat of my heart hammering in my chest.

I rush into the kitchen and pull my phone off the charger, frantically trying to unlock the screen to dial Madden's number.

"Who the fuck are you?" a man growls from behind me. I twist my arm behind my back to hide it, dropping it onto the counter as I spin around.

I hold my hands up in the air when I hear the muffled voice coming from behind me, thanking God that I managed to click the call button right as he interrupted me.

"I don't live here. I'm just visiting. You don't have to worry about me. Take what you need, whatever you're lookin' for, and go. I won't tell anyone you were here," I say loudly, attempting to cover up Madden.

I cough, pretending to clear my throat, to disguise Madden shouting my name. I press my back against the counter, praying like hell the man doesn't hear him.

He's dressed in a pair of denim jeans that look like they've seen better days and a burgundy T-shirt with a pack of smokes stuffed in the front pocket. There's a hole in the knee of his jeans and dried mud caked along the front. His boots are worn, much like his pants, as if he just got done pulling a long shift at work and came immediately over here after.

He chuckles low, reaching his hand into his back pocket and pulling out a walkie-talkie. He pushes the button on the side and lifts it to his mouth.

"Houston, we have a problem."

I hold my hands up and wave them. "No, you don't. I swear you don't."

His eyes drag down my body, and it dawns on me I'm dressed in a pair of cotton shorts and one of my tank top halters, showing off my stomach. I pull my cardigan around me, attempting to cover myself up.

"Hanna's gonna have a field day when she sees this."

I swallow hard.

"I swear, I won't tell anyone you're here. I promise."

"Like fuckin' hell you won't. I don't believe a word this dumb bitch says," a sweet voice replies from behind me, and my body steels itself. "Well, if it isn't fuckin' blondie who waltzed in here and fucked everything up."

I shake my head, looking between her and back over to the man.

"Whatever you're thinking, I can assure you I never meant to interfere between you and Madden. We're just friends."

She throws her head back and laughs. It's maniacal and terrifying, sending a shiver down my spine.

She's standing near the stove in the kitchen and turns as if she's going to walk out of the room to leave when she leans over across the counter and pulls out one of the knives from the butcherblock.

"You think I'm supposed to believe a damn word that comes out of your mouth?" she asks, waving the knife between the two of us and laughing again.

"Jesus fuckin' Christ, Hanna. Will you calm the hell down? This isn't what we talked about. Put the knife away." The frantic guy charges toward her. "You're fuckin' pregnant. The last thing you need to do is go after her wielding a goddamn knife."

"Hanna, I don't know what you think you know about me, but I promise you I'm not trying to get between you and Madden," I lie. The words are all lies.

I'll tell her whatever she wants to hear if it means I get out of here alive, and right now, I don't trust her to ensure it'll happen.

"Whatever it is you're looking for, whatever you want, you can have it. Okay? You need money? I'll write you a check right now."

She cackles. "You think you can give me what I want?"

She has no idea how much money I have in the bank, which is unfortunate for me, because if she did, she probably wouldn't be reacting that way.

If she doesn't want money, though, what does she want?

There has to be something else, some other reason for her to break in here again.

"What is it you want? What are you looking for? Maybe I know and can help you."

"You think I want your help? You think I want anything from you?"

She charges at me and shoves me against the corner of the granite countertop, and I hunch over, howling in pain.

Madden must hear me on the other end of the line and goes frantic, shouting my name into the phone.

Hanna stops in her tracks, glancing around, picking up on the faint sound of Madden's voice before her eyes land on my phone where I dropped it on the counter.

"No, no, please," I beg, trying to stop her.

She reaches for the phone, lifting it to her ear as she stares at me. Her chest heaves, her breathing coming out in heavy pants, as she turns to glare at me.

"You shouldn't have let the bitch come between us, Madden." Her cynical voice drops low. "Now, it's not just you who will take the brunt of it, but it's her too. It's too bad you're nowhere around to help her."

She laughs again, and the delirious sound will forever be ingrained in my memory.

She smashes the end call button and chucks the phone across the room, shattering the cabinet in the dining room, sending shards of glass clattering onto the floor.

"Now look what you did," she retorts. "You're constantly destroying everything. You had to go and try to call Madden in hopes he'd come in on his white horse and save you. What does he even see in you anyway? You look like an uptight little bitch. Like you could possibly know anything about what a man like him wants, what a man like him needs."

I swallow hard, shaking my head.

I don't know how to answer it because, truthfully, I have no idea what he sees in me.

"We need to hurry up," the man says, stalking across the room. He pulls the curtains away from the window, peering outside, before turning back toward us. "They know we're here, and they're gonna call the cops. It's only a matter of time before they arrive."

"Goddammit." She grits her teeth and shakes her head.

"Go back into his office and try again. There's gotta be a way to get in there. I know it's where he keeps everything locked up."

"We don't have enough time, Hanna. That's what I'm fuckin' telling you." His voice turns sinister, angry.

They're backed into a corner, and there's no way to tell how they'll react.

Hanna paces back and forth in the kitchen. She stops, turning to rest her hands against the edge of the counter. Her head sags between her shoulders in defeat.

"What do you need, Hanna? Is it money? I promise you I have more than enough money if that's what you need. I'll write you a check right now. You can take it and go, and I promise we'll keep it between us."

She lifts her head, her eyes locking on the bouquet Madden surprised me with this morning after telling me he loved me last night.

I grit my teeth, knowing it doesn't matter what I say now when she grabs the card and turns back toward me.

"Friends, huh?"

I clench my jaw when she holds the card up, pointing at the handwritten message.

"You think I'm going to believe a damn word you say to me when you can't even be honest about your relationship?"

A voice comes over the walkie-talkie. "We've got blues comin' in hot a mile away. You need to get out of there. You hear me? You need to get out."

The man lifts the walkie-talkie, presses the button, and mutters, "10-4," before turning back to us.

"I told you, Hanna, we gotta get going."

She flares her nostrils while staring at me and shakes her head.

"All right, I'm right behind you," she mutters as he crosses through the kitchen into the entryway.

She shakes her head, pretending to follow him when she reaches for the vase. I don't even see it coming at first. The flowers spilling onto the floor catches me off guard before I have a chance to lift my hand in an attempt to block her.

When the bottom of the vase slams against my head, all I picture is Madden's face when he walks through the door before everything goes black.

CHAPTER TWENTY-FIVE

MADDEN

I've been on edge since I got the call Brielle was being rushed to the hospital. Abel drove separately and hadn't made it to the meeting yet, so he got back to the house before I did. I've only managed to get a few hours of sleep the past couple of days.

The media was going crazy when word got out about my house getting broken into, and rumors about a woman staying with me being injured. It's only adding fuel to the fire after the article lying about my reaction to Hanna's pregnancy rumor.

After they ran test after test, scan after scan, making sure Brielle didn't suffer any lasting effects, she was sent home with a minor concussion and strict orders to get some rest.

She's been fighting a pounding headache. I'm still struggling to look at her without letting my own anger seep in when I see the goose egg she's sporting on her forehead.

Abel stands near the front door when I jog down the steps after I get out of the shower. He's pacing back and forth, staring down at his phone.

"Everything all right?"

He tenses, locking his phone, and slips it into his pocket. When he notices my eyes narrowing on him, he clenches his jaw.

"Everything's cool, man, I promise."

"It doesn't look like it. I know you better than to think there isn't something more going on."

Abel has become one of my close friends after joining us out on tour. His stint working with us was supposed to end after the tour wrapped up, but then shit went down with Trey and Layken, and he's stuck around to watch over us.

We weren't prepared for all that came along with life in the public eye. I have to admit, it's been nice having him here to help me through all this shit with Hanna.

"Is this about Hanna? Any word on where she disappeared off to?"

Brielle mentioned she was with some guy, but since the video surveillance from when she was here has also turned up missing, we are short on clues as to who it was or what happened.

The police have reassured us, even with Abel and me calling them several times, that they're looking into it and will let us know when they have more information.

It's driving me crazy waiting, wondering where they're at or what else they could end up doing.

"It's not that, man. I swear. It's just shit with my personal life is all."

This is the first time he's ever mentioned his own shit going on, and I feel bad thinking about how much I've leaned on him lately without considering what he's left behind.

"Do you need to take off and head back home? I'm sure we can find someone else to come in and help us out."

He waves me off and shakes his head. He stares down at the floor, running his hand over his beard.

"Nah, it's not anything like that at all. I don't have shit to go home to anymore."

The way he words it clues me there's something deeper goin' on.

"I, uhh, found out my ex got engaged is all." He shrugs. "I guess I wasn't expecting it."

I clap him on the shoulder, and he clenches his jaw, pasting a forced smile on his face.

"I'm sorry to hear it, bro. I truly am."

He shrugs. "I can't even be mad, though. It's my fault it ended, and it sounds like this new guy could give her more than I ever could. I'm happy for her."

I don't believe it for a second, but the pain in his voice doesn't give me the feeling there's anything I could say that could ease the hurt.

"You won't get me to believe that, not even for a second." I attempt to reassure him.

"Thanks, man." He nods. "I talked to Kyla about an hour ago. She told me to tell you she's still working with PR to do damage control. They'll be putting out a public statement at some point today."

I drag my hand over my scalp. As much as I know this is the right step, I hate that we even have to say anything at all.

His phone vibrates, and he pulls it out to check the screen.

"I'm gonna go check on Brielle. Let me know if you hear or need anything."

He nods, answering the call, and I saunter into the kitchen to find Brielle seated at the breakfast bar with her laptop open in front of her.

She's wearing one of my T-shirts and a pair of gray sweatpants, with her hair pulled up out of her face.

"Don't you think you should be curled up on the couch watching a movie or taking a nap?" I ask, leaning against the counter across from her.

I cross my arms over my chest, and her eyes wander down my body, pausing on my arms before meeting mine again.

"I just logged in to try to get some work done. I'm not feeling too bad right now."

"You're supposed to be off work for the rest of the week," I gripe.

She rolls her eyes and shakes her head.

"Excuse me," I grunt, pushing off the counter and rounding the island.

She turns to face me, mimicking my movement to cross her arms, trying to stand her ground.

"Don't you roll your eyes at me," I mutter, gripping her chin before I lean down to kiss her.

"Or what?" she whispers against my mouth. "I thought all the good stuff was off the table until I'm healed."

I clench my jaw. She has a point. I told her we weren't messing around until her symptoms and the bump on her forehead went away.

This has only seemed to spur her to up the ante when it comes to trying to tease and torture me. All morning while we were lying in bed, watching a movie, she kept running her hand over my chest down to the waistband of my shorts.

She'd played innocent when she arched her back and grinded her ass against my dick, pretending it was an accident when I warned her to stop brushing her hand over the front of my shorts.

It didn't stop her from laying into me about not wearing my "dick showin' pants" if I was leaving the house. I told her I was stopping by my lawyer's office. She wasn't the least bit impressed by the thought of me wearing my sweatpants there.

The same ones she later snatched and is now wearing herself before my appointment was rescheduled.

"How about I make you an early dinner, and you take a nap while I run to my meeting?"

She sighs, slipping off the barstool, and wraps her arms around my waist.

"Who would've thought you'd be here taking care of me." She sighs, resting her cheek against my chest.

I run my fingers into her hair at the base of her neck, and she hums in appreciation.

"Of course, I'm gonna take care of you. There's nothing else I'd rather do."

We've had a few conversations over what happened when Hanna broke in. We still don't know what they were looking for or why they were here.

It bothers her she couldn't warn me sooner or try to stop them. They thought the house was empty, and they certainly hadn't expected Brielle to be here.

"I'm not used to this," she whispers. "My parents weren't exactly around growing up. My mom was too busy keeping up with the Joneses, and my dad practically lived at work. I guess I'm just used to taking care of myself or having the people they hired to look after me do it."

"Well, now you have me, and I want to take care of you."

Her face softens, and she nods. "Now I have you."

"What sounds good to you?"

She narrows her eyes, lost in thought. "Do you have soup? I could go for a grilled cheese and tomato basil soup."

"I think I can figure it out." I smirk. "You go upstairs and crawl into bed, and I'll be up with your food when it's ready."

She leans up on her toes, sliding her arms around my neck to pull me closer, and kisses me. When her tongue swipes across my lip, I grunt, breaking the kiss, and step back, shaking my head.

"You're not gonna get one over on me," I quip, earning me a smirk. "Get your sweet ass upstairs."

She huffs, shaking her head and stalks out of the room, leaving me with a grumbled, "You're no fun," under her breath.

I'm relieved to find we have all the fixings for what she asked for. Otherwise, I was going to have to order it for delivery. I fire up the stove and lean against the counter again, pulling up Hollywood Tea on my phone to see what garbage they're spewing now.

There's a doorbell sound, and I glance up, wondering where the noise came from, when I realize it's from Brielle's computer.

I look over to where she left her laptop on the bar and decide to pack up her stuff and bring it upstairs with her dinner, when I spot who the email message is from with my name printed in the subject line.

Why would Brielle be emailing Hollywood Tea?

I glance back down at the list of articles on my phone, each one posted over the past few weeks, several of them spewing more lies and garbage about me and the guys.

I walk through the dining room into the entryway, debating whether I want to go upstairs and ask Brielle about it now before I let my curiosity get the best of me. I stalk into the dining room, staring at the laptop screen before moving the mouse to click on the email.

From: Clive Teller <cteller@hollywoodtea.com>

Date: April 25th, 2022

To: Brielle Silvers <bsilvers@limelightmag.com>

Subject: Madden Cole

Brielle,

Well, well, well... I certainly hadn't expected this email or all the juicy details. You and Madden Cole? Let's just say, you've piqued my interest.

We can meet at Granite on Monday at 3 p.m. Until then, you have my word not to let anything shared hit publication.

Clive

PS – The offer still stands if you ever decide you want to come back to Hollywood Tea. We miss you here.

My eyes read the last line over and over.

The offer still stands if you ever decide you want to come back to Hollywood Tea.

Brielle worked at Hollywood Tea?

I grit my teeth and slam the laptop shut, pacing back and forth in the kitchen until I realize I've left the soup simmering on the stove unattended.

I quickly turn off the burner and set the pan in the sink.

What the hell do I do?

On the one hand, I want to stomp up the stairs, demanding her to explain the email. What juicy details? Why is she meeting him at Granite on the day she's supposed to be flying back to New York?

Most of all, why, after all I've told her about being screwed over in the past, did she not tell me about her history with Hollywood Tea?

I press my fingers into my temples, attempting to massage them to ease the pulsing tension.

She's still recovering from what happened, and the last thing she needs is for me to snap.

I don't even know what to say to her right now.

All I do know is I can't be here with her. I can't face her and try to pretend my heart isn't crushed into a million pieces thinking about her betraying me too.

The guys were right. I shouldn't have opened myself up, I shouldn't have gotten close to her.

How could I let myself fall for someone who only came into my life to use me?

"Madden, everything okay?" Kyla says, when she answers my call.

"No, it's not," I mutter low. "I need you to get over here as quick as you can. Please."

"Shit," she exhales. "Yeah, of course. You got it. I'll leave here in a minute and be right there."

"Thank you," I whisper.

"Madden, are *you* okay?" she asks. She knows I've been on edge with everything going on. "Brielle?"

"Physically, yes."

"Okay, I'll be there in a minute."

I sag in defeat. Betrayal hits hard no matter who it is, but the pain when it's someone you love hurts on a whole other level.

I don't know if I have it in me to look at her to even say goodbye.

CHAPTER TWENTY-SIX

BRIELLE

I don't know how, but somehow with everything that's happened, it's only brought Madden and me closer together.

I ended up crawling into bed and crashing after he sent me upstairs to get some rest. Mentally, I hate being in bed, but physically, I know it's what I need right now.

The light on the nightstand is on, but through the sheer curtains overlooking the backyard, the sun starts to set in the distance. The clock reads after seven.

I push myself up against the headboard and glance around the room.

Madden sent me upstairs with strict orders to relax until he brought me dinner. Somehow, I managed to sleep for three hours, and he never bothered to wake me.

He's been getting on me about resting, though, so maybe he didn't want to wake me when he found me asleep.

I climb out of bed and glance over the balcony looking down into the entryway. The lights are off, and the house is quiet.

It's my first clue something is not okay.

I quickly dart into his bedroom and pick my phone up off the charger. I have a couple of new emails that came through, but no missed calls or text messages.

I decide to head downstairs in search of Madden. I'm telling myself the break-in has my defenses up and I'm on edge, but I can't escape this feeling something's not right.

Tysin sits at the breakfast bar when I walk into the kitchen, and Kyla stands across from him, leaning against the counter. Any time I see her, she's always greeted me with a warm smile. This is different. The look on her face says she's gearing up for an argument.

"Hey," I say, glancing from Kyla over to Tysin, then back to Kyla again. "Where is Madden? Is everything okay?"

She stares at me blankly and shakes her head.

"He's not here."

"Oh, okay. Well, is everything all right?"

The bread still sits on the counter. I walk past her into the kitchen, opening the cabinet to get a glass of water, and notice the pot with tomato basil soup left sitting in the sink.

Something is definitely wrong. It's as if Madden took off in the middle of cooking, leaving everything right where it was.

"I don't know, Brielle, why don't you tell us?"

I set the glass on the counter and turn toward her.

"What do you mean?" I narrow my eyes, confused by her sudden change in tone and demeanor. It's like everything about the Kyla I've gotten to know is gone with a snap of my fingers, replaced with someone cold and distant.

"Should I even call you Brielle? Is that even your real name?"

I swallow hard. I've already told Madden about why I chose to change my last name and go by an alias. This isn't a secret, and he told me he understood. Why is this an issue now?

"Yes, my name is Brielle." I shake my head, still confused. "Let's just cut the bullshit, Kyla. What the hell's your problem? Why do you seem upset?"

She curls her lip and chuckles, tilting her head as she glances over at Tysin.

Whatever has her upset, she's clearly pissed off. Fuming.

"You can cut the bullshit already, Brielle. Madden knows. We all know."

"Knows what?" I snap, waving my hands around. I wince, and the pain hits like I got knocked upside the head all over again.

"You didn't think he would find out about your history at Holly-wood Tea sooner or later? Really?" She smirks. "Did you not think that's something you should tell him?"

I clench my jaw and force myself to breathe.

"I have no idea what you *think* you know about me, but this is all a huge misunderstanding."

She chuckles and shakes her head. "You're not gonna sit here and lie and think it's all going to be swept under the rug. It's over. He's done. He left and doesn't want to see you. I owe him a favor, so when he asked me to see to gettin' you back home, I told him I'd take care of it. So you're left with me."

Kyla smirks, dropping her arms to her waist.

"I understand you're not feeling well after what happened, so I've made arrangements to put you up at a hotel. You can stay there if you'd like until you fly back to New York. If you'd like to move your flight up, I can take care of booking you a new one instead."

My mouth drops open. Is she serious?

I shake my head. "I'm not leaving until I talk to Madden."

I reach for my phone and pull up his name.

"Don't bother wasting your time. He doesn't want to see you, and he doesn't want to speak to you. Don't you get it? He's done."

"No, I don't get it because he's wrong. It's not what he thinks."

"So the email he saw from Clive Teller, talking about his offer still stands if you ever decide you want to come back to Hollywood Tea, is all a big misunderstanding? I don't know, Brielle, but it seems pretty clear to me."

The email I sent to Clive.

I squeeze my eyes shut and shake my head. There's no holding back the tears filling the brim of my eyes. After everything that's happened over the past couple of weeks, I don't even bother trying to reason with her.

It's clear Kyla's already made up her mind about me, and I don't have the energy to fight with her right now.

"I'll just get my things, and I'll be out of your way."

She doesn't say anything as she watches me circle the bar to grab my laptop.

"Just tell me one thing," Kyla retorts. "Were you behind all the articles printed about any of us on Hollywood Tea?"

I glance up at her. No, I wasn't. I've never written a bad thing about any of the guys, and I meant what I said the day I showed up here for the interview, when I told Madden I had no intentions of doing anything to hurt them.

"No. I never have, and I never will."

She nods slowly, glancing over at Tysin and shrugging. I don't think either of them believes me, but at this point, I don't care anymore.

After I'm back home in New York and all the shit settles down, and I'm left with picking up the pieces, I'm sure this falling out with his sister will hurt too. Right now, though, I can't let myself focus on the ache in my chest.

"From the moment I came in here, I know you all expected the worst. I overheard you talking to Madden after we first met the day of the interview. I even heard you and Brix warning him to be careful after he invited me out to Whiskey Barrel," I say to Tysin. "There's no point in me sitting here trying to explain or defend myself, when you all have been set on thinking the worst of me from the moment I stepped through the door."

"Were we wrong, though?" Kyla scoffs. "I mean, I think it's safe to say our suspicions were correct, wouldn't you agree?"

I shake my head. "No, in fact it's the furthest from the truth. I have no idea what you think you may know about me or what lies you've filled your head with as to why I was talking with Clive at Hollywood Tea. What I will tell you is I was doing it to try to protect Madden. That's all I've ever tried to do. It doesn't matter, though. Like I said, I'm not gonna sit here and try to defend myself to people determined to only see me from their point of view."

Kyla nods her head and watches me pack up my things.

It isn't until I climb the stairs to Madden's bedroom that I let the emotions hit me. There's no holding them back now.

I pull up my messages with Madden, reading the last one he sent me saying "I love you" when I was in the hospital. I quickly type out a text to him before I think better of it. Who knows if he'll see it, and if he does, if he'll bother to read it.

Me: What happened to not pushing me away and us getting through anything? You couldn't even give me a chance to explain?

I force myself to quickly pack up my things in my suitcase while I order an Uber to pick me up. Kyla offered to put me up in a hotel, but the last thing I'm going to do is accept anything from them.

I'm going to collect my things, head straight to the airport, and fly back to New York. All I want right now is to get home and as far away from here as I can get.

CHAPTER TWENTY-SEVEN

MADDEN

"If you're gonna tell me 'I told you so,' you can save it. I don't want to hear it," I grumble when Brix opens the door.

He steps back to let me in and presses his lips into a firm line, shaking his head. Although he doesn't say anything, the words are on his face as plain as day.

"Where would be the fun in that? You just took the wind right out of my sails."

"Shut the fuck up," I grunt.

Ivy stands in the kitchen when I walk in, dicing onions. There's food cooking on the stove. She drops the knife when she sees me and wipes her hand on a towel.

"Kyla told me things with Brielle were over. She didn't tell me why, just that she wasn't who you thought she was," Ivy says, her face softening. "How are you holding up?"

She grew up running around with Kyla and was like a sister to me long before she got engaged to Brix.

I climb the barstool across from where she's working and fold my arms on the bar. I can't even wrap my mind around everything. There are so many questions, not enough answers, and I don't know if I'll ever want to hear them.

Even if she came clean and told me the truth about her past with Hollywood Tea, why didn't she tell me to begin with? Why is this how I'm finding out?

I'm angry and hurt, especially when we've had countless conversations about my lack of trust when it comes to people in the industry. Hollywood Tea is known for being one of the first and only to smear our names across their headlines any time they think they've stumbled upon some dirt.

All they care about are getting clicks and lining their pockets. They don't give a shit who they hurt or about the lies they spread in the process.

"I'm still sorting through how I feel, if I'm being honest. Angry, hurt, betrayed, to name a few."

She sighs and nods. "Well, you're welcome to stay here for as long as you need. Kyla said she was working to arrange a hotel for Brielle to stay at, but if you want to stay here tonight, I can make up a bed for you."

I hold up my hand and shake my head. "I'll be fine. I can't hide away forever, so even if she's still there when I go home, it is what it is. I wouldn't mind taking you up on whatever it is you're cooking, though. It smells delicious."

She smiles. "I think I can make that happen."

Brix leans against the counter next to her. He doesn't say anything, but I know him well enough to figure out what he's thinking.

"I guess she worked for Hollywood Tea," I mutter under my breath, wincing at the shooting pain in my chest.

I love her and believe she loved me, but it wasn't that simple.

"Shit," Brix grunts. Ivy joins me on the other side of the break-fast bar and wraps her arms around my shoulders in a hug.

I lean my head against hers, and Brix grumbles under his breath, "That's enough," and I return it with a smirk.

"She was talking to the editor-in-chief, Clive Teller, in an email. Something about meeting up with him when she's back in New York. All I saw was the response back to her, and he mentioned that if she's interested in coming to work for him again, the offer is on the table."

"Maybe it's not what it seems," Ivy suggests, turning toward the pantry to pull out a box of pasta. "I know it may not seem like this now, but try to put yourself in her shoes. Maybe she was trying to help you in some way, using her connections to curb all the swirl about Hanna."

"I don't need her fuckin' help," I grunt, shaking my head.

"I know you don't, but let's be honest, if she offered to use her connections, would you even let her? You guys can be so damn stubborn and hardheaded sometimes. Listen to you now."

I roll my eyes. "The last thing I'd want her to do is try to make negotiations on my behalf with those scumbags."

"I know that. Hell, we all know it, but I still believe she thinks she's doing the right thing. I've seen the way she looks at you, Madden. That girl loves you, and I know it may not be what you want to hear, but I think you owe her a chance to explain herself."

My phone vibrates in my pocket, and I pull it out to see an unread message from Brielle and Kyla. I don't have it in me to read Brielle's message right now, so I click on my sister's.

Kyla: She's gone. You can come back whenever you're ready.

"It doesn't matter now anyway. She's gone. On her way back to NYC, I'm sure."

"It does matter, even if you don't see it now. You love her, and she loves you, and you can't tell me if the roles were reversed, you wouldn't want her to give you a chance to explain."

I shake my head. "The roles wouldn't be reversed. You see, the difference between the two of us is I'd never betray her to where it'd put me in the position to lose her."

I guess I was wrong to think I could trust Brielle.

I thought we were a perfect match, but matches burn, and we went down in flames.

I stick around for dinner and catch the Miami Blaze play Chicago in the NBA playoffs. There have been a lot of rumors and speculation around the two teams with the ongoing beef between Jaxsen Wild and Crew Savage.

When the game is over, I thank Ivy and Brix for dinner and slip out, wanting to get home.

I'm surprised to see Abel standing in the entryway when I pull up. He pushes the button on the wall near the doorway to turn on the security system again.

"I'm sorry to hear about what happened with Brielle," Abel says, ducking his head.

I shrug. "What can I say? I guess I know how to pick 'em, huh?" I try to laugh it off, but the ache in my chest makes it hard to breathe through.

He gives me a sympathetic pat on the back, and I motion for him to follow me into the kitchen. The only thing I need right now is something to help me numb the ache.

I hold up the bottle of whiskey, and he shakes his head. I guess it makes sense. At least one of us needs to have our wits about us in case of other incidents. Although I don't think I have any more fight left in me right now.

I set down a shot glass and fill it up, tossing one back before filling another.

"You wanna tell me what's goin' on?" I ask, gritting my teeth when I slam the glass back on the counter.

"What do you mean?"

"Well, you were waiting for me at the door like you have something you want to say. So let's hear it."

Abel nods. "Well, I got some good news and some bad news. The good news is, I talked to the surveillance company and they think they might be able to recover the footage. So even though they took all the hard drives, we may still have access to what's on them."

"All right, now what's the bad news?"

"Well, aside from the fact Hanna has the hard drives and she's still out on the run, doing God only knows what with them. I caught up with Brielle while she was packing up her things to leave, and she said a camera she had with her was missing. She seemed pretty distraught over it, wouldn't tell me any details, just said there were some private photos of the two of you together."

"Dammit." I grit my teeth, dragging my fingers through my hair.

It's one thing for the camera to go missing and have Hanna threaten to destroy me, but something about knowing those intimate moments with Brielle could be leaked online has anger surging through me.

Not to mention, she has footage of the two of us together in the house too.

Lord knows what she could do with it.

"I need you to get on the phone with the sergeant and figure out what the hell is going on and where they are at with finding her. What the heck is taking them so damn long?"

"I've been on the phone with them already, man. I talked to them right before Brielle left and assured her I'd let her know as soon as I heard anything."

I turn back around, pouring myself another shot before taking a heavy swig directly from the bottle.

"Hey, hey," Abel says, grabbing me by the shoulder and reaching for the bottle to stop me. "I think that's enough for tonight."

The emotions well up in my eyes, and I hate how this seems to be only piling more and more on top of me.

To make matters worse, the only person who could make it any better is likely on a plane traveling thousands of miles away, and who knows if or when I'll ever see her again.

I wave Abel off and shake my head, stalking out of the room.

"Just let me know when you have some fuckin' good news for me. Something, anything."

I stomp upstairs to my bedroom but regret coming up here the moment I do. The blankets are still pulled back on the bed from where she was sleeping earlier. Even with her gone, I can still smell the faint scent of her perfume and feel her energy in the small space.

I'm frozen, staring at the bed we've shared together the last few days, thinking back to the other night when we made love right there after I told her I love her for the first time.

How can everything change so quickly? Like the flip of a switch and now she's gone.

I take a seat on the edge of the bed, and my head sags between my shoulders before I collapse on the mattress. It only seems to make it worse because it's as if her smell surrounds me.

I angrily push myself up and rip off the blankets and sheets, tearing everything off down to the mattress. I toss them in a pile in the corner of the room, telling myself I'll do something with it in the morning.

I slug along into the bathroom, flip on the water, and rip my clothes off, adding another pile to the floor.

It's as if I want to scrub every trace of her from my body and my memory, and this is the only way I know how.

I don't bother waiting for the water to warm up before stepping into the shower. Leaning against the wall, I let the stream cascade down on me.

When I squeeze my eyes shut, she's all I see.

Her long blond hair, those crystal-blue eyes. She's here, everywhere, torturing me.

Even when she's gone and I'm left with the memories of her, I'm still turned on by the thought of being with her again.

I wrap my hand around my dick and release a low hiss, squeezing my eyes shut.

I let my mind flutter back to the morning of the incident before everything was flipped upside down.

She had been waking up early to start her shift long before I dragged my sorry ass out of bed. That morning she was insistent on waking me up with her, and dammit, what an amazing wake-up it had been.

For that moment, I let my mind drift back to her.

"What the hell do you think you're doing?" I grunt, lifting the white cotton sheet to find her grinning at me from between my legs.

"Trying to get you up." She snickers, swiping her tongue over the tip of my cock.

I toss my head back and thrust my hips toward her, desperately wanting more. All thoughts evaporate when she takes me deep into her mouth, and I push the sheet away, tucking my arm under my head to give me a better view.

"You sure know how to make a man weak, baby."

Her eyes glimmer with satisfaction, never taking them off me while she forces me deep in her mouth. Her hand follows along with her as she bobs up and down.

At this rate, if I don't stop her now, this will be over before I have a chance to be inside her, and I know I don't have a lot of time to drag this out.

I pull her up, and she narrows her eyes, sighing in disappointment.

"C'mere, baby. You won't be mad at me for long, I promise."

She crawls up my lap, and I roll her over, pinning her arms to the mattress. Her legs circle my waist, and I grind against her, hating how she's still wearing her panties and the lace top she put on when she climbed into bed last night.

I pull the material down to reveal her nipple and suck the beaded flesh into my mouth. I nip and flick my tongue over the bud, releasing it with a pop.

I lean back onto my haunches and move her panties to the side, brushing my finger over her clit down to her pussy.

"Mmm," I hum. "So wet and ready for me."

Her body shudders, and her breath hitches.

"Please, Madden." She arches her back. I line myself up at her entrance and slowly enter her before leaning over her again.

She circles her arm around my neck, pulling me in to kiss her, and I'm lost.

My mind snaps me out of the moment, and I'm left with the searing pain in my chest knowing what we had will never be the same.

I tighten my grip on my dick, squeezing my eyes shut, desperately trying to bring myself back to that morning with her.

The sight of her legs spread open for me, her soft moans, and hell, even her breath against my ear.

I need her. I want her. Fuck, I love her.

I brush my finger over the tip of my dick, and the familiar tingle at the base of my spine causes my whole body to tense, but I don't let up. I fist my dick hard and fast until my release shoots against the wall, and I sag in relief.

Then I open my eyes, and once again, I'm reminded she's gone.

CHAPTER TWENTY-EIGHT

BRIELLE

"I gotta admit, I was shocked when I saw your email in my inbox. From *Limelight* no less."

Clive sets his briefcase down on the chair beside us and takes a seat across the table from me.

He's aged quite a bit since I last saw him two years ago. His dark hair is cut short, and he's still sporting the clean-shaven look.

He's dressed in a pair of black slacks and a sport jacket with a white button-up underneath.

I have to admit, he's always given off the vibe that he grew up being picked on and his career at Hollywood Tea was getting payback on all the celebrities who managed to get the attention from the women he's desperately wanted.

I understand where Madden's coming from when he says he finds it hard to trust people.

Clive Teller is a perfect example of the type of men you want to steer clear of, which makes this sit-down with him hard to do.

Especially now when I know it's what led to my relationship with Madden crumbling to the ground.

"Yeah, I started working at *Limelight* a couple of months ago."

His eyes glisten, like I've just piqued his curiosity.

"Have you given my offer any thought? I saw your feature in *Limelight* a few months back about A Rebels Havoc. I'm assuming that's why you wanted to meet today, right?"

"Actually, I have, and you're right, that's why I asked you to meet me here today."

He nods, narrowing his gaze as if he's expecting and waiting for me to spill all the tea I didn't divulge in my interview with them.

We both know there's a difference in the content we print at *Limelight* and the type of dirty gossip Hollywood Tea is known for running.

It's exactly why when I finished my internship with them, I wanted to leave my time there in the rearview.

It's just another reason I chose to go by an alias when I started my career at *Limelight*. While I was never the one sitting behind the keyboard, writing the articles on their site, I was responsible for feeding them the tips that came through.

The further I get into this industry, the more I start to see the ugly sides that come along with it, and it's had me questioning everything I thought I wanted in my career since I started dating Madden.

"Do tell." He shimmies in his seat, leaning on the table, urging me to continue.

"Well, it's no secret to you now that I've gotten close to them over the past few weeks, particularly Madden. I appreciate you giving me the respect to meet with me today and hold on publishing any new content until we had a chance to talk."

He nods, flashing his eyes around us as if checking to see who might overhear.

He's not looking out for anyone but himself. He thinks whatever I'm about to share will be juicy, and he wants to be the first to put it out there.

"I need you to make a deal with me, and I want you to give me your word."

His eyes narrow on mine. "What are the terms exactly? I need to know what it is you're asking of me before I can make any agreements."

I tilt my head to the side. "You know I wouldn't be asking this of you if what I have wasn't juicy." I smirk.

"All right. I agree, but let me know what I'm up against, and you have my word I'll uphold my end of the deal."

"The shit you guys have been posting about the band is not all true, especially the news recently about Madden finding out he's expecting a child with Hanna and he became angry and broke a window."

He nods slowly. "Before I show you what I'm about to show you, I need you to promise me that you will come to their PR team and validate whatever you post before you print it. What you are failing to understand is the misinformation you're spreading hurts people. You're taking the word of one person and running with it."

He chuckles and shakes his head. "Listen, I know you came into this world with rose-colored glasses on, not fully understanding the cockroaches living underneath the surface. This is the price you pay for fame."

I shake my head and pick up my bag, pulling the handle over my head.

"I guess we can agree this conversation is over."

"Whoa, whoa. We had a deal, and like I promised, I'll hold up my end. You want me to come to his team before I run anything. I'll do my best to make it happen."

"Your best is not good enough. I need you to give me your word. We both know I could dig up my fair share of secrets from my time at Hollywood Tea. We both know cockroaches don't like having light shed on them."

Like the rumors about how he landed his job to begin with.

He sighs, leaning back against his chair. He steeples his fingers in front of him and nods.

"All right, you have my word."

"Well, for starters, the article about Madden getting angry after finding out Hanna is pregnant is total bullshit. I was there the weekend the window was broken, and it wasn't by Madden. It was by an unknown man they caught on his video surveillance, and I suspect it's the same man who was with her when she broke into his house and assaulted me."

Clive's eyes widen, and he leans forward as if he's not sure he heard me correctly.

I pull back the scarf I'm wearing around my head, used to style my hair. It's the only thing I could come up with to try to hide the hideous bruise leftover from the goose egg.

The swelling has started to go down, though.

"I still don't know what she was looking for exactly, but what I do know is the baby she's expecting is not Madden's."

"How do you know? We have sources who've confirmed they've been intimate together before."

I grit my teeth and nod. I hate thinking about the two of them together, but it's a part of Madden's past, and considering how we met, it's not one even I can deny.

I pull out my laptop and click on the files I transferred earlier today.

"I was at Madden's alone when the break-in happened. In the midst of everything going on, I managed to start recording a voice memo on my smartwatch. This clip is from after she hit me on the head with a vase, and I was knocked unconscious."

I hand Clive my headphones and press the play button.

He stares blankly at the table, listening intently as the audio picks up the conversation.

The police were on their way, and they knew they weren't far when it all happened. I hadn't expected for the audio to pick up much of anything, assuming they took off after.

When the audio clip cuts off, he pulls off the headphones and shakes his head.

"So the baby isn't his? What's her reason for pinning it on him? All because he chose you over her? What was the point of breaking into his house?"

I shrug. "It's all about money for her. Either she knows when he finds out the due date, it won't line up with when they were together or it's been a setup from day one. I think she knew with the band's history of having their names splattered in the press, he'd buy her silence to keep the rumors from spreading."

I still don't know what she was looking for when she broke in. She stole my camera, and his hard drives. Who knows what she'll do when she figures out what she has on them.

I've spent the past few days mentally preparing myself for when the photos of my most intimate moments with Madden are leaked online.

All I can hope now is she'll be caught before it happens.

"Man, I'm sorry you've got tangled up in this." He reaches his hand across the table, patting me on the arm.

"She'll come to you and use whatever she has as leverage to try to smear his name again. I need you to help me stop her before she does."

He sighs, sitting back against his chair, and nods.

"You have my word, I won't run any articles if she's my source, and I'll go through their PR team before anything hits publication."

"Thank you."

The weight sitting on my chest eases some. I've felt helpless over the past few days, trying to piece everything together.

There's not a lot I could do, but this, this I could.

Even if I never get the chance to see or speak with Madden again, I will always love him and want to protect him in any way I can.

After my meeting with Clive, I swing by the small grocery store on the corner near my apartment and pick up the essentials on my way home.

I've been working from home still and have run low on a few things, the more important being the heartbreak cures like ice cream and wine.

"Helloooo," Serena sings when she steps off the elevator into my apartment, her heels clicking on the floor.

She stops when she turns the corner, finding me on top of the counter.

Her brows deepen, and she tilts her head to the side.

"What are you doing? You do realize there are chairs around here, right?" She holds her hand out, motioning to the barstools and sofas in my living room as if I somehow missed them all.

"I needed to change the light bulb," I mutter through my spoonful of ice cream, pointing up at the light fixture above. "I didn't feel like getting down after, so I just made myself at home here."

She nods slowly. The worry and concern evident on her face, but I shrug.

We both know what's going on with me, so no further explanation is needed.

She bends down and unhooks the strap of her heels, kicking off her shoes.

"What are you doing?" I smirk when she hitches her leg to climb up on the counter next to me.

"What the hell does it look like I'm doing?" She quirks her brow. "My sister is goin' through some shit and wants to eat up here, and I won't let her do it alone."

I smile, leaning over the side to open the drawer and grab another spoon. She mutters a quiet thank-you when I hold out the carton to her, and she digs in, taking a bite of her own.

"How are things going? Any word from the rebel?"

I shake my head. The thought of reaching out to him makes my heart feel like it's dropping into the pit of my stomach.

"I still haven't heard from him since I texted him the night I left. I'm trying to wrap my mind around the fact this is the end of it. No conversation, no chance to explain. It's just over."

The last time I was with him, everything felt perfect. We were standing in the kitchen, our arms wrapped around each other.

If only I had known it was the last time we'd be together, I'd go back and relive it all over again.

"So that's it? You're not going to fight for him?"

"Why do I have to be the one to fight for him?" I scoff, letting the anger and frustration seep through my tone. "I sent him a text the night I left, telling him I couldn't believe he was going to push me away and not give me a chance to explain. He promised me he wouldn't run, but he did. I understand he's hurt, and he questions if he can trust me, but every time he's needed me, I've come running to be there for him."

She sighs and shakes her head, scooping another bite of ice cream into her mouth.

"I've thought about sending the audio file I shared with Clive to Kyla. I still have her email from when we arranged the interview."

"Do it, if nothing but to give Madden the peace of mind."

"I just know they'll question how I got the recording. It seems like everything I do, they think I'm doing it to hurt Madden and the guys."

She scoffs, tossing the spoon onto the table and climbs off the counter.

"What?" I chuckle, not sure what's got her all riled up now.

"I'm just pissed they constantly assume the worst of you. You're the most honest and loyal person I know. He's going to regret this, Elle." She squeezes my arm. "Some men don't realize what they've lost until reality smacks them upside their head."

The familiar twinge in my chest returns, and I shrug.

"He made his choice, and he chose not to let me explain. I guess this is how it ends."

CHAPTER TWENTY-NINE

MADDEN

I've noticed Abel and Kyla checking on me more than they did with the break-in. I'm starting to think they're waiting for me to go off the deep end.

To be honest, I am too.

Everything is slowly starting to pile up on me. They are still searching for Hanna and all the shit they stole out of my house. Rumors have been swirling about who was helping her.

Abel keeps telling me to be patient, to let the police do their job, but I'm running out of patience.

Then, there's Brielle.

All weekend, my mind was a fuckin' mess over her. I read her text message, and dammit, she was right. We agreed to talk things out, and I made a promise to her I wouldn't run away when shit got hard.

At first, she wasn't honest with me about who she was. I didn't even blame her. She wanted to separate herself from the Granite name and the pressure that came along with it.

If I could understand anything, it was that feeling of all eyes being on you. She wanted to stand on her own two feet, and I respected the hell out of her for it.

Why did she have to lie to me about this, though?

Not only did she work for Hollywood Tea before starting at *Limelight* but she was sneaking behind my back.

For what reason? Was she feeding them information on me and the guys?

I exhale a heavy breath, pressing my elbows to my knees and burying my face in my hands.

"You good, man?" Abel croaks.

"I'm fine, Abel. I just want to be left alone."

He stays silent for a minute. "I understand, and I'll leave you to it, but I have an update. You told me to tell you when I finally have good news, and I think you'll want to see this."

I exhale, dropping my hands to sit up. Something about his indifferent expression doesn't make me feel any better.

"What? Just tell me."

"I got a phone call from the police sergeant. They found Hanna and the two guys who helped her and brought 'em in. He said they believe they were able to recover what was stolen."

"Are you fuckin' serious?" I say, letting out a shaky laugh. I press my palms against my eyes, feeling like I've finally taken a deep breath.

"Even better, you remember how I told you I talked with the security company and they told me they may be able to retrieve the footage?"

"Okay, and?"

"They managed to extract the surveillance footage from their cloud backup. So even though they stole the hard drives, we were still able to recover it all."

I pipe up then. "Well, that's good to hear. At least we can retrace their steps and see what all they took while they were here."

He nods. "There's more."

"What?"

"C'mere, I want you to see for yourself."

I push myself to stand and stalk behind him through the house to the office. Abel took care of increasing the security after the first break-in, equipping us with full video surveillance around the property, covering damn near every inch and angle of the house.

He takes a seat at the desk and starts scrolling through the footage, stopping on Brielle in the kitchen with Hanna. I wince at the sight of her, dressed in her cotton shorts and her tank top.

Abel presses play to when Hanna snatches her phone out of Brielle's hand and lifts it to her ear.

I grit my teeth, recalling this part of our conversation.

"I don't want to replay this, man." I shake my head, knowing what's about to come next.

He fast-forwards past the part where she slams the vase against Brielle's head. She's lying on the floor in a pile of glass, leftover from where the built-in shelves shattered all over the floor amongst the shards from the broken vase.

"Are you fuckin' crazy, Hanna?" the unknown man shouts. "What did you do that for? All this because you're jealous some man who doesn't even want you chose her?"

She turns her cold gaze on him. "You shut the fuck up."

"No, you shut up! Look at yourself. You think he isn't gonna find out you're lying, and that kid isn't even his?"

"I said shut up. Let's go, the cops are gonna be here any minute."

She shoves him, pushing him toward the doorway out of the kitchen, leaving Brielle motionless on the floor.

My stomach drops, and Abel hits pause, turning in his chair to stare up at me.

"She was lying all along."

I shake my head, dragging my hands through my hair, pulling on the strands. It doesn't help relieve any of the tension coiling in my body. If anything, it only makes the headache I feel coming on worse.

"Why the fuck would she lie about something like this?"

Abel shakes his head because he's at a loss too.

"She was trying to get back at you for choosing Brielle over her," Kyla pipes in from the doorway.

There's anger on her face, no doubt over the fact Hanna used a child as a pawn to hurt me and drive a wedge between me and Brielle.

Too bad Brielle took care of that all on her own.

"She was probably doing it to hurt you and your relationship. Maybe she didn't think you'd demand a paternity test or you'd just pay her off to get her to shut up."

"Well, we have the proof we need now. It's on video, along with the footage proving the window wasn't broken by me in a fit of rage."

Kyla nods, taking a step toward me, and wraps her arm around my waist.

"I'm sorry you're going through this," she mumbles against my chest. I return the hug, slipping mine around her shoulders.

"Me too," I whisper.

She steps back, releasing my hold, and we turn back to Abel.

"I'll take care of sorting through the footage to figure out what was taken and get this over to the police to make sure they recover it all."

"Thanks, man. I appreciate it, both of you."

I duck my head and slip out the door. Kyla shouts my name down the hall, chasing after me.

I'm waiting for her to ask me when she—

"How are you handling everything?" she probes.

I knew it was coming. I don't answer immediately, letting her follow me into the kitchen.

We finally got the new window installed, but they left a bunch of other shit damaged in their wake.

"How do you think?" I let out a self-deprecating laugh. "How would you handle a shitstorm like this?"

"Terribly, which is why I'm checking on you." She crosses her arms and studies my face. "I'm the same way you'd be with me."

She's right. When she was admitted into the hospital, back before I knew the truth about her relationship with Tysin, I was next to her every step of the way. I would've never let her go through it alone, and I know she's only trying to do the same.

"You know what? I think I'm more hurt about Brielle than I am any of this. I don't give a shit about them breaking into my house and stealing my stuff. The drums and guitar piss me off, but I can replace them. All the damage in the house can be fixed. How am I supposed to fix the giant hole in my chest?"

"Have you talked to her at all? Maybe Ivy is right and this is all a misunderstanding."

"It doesn't matter now. And if it was, why couldn't she come out and tell me herself? Why did I have to find out by reading an email?"

I scoff, stalking over to the refrigerator, and snatch a beer off the shelf. I untwist the cap and take a drink.

"It's two o'clock in the afternoon," Kyla mutters. She shakes her head, causing her purple hair pulled into a messy bun to bounce.

"I ain't got shit to do around here. Who cares what time it is? If it helps me numb the pain and drown everything out, I'll take it."

"What should I do if she reaches out to me?"

I slam the bottle down and rest my palms on the counter. I let my head sag between my shoulders and shrug.

"She won't," I mutter. "I sent her away already. She's too stubborn to try and fight it now."

Kyla sighs. "Two stubborn people, a true love story." She snickers.

I glance over at her, rolling my eyes, and push off the counter.

"If she does, I don't want to hear about it. Better yet, let's not talk about her at all anymore, okay? Leave me and the topic alone."

I stalk out of the room, and she shouts behind me, "Okayyy, ya fuckin' grump."

That one manages to get me to crack a smile.

I'm a few beers deep when I hear a knock on the door. Abel must've let whoever it is past the gate. I swing it open to find Brix and Tysin standing on the front step, both wearing a smirk.

"Heard you could use some company." Tysin grins, slinging his arm over Brix's shoulders.

I guess I told Kyla not to talk to me about it, but I never specified getting the guys to leave me alone too.

"We're here to kidnap you and haul your ass down to Whiskey Barrel," Brix says, giving me a once-over before meeting my eyes. "I guess to get you more drunk than you already are."

I haven't showered all day, and no doubt my hair shows it. I didn't sleep for shit last night either.

"Nuh-uh, I ain't goin' anywhere."

"Like hell you're not. You wanna sit around and mope all night, you can do it from a barstool with us. C'mon, let's go," Brix urges.

I jerk my arm away and step back, shaking my head.

"We don't have Trey here to help us, but if we need to, we'll haul your ass out this door."

No way will they accept no for an answer. I shake my head and concede. "Fine, give me a few to at least clean up. The last thing I need is another headline speculating I'm spiraling out of control after showing up disheveled at the bar."

I move to shut the door on them, before one of them reaches their arm out to stop me. I don't stick around to find out who, stalking up the stairs to wash my face and change.

The bar is quiet, and the crowd is thin, but it's a Monday, after all.

Abel tagged along with us, muttering something about wanting to keep an eye out.

I didn't have it in me to fight with him anymore, so I let it go. As much as I resisted the idea, I'm glad they dragged me out of the house.

I hate to admit it, but I needed to get away and out of my own head.

"You still haven't heard from her?" Brix asks.

I shake my head. "Not since she texted me before she left."

"What is it that bothers you the most, the fact she worked for Hollywood Tea or the fact she didn't tell you about it?"

"Both, but more so that she hid it from me. We've had conversations about my feelings on it, how Hollywood Tea has made a business out of dragging people's lives through headlines. Come to find out, she's one of them."

I take another swig of my beer. "It's not even the first time she's hid from me who she is either."

Tysin's brows deepen. "What's that mean?"

"She goes by the name Brielle Silvers, but it's an alias. She uses it at *Limelight*. Her real name is Brielle Granite."

"Wait, Granite? Where have I heard that name before?" Brix questions. "As in Granite hotels?"

I nod, and Tysin mutters, "Shit," under his breath.

"I met her father when we were in NYC doing press on *Come Hell or Havoc*. He showed up at her house the morning we flew back. That's why I was late that morning. We were butt-ass naked in her bed when he strolled into her apartment."

"Damn, that fuckin' sucks." Tysin smirks, and I dart my eyes over at him.

"Not as bad as catchin' your ass with my sister in the fuckin' pool," I retort, and Brix barks out a laugh.

"Well, if it makes you feel any better, at least you know she wasn't after your money. I bet she's worth more than the three of us combined," Brix adds.

Yeah, I thought so too. In fact, she turned down the chance to work for her father, which would only line her pockets more.

Which begs the question, what would she get out of going behind my back to contact Hollywood Tea?

CHAPTER THIRTY

BRIELLE
THREE WEEKS LATER

"What are you still doing here?" Davis asks, peeking his head into my office.

I glance down at the clock for the first time in a while and am surprised it's so late already. It's a quarter to five, so most of the office has started to clear out for the day.

I've been putting in extra hours, living and breathing my job. I'll be honest, it's not at all because I want to be here. It's the only thing helping me get through the days by keeping my mind off Madden.

"I guess I should probably get packed up and take off, huh?"

"If you want to go out for dinner or grab a few drinks tonight, let me know. I can stick around, and we can hit up Blackbird."

I nod, trying to consider it. What else do I have to do?

Nothing. I'm sick of going home only to drown myself in a glass of wine and sob into a bowl of ice cream.

Sooner or later, I need to come back down to earth and accept reality.

Starting now.

I've had a lot on my mind over the past week, and I've made a big decision. One I've been dreading sharing.

Change is hard for me, especially when I'm dipping my toes into the wild unknown. Maybe it's from growing up around my father, listening to him drone on and on about making something of myself when I grow up.

Living up to him and his incredibly high expectations have made me constantly fear failure. Which explains why I've spent the entire week sticking my head in the sand, focusing on work, when I know it's why I'm not happy anymore.

"Actually, I'll take you up on it. Dinner and drinks sound great. Before I go, though, do you know if Sawyer is still in her office?"

He nods. "She's finalizing the submissions for the June issue."

I push my chair back from my desk and force myself to get this over with. I can't keep living my life in fear. This next step may feel unsteady, but I know it's the right move to make.

If it'll bring happiness back into my life, it's what I need to do.

"I'll meet you down in the lobby," he says.

"You know what? Let's plan to meet at Blackbird in an hour. I have some things to wrap up, and I don't want you waiting on me."

He nods, leaving me with a wave. I exhale a heavy breath and shake out the nervous jitters before making my way to Sawyer's office.

"Sawyer, do you have a moment?" I ask, popping my head in, finding her buried in her laptop.

I try to force some energy into my voice, but even I can hear the apprehension.

She smiles up at me and nods. "Of course, have a seat."

She spins her chair away from her computer to face me.

The one thing I've loved about working with her is how easy she is to talk to whenever I've come to her. Especially now, when I've been dreading this conversation and replaying it over and over in my mind.

"I've actually been meaning to talk to you," Sawyer interjects.

"Okay, sure. How about you go first?"

"Well, I have to admit, I was a bit taken aback by your submission for June. Your interview with Isla Grace was incredible, and your photos were stunning. I know you told me you wanted creative freedom for the article, and you were right. Everything came together perfectly."

Isla Grace is a country singer taking the music industry by storm. She was discovered on TikTok and blew up practically overnight.

"Thank you." I smile. "I'm so glad to hear you liked it."

"Liked it? Girl, I loved it. You blew me away, and I have to say it's drawn some attention around here."

I swallow hard. "Really?"

She nods enthusiastically. "Absolutely. I planned on having this conversation with you tomorrow after we hit our deadlines, but since we're sitting down together, I might as well talk to you about it now. As you know, we've recently made some changes, and I was offered the position as editor-in-chief. I wanted to know how you felt about taking over my role as managing editor."

I sit up in my seat and attempt to smooth over the surprise I know is written all over my face. This is the last thing I expected to hear when I walked in here.

Hell, I only started my job at *Limelight* a few months ago. How have I been offered this opportunity in such a short time?

"Wow, I have to admit I hadn't expected this. Thank you for the opportunity and for believing in me."

The smile on her face is beaming. How is it someone I've only recently met seems to be prouder of me than my own parents?

Something about that thought seems to make the weight of what I'm about to say even harder.

"Does that mean you'll take it?"

I fold my hands in my lap, squeezing them together before forcing myself to say the words.

"I truly do appreciate the opportunity and am so grateful to have worked with you. It honestly makes what I'm about to say more difficult, but I've made the decision to resign from *Limelight*. This will be my two-week notice."

Her face falls, and I think she's as shocked now as she had me a few minutes ago.

When she follows it up by asking me if something happened, I don't know where to even start. So I start from the beginning, from my first interview with A Rebels Havoc all the way up to the end.

By the time we wrapped up our conversation, I'm even more mentally drained.

It's been weighing on my mind knowing A Rebels Havoc's tour starts this weekend, which means Madden will be in the city.

I pack up my things and debate canceling my plans when I enter the elevator, before reminding myself why I agreed to join Davis in the first place. I need to get out and keep my mind occupied on things besides how much I miss Madden.

I don't notice Kyla and Ivy when I step out the doors of Limelight until I hear them shout my name down the sidewalk. I stop, turning around in search of where the sound came from, when I spot them standing near a black SUV with Abel.

Kyla yells for me to wait, before taking off running toward me. Ivy is hot on her heels, and Abel follows them.

What the hell are they doing here?

Kyla presses her hand against her chest to try and catch her breath when she reaches me.

"Jesus, I should know better than to try and run in four-inch Jimmy Choos," she snickers.

I notice the change in her demeanor from the last time I saw her, and I wonder if it has anything to do with the audio file I emailed her a couple weeks ago.

I force a smile and twist the ring on my hand, trying to avoid showing how anxious I am over why they're here.

"Is something wrong? Is Madden okay?"

They glance between each other and shake their heads. My face falls, and Kyla darts her hand out to stop my line of thought.

"No, no, he's *okay*, in the physical sense, but he's not my brother."

The familiar ache in my chest is back at her admission.

"He hasn't been handling things well. Hell, with the drama with Hanna, the break-in, and all the damages, it's been a lot for him to deal with, but I think the part he's handling the worst is losing you."

I wince, flicking my gaze to the concrete. "That makes two of us."

"Brielle, I owe you an apology. I got your email, along with another one from Clive Teller at Hollywood Tea. He didn't go into detail, but did share he had a conversation with you, and whatever you did seems to have changed their tune in terms of what they're posting about the guys. He's reached out and offered to share Madden's story, the truth about what happened. I have to believe it has every bit to do with you."

"I told you that night, and I've told Madden repeatedly, I never wanted to hurt him," I say. "I didn't give him any reason not to believe me. From the moment I stepped foot into his home, it seems like everyone's thought the worst of me, drilling it in his head he can't trust me, without giving me the benefit of the doubt or a chance to defend myself."

"I'm sorry," Kyla admits, and Ivy nods standing next to her.

"If there's anyone who understands what it's like to date one of the guys while trying to have a journalism career, it's me, Brielle," Ivy pipes in. "You have to know, it was never any of our intentions for you to feel we couldn't trust you. It's just, we've been through a lot the last year, the guys especially."

I nod. I get it, I've heard it countless times. What they are failing to remember is none of that was my fault, but I'm somehow paying the price for it.

I'm not the enemy.

"We're in town for the next couple days, the guys start their tour and play their first show tomorrow night and we were hoping you'd come by the venue. Maybe it would give you guys the chance to talk. I think there's a lot that needs to be said between the two of you."

I shrug, shaking my head. "Listen, I respect and appreciate you guys coming here to talk to me. Thank you for your apology. I hate to hear Madden's been struggling because I have too. I tried talking to him before I left town, and he chose not to reply to my text message. I've always been the one who runs to him, to be by his side when he needed me. If he wants to talk or see me, he knows how to get in touch and where to find me."

I tilt my head, giving them a forced smile. "Now, if you'll excuse me, I have dinner plans, and I don't want to keep them waiting."

The lights are dim with jazz music playing when I walk into Blackbird. I text Davis when I pull up outside in my Uber. His eyes are trained on the door when I walk in, his hand shooting up from where he sits, chatting with a woman I don't recognize sitting next to him.

By the looks of it, he's already one glass in when he lifts his drink to his mouth, finishing it off.

He waves over the bartender when I join him, asking for another French martini, and I hold my fingers up to make it two.

"You want to tell me what your important meeting with Sawyer was all about?"

I hang my purse over the back of my barstool chair, tucking a strand of hair behind my ear. How am I going to break this to him now?

I guess it's easier though, than it is to open up about Madden.

"She offered me her job."

He gasps, his mouth dropping open, slapping his hand down on the counter in the process.

"You're kidding me. What? I'm so damn happy for you. Look at you fuckin' go. You just started, and you're already kickin' ass."

"I put in my two weeks."

Turns out, I'm shocking the hell out of everyone today.

"Wait, is this a joke?"

I shake my head. The bartender sets our drinks down, and I leave Davis to wrap his mind around what I've shared with him while I work on getting caught up to where he's at.

He stares wide-eyed at me, when I lift my drink in cheers before taking a sip.

"You want to tell me why? This is an incredible opportunity, and you're just gonna walk away from it?"

I shrug. It's something I've been thinking a lot about over the past few weeks.

As much as I've appreciated the opportunity, knowing without it I would've never met Madden, I've come to terms with the fact this isn't what I want to do anymore.

On the nights when I've been alone and lonely, I've sat down with my laptop, and I started writing. I didn't really know what I was doing at first. It's been years since I've written anything outside of work.

It started off as me going back to when I first met Madden. What began as me journaling our story quickly evolved into me writing the ending we never got to have.

"You know, I think I just came to terms with the fact I've been chasing a career to prove to my father I can make something of myself without him carving a path for me. I've learned through my relationship with Madden, that I don't want to live my life according to other people's opinion of me, and I certainly don't want anything to do with spreading lies and gossip about people either."

Davis folds his hand over mine, squeezing my fingers.

"As much as I've loved being Brielle Silvers, it's not who I am."

"Well, it doesn't mean you're a stranger either. You better not leave us and disappear on me."

Disappear.

There's that word again. It's been tormenting me coming to terms with the fact Madden abandoned me and everything we had.

Like our relationship wasn't worth fighting for, so he walked away.

"I'll never be a stranger to you," I reassure him.

He must pick up on the change in my emotions. He lifts his hand to signal to the bartender again we need another round of drinks.

"I figured you'd be ready for your next one." He smirks. When I don't say anything back, he asks, "Have you heard from him at all?"

I shake my head. "It's probably better this way. Don't you think? It's like a death. You have to work through the stages of grief in order to move on. Talking to him or seeing him would only set me back."

That's what I told Serena too when I mentioned selling my ticket for tomorrow night. I never thought when I bought it, we'd end up in this place.

"I tried talking to him when I left, and he hasn't taken the initiative to respond back to me. It's only going to hurt more going and seeing him, and even worse facing him reject me again."

I'm starting to understand what Hanna felt when he ended things with her. Even though he insisted they were never together, I guess neither were we.

I know what I felt when I was with him, and my heart breaks to think when he told me he loved me, he never truly meant it.

Even more, I hate how easily he could toss what we had to the side.

CHAPTER THIRTY-ONE

MADDEN

I've been anxious to get back out on the road.

Life has gotten crazy the past couple of months from meeting Brielle, the album release, drama with Hanna, and Trey and Layken having their daughter and getting married. It's been one roller coaster ride after another.

Now, it's time to board our bus and head out on tour.

A lot has changed since our first tour last summer. For starters, they don't have us crammed onto one bus. Thankfully, it didn't take much convincing for our label to agree on two buses.

Brix and Tysin are on one with the girls, and I'm on the other with Trey, Layken, and their daughter, Leanna.

They decided to try bringing Leanna out on the road for as long as they could. I never would've thought last year I'd go from hitting up nightclubs with the guys to this, but I'm rollin' with it.

I have to admit, watching Trey with Leanna has me thinking about all I'm missing out on these days.

I've considered reaching out to Brielle countless times. Especially in the days leading up to our tour, knowing our first stop was in NYC.

There's something about knowing we're in the same city together that makes me wish I could see her. Thinking about how much I miss her leaves a hollow feeling in my chest.

I never would've thought the one person I shouldn't want is the one I can't live without.

We got into the city a couple of hours ago, and I'm already going stir-crazy. I'm sitting in my bedroom, messing around on my drum practice pads. My headphones blare one of our songs when the door swings open, and Kyla pokes her head inside.

She's wearing a concerned expression when she nods toward my headphones. I move one of the speakers off my ear and press pause.

"We're goin' to grab dinner if you wanna join."

I nod. "Give me a few to get cleaned up, and I'll be ready."

She gives me a sympathetic smile and ducks her head, pulling the door shut behind her.

I have zero interest in doing anything tonight. I keep telling myself the tour is what I need right now to keep my mind off Brielle, but it's been impossible.

My eyes zone out, staring absentmindedly at a painting hung on the wall, twisting my drumsticks in my hand.

"Well, did you try giving her a ticket for tomorrow? Maybe if she came to the meet and greet, we could get them together and force them to talk. I mean, it worked for you." Brix suggests.

"Thank fuck, too," Trey quips.

What the fuck are they talking about?

"What else did you expect us to do? Kidnap her? She doesn't want to come," Kyla insists.

"I can't say I blame her either," Ivy joins in. "She was only trying to help him, and he practically forced her out the door."

Are they talking about Brielle?

I toss my sticks on the table where I dropped my backpack earlier. I've learned not to bother with suitcases since we'll pack up and leave town before long anyway.

"It's not like any of us knew she was conspiring *for* us and not *against* us."

Kyla must not have realized she left the door cracked. I reach for the handle, jerking it open, causing her and Ivy to jump.

"Jesus, Madden! You scared the shit outta me." Kyla holds her hand against her chest. She exhales before it clicks in her mind I could hear their conversation, her gaze snapping to mine.

"Who the hell were you talking about?" My eyes bounce from the girls, over to Brix and Trey.

Trey holds his hands up and backs away, always trying to steer clear of the drama. Ivy and Kyla exchange concerned glances before Brix shrugs, shaking his head.

"Does someone want to spit it out, or are you gonna play stupid all night? Should I pretend to shut the door and let you finish?"

"Brielle," Kyla says on an exhale. I still at the sound of her name. "We were talkin' about Brielle, okay?"

They all study my face, waiting for the reaction they believe will soon follow.

"You remember the email I told you I got from Hollywood Tea wanting to share a story about what happened with Hanna?" Kyla continues.

Yeah, I remember. They asked if we wanted to review a story they were running about how Hanna was behind the break-in and how the pregnancy claims were all a setup.

When have they ever given us a heads-up before?

Never.

"What about it?"

Kyla swallows, flashing her eyes over to Ivy. "Brielle wasn't trying to hurt you when she reached out to Hollywood Tea, Madden. I understand how it looks, and I get why you were upset, but she wasn't doing it for reasons, you think."

My brows knit together and Kyla adds, "She was the one who gave them the story to print. She was trying to clear your name."

She pulls her phone out of her pocket and presses play. The muffled audio is hard to hear, but I'd know that conversation anywhere.

It's the same one we heard when Abel recovered the footage.

"How'd she get the recording of them in the kitchen saying the baby's not mine?" My brows deepen, shaking my head in confusion. "We saw the recording. She was unconscious on the floor."

It's not making any sense. Why didn't she tell me before?

"She didn't realize it at the time, Madden, but her smartwatch recorded a voice memo. She's had it this entire time."

She was trying to help me by reaching out to Hollywood Tea, and she knows the baby isn't mine?

"Madden, you need to go talk to her," Ivy says, squeezing my forearm. "She was doing what any of us would've done, if we had the connections and thought it would help."

I push past Brix to pace back and forth across the room. Kyla chews on her lip, and I can see the worry on Ivy's face. I drag my hand through my hair, tugging on the strands.

How could I think she'd ever hurt me?

How could I ruin the one good thing in my life that was all mine?

"I need to go see her. I need to talk to her before it's too late."

The temperature has dropped since we pulled into town, and the sun has disappeared into the horizon.

I lean against the brick building outside Brielle's apartment, tilting my head to stare into the dark night amongst the tall buildings and skyscrapers making up downtown.

Each time someone shuffles down the sidewalk or another car drives past, I hold my breath in hopes it's her.

Every time I've been left disappointed.

I tried going inside to talk to her doorman, who reassured me she hasn't returned home for the evening. For all I know, she could be out of town or have other plans for the night. Who knows when she'll be home.

I don't care. If I have to, I'll wait here all night.

What if she's on a date?

I shake my head. She wouldn't move on already. I refuse to let myself think of her with someone else.

Abel exhales a heavy breath, and I roll my head to look at him. "Maybe she's not coming home tonight, man."

"I don't care," I grunt. "I'm not going anywhere. So you can either wait with me or leave. Take your pick."

He holds his hands up, and I clench my jaw.

"She'll be back here sooner or later. When she does, I'll be right here waiting."

He folds his hands in front of him and nods.

The longer we stand here, the more my thoughts plague me, replaying the conversation I overheard back at the hotel.

They went to see Brielle to try and convince her to come to the show tomorrow, not knowing she originally had a ticket to come. At least that was the plan she told me.

Maybe she changed her mind though.

What will she say when she gets home and sees me waiting for her? Will she give me a chance to explain after refusing to talk to her before?

"Madden?"

For a second, I wonder if I'm dreaming until I turn my head to search for her, finding her standing at the end of the block.

She blinks slowly, almost as if she can't believe I'm here either.

"Yeah, baby, it's me."

She flinches, noticing Abel standing across from me.

"What are you doing here?" she asks. Her heels click on the concrete, the words spoken more stern than a moment ago.

"I'm in town for the concert tomorrow. Kyla and Ivy told me how they talked to you and tried convincing you to come to the show so we could talk."

She nods. "So you only came all this way because I refused to go? What, did you think you could send out the call and I'd come running again?"

She scoffs, shaking her head, and moves to pass by me.

"Wait, don't go." I reach for her hand and she snaps it away.

I swallow hard. "I get it, okay? I don't deserve for you to hear me out or forgive me."

Her expression softens. There's an internal struggle playing out on her face; she doesn't know whether she should push me away or if she wants to give in and hear me out.

The sound of tires squeals around us. Abel reaches for my arm.

"I think we should continue this conversation inside if we can. The last thing we need is someone to recognize you and for this to make another headline."

"Abel, you can wait in the SUV, but I'm not leaving until I talk to her," I growl, keeping my eyes trained on her. "Do you hear me, Brielle? I'm not going anywhere. I shouldn't have run in the first place, but I'm done running now. I'm here, and I'm fighting for us like I should've been the whole time."

Tears fill the brim of her eyes and I take a step toward her, closing the distance between us. I don't miss the subtle sound of her breath hitching or the way her body relaxes when I wrap my arms around her.

I push her into the small alcove, pinning her against the wall and press a kiss to her forehead. The smell of her engulfs every one of my senses, and I squeeze my eyes shut at the emotions having her with me evoke.

"Madden," she murmurs.

I lean down, running my nose along her cheek to her ear.

"What, baby?"

"I think we should talk first, don't you?"

I pull back. "Sorry," I say dejectedly, giving her space.

"No," she scolds me, gripping the front of my shirt. "You can't expect me to come running into your arms and pretend like the past few weeks never happened."

She's right, but dammit if I don't wish I could hold her for a minute and forget everything for a while.

"C'mon," she nods, and I glance over my shoulder to Abel, holding up my hand to let him know I'll call him. I don't care about the logistics, all I want is to be with her, to figure this out together.

When it's just the two of us in the elevator, I reach for her hand again.

"I just need to feel you right now."

She stares down at our linked fingers and sighs. "Yeah, me too."

The bell dings when we make it to her floor. I press my hand against her spine, following her into her place. She drops her purse and laptop bag on the island, avoiding eye contact, as if she's nervous to have me here with her again.

It's hard not to be in this room and think about the memories we shared here not long ago. For the first time since seeing her again, I'm able to make out the sadness in her eyes.

"Why didn't you tell me you worked for Hollywood Tea?"

"It's not what you think, Madden," she admits. "You're right though, I still should've told you. I guess, at first, I didn't think it mattered. My junior year, I was taking a journalism class and we had a list of places available for internships. All my top picks were snatched up by seniors, so by the time they got to me, there wasn't much to choose from. I ended up with Hollywood Tea."

I run my hand over my jaw, listening intently.

"It was for three months, and my job was to weed through hot tips that came in. Was it my first choice for internships? No, but I learned a lot about myself during the time I was there and met some nice people. When it came time for my senior year, I knew I wanted to do something more like what I do now at Limelight, and I thought this was it."

"I think for so long, I've been focused on finding a successful career, one that would pull me away from the path my parents laid out and prove to them I could stand on my own two feet without them. I hadn't really stopped to consider if what I was doing made me happy. At least, not until now."

I take a step closer to her, pushing her back to the edge of the counter, and she exhales a shuddered breath.

"Until now?" I ask, tucking a strand of hair behind her ear. "What would make you happy now?"

She raises her chin to meet my gaze. "I guess it depends."

"On what?"

"On you."

I find myself exhaling a sigh of relief, linking our hands together, lifting her fingers to my mouth.

"You make me question everything I thought I wanted in life," she admits.

"Why do you say that?"

"I quit my job."

"Wait, what? Why?"

She nods. "I love working at Limelight. It's fun, they've given me more creative control, and I'm good at it." She stops, contemplating her next words. "I love my job," she repeats, "but I love you more."

And there it is.

Those three words I thought I'd never hear her say again.

I cup her face and grip her chin, forcing her eyes to meet mine.

"I love you too," I whisper.

Her eyes glisten, lifting her lips and waiting for me to kiss her. When I crash my mouth on hers, she moans, digging her nails into my waist as she holds onto me.

The feel of her lips on mine, the sounds she makes, and the warmth of her body in my arms has me never wanting to come up for air.

It's so easy to get lost in her and forget everything.

"I don't want you to quit your job for me," I whisper against her lips when I pull back.

"It's not for you, Madden. You've opened my eyes to what makes me happy. It's not the job or the beautiful apartment overlooking New York. I've come to terms with the fact this isn't what I want to do anymore. Hell, if it wasn't for Serena, I probably would've packed up my bags already and got the heck out of New York."

"I'm not giving up on my passions. There are other creative ways I can do what I love that won't hurt anyone, especially the people I care about. I've always wanted to write a novel and get back into photography. There are so many things I can do. I'm not going to rush to figure it out simply because I'm avoiding my father pressuring me to work for him. I'm going to do what I want and what makes me happy.

"I understand why you were upset with me," she says, pressing her hand against my chest. "I don't blame you for not trusting me, for pushing me away. I meant what I said in the very beginning though, I never wanted to hurt you."

"I never wanted to hurt you either." My voice breaks. "I've been wrong about people in the past. I felt like the ground was crumbling beneath me. I didn't want to look at you, and know how much I love you, and be forced to face the fact I was wrong. Now I realize the only thing I was wrong about was thinking I could ever walk away from you."

"All that matters is you're here now, right?"

I nod, pressing another kiss against her lips. I bend down and lift her into my arms. She giggles, wrapping her arms around my neck before I set her down on the edge of the counter.

"I'm here now, and baby, I'm not ever letting you go again."

CHAPTER THIRTY-TWO

BRIELLE
FOUR WEEKS LATER

"You do realize we can't stay in here all day, right?"

We pulled into some town in Iowa late last night. They don't have to be at the venue for a few more hours, and Madden's dead set on spending every last second we have this morning in bed.

"Like hell we can't," Madden mutters. Rolling over on top of me, he buries his face into the crook of my neck.

I giggle, attempting to push him away, but it's impossible with the weight of his large frame on top of me.

It wasn't long after we got back together the news broke about our relationship, connecting me to the mystery woman a few months back. Rumors started online, speculating who I was and how long we've been together before the pieces fell into place and my true identity came out.

Soon, Sawyer called me into her office, and my father was on the phone asking questions. Especially when he found out I was heading out on tour with them, quitting my job and apartment in the city behind.

It didn't matter anymore, though. I wasn't hiding behind secrets, and I wasn't going to hold back from letting the world know we were together or how much I loved him.

Clive stood by his word, reaching out to their PR team before running the story. All I asked was that he held up his end of the deal. We both know if he didn't, I had the connections and resources to send his world into a tailspin.

As rocky as it was early on, especially with the guys questioning our relationship, they seemed to put it to rest after finding out the truth behind my conversation with Clive. Any doubts that lingered were put to rest when Madden told them I was leaving my career with *Limelight*.

"You think I haven't watched every single one of them disappear on me, especially early on in their relationships? I've been the last one in the group to find someone, so I've been waiting for my time to drag my woman away and tell them to fuck off."

The low rumble of his laughter vibrates against me, his facial hair brushing over my skin, and I shudder, trying to get away from him.

"Where do you think you're going?" He pins my arms to the mattress, rubbing his face over mine until I yelp and beg for him to stop.

"Fine, fine. You win, okay?" I yelp, out of breath.

"I win." He wags his brows, leaning over me. "What do I win exactly?"

He drags his finger over my lips and down my chest, tugging on my lace top to reveal my breasts.

"What do you want?" I quirk my brow.

A salacious smile curves the edge of his mouth. I know that look. Whatever he has on his mind looks like trouble in only the best way.

He reaches for my hand and hauls me up with him, gripping my chin between his fingers as he kisses me hard.

He moans against my mouth. I open mine, swiping my tongue over his lips, silently begging for more.

"Lift your arms for me," he mutters, and I obey his orders.

He clenches his jaw, dragging his gaze down my body. He sucks his thumb into his mouth and brushes it over my nipple, causing it to harden.

I watch him intently as he slips off the bed, yanking my panties with him before he climbs off the bed, shedding his shirt and shorts in one fell swoop.

He wraps his large hand around his length, and the sight of him does crazy things to my insides.

"Open your legs," he grunts, and I do.

The heat in his stare, mixed with the sight of him jerking off, causes my body to warm. I know without looking that my cheeks are on fire.

"Tell me what you want," I whisper, tracing my hand over my stomach down to my pussy.

His nostrils flare when I brush my finger over my clit. A low growl vibrates around the room when I roll my eyes closed.

"I want you in every fuckin' way I can have you."

"Well, we don't have all day." I smirk. "So you're gonna have to pick one."

I push myself to kneel and crawl toward him. He drags his lip between his teeth, his eyes darkening when I lift my breasts into my hands, tweaking my nipple.

He seems to have forgotten what I said, staring dazed at me while I trail my hand back down my body, disappearing between my legs.

I press my lips together, fighting off the urge to smile when he grips my wrist and lifts my fingers to his mouth. He licks and sucks them, closing his eyes while his loud moan shudders against me.

When he releases my hand, he studies me as I turn to press my chest against the mattress. My hair fans out around me, and I arch my back to give him a better view.

"How about this one?" I drag my lip between my teeth.

"We have to be there in twenty minutes," Kyla shouts from the other side of the door.

His head snaps up, glaring in her direction, and I giggle at the sight of him all wound up.

"I guess we'll have to make it quick."

"Like hell, we will," he grunts. "I'll take my sweet fuckin' time devouring every inch of you."

"Mmm," I hum.

He brushes his fingers over my clit from behind before moving down to thrust his long digits into my pussy.

I bury my face into the crux of my arm, attempting to muffle the moan.

"Fuck, I need to feel you so bad." He wraps his hand, still slick with my wetness, around his dick, jerking it hard before lining up at my entrance.

When he attempts to enter me slowly, I give in and rock backward, slapping our bodies together. He grips my hips, burying himself deep inside me.

I push myself up on my hands, upping the tempo and meeting him thrust for thrust.

Glancing over my shoulder, I get a glimpse of him, his shoulders and arms tense with need. His eyes burn into where our bodies meet, and he widens his stance, his strokes growing harder.

"Fuck, you're taking me so good."

My mouth drops open, my breaths coming out in heavy pants.

"You like that, baby? You like when I tell you how good this tight pussy feels."

"Madden," I cry.

"Tell me," he grunts, slamming into me harder.

"Yes," I say on an exhale. "Yes, I love when you tell me how much you want me."

He pulls me up, meeting me halfway, and wraps his hand around my throat. Tilting my head back, he kisses me hard, and I moan against his mouth as he buries himself deep.

"I want to claim every inch of your body. You're mine. Forever."

Tears prick my eyes, and I squeeze them shut.

Every nerve ending is alive. My emotions are hitting me all at once.

He drops his hand, moving back to grip my hips.

"This is only for you," he groans. "There's no one else for me. You hear me? I'm yours."

His arm circles my waist, his fingers finding my clit, and it causes me to jolt. This time, I can't hold back or contain the moan from slipping out of my mouth.

"Right there," I mutter, tilting my head back against his shoulder.

"Let me feel my pussy come for me, Brielle."

He thrusts deep. His lips skate across my shoulder, nipping and biting at my skin. My vision goes blurry when he flicks his tongue over my ear and my body tenses.

"Oh fuck, that feels so good." Madden groans, thrusting into me one final time.

"I'm not kidding, Madden. If you two don't hurry up, we're gonna leave without you." Kyla pounds on the door.

Our moans echo around us, and we collapse onto the bed. Our bodies tremble, the aftermath of our release drains all the energy out of me, and I relax into him.

I don't want to ever lose this feeling with him.

It's hard to believe we're already in the second month of their tour.

I don't know what I expected life on the road to be like with a rock band—traveling from city to city. If we're not sleeping on the bus, we're crashing in a new room every night.

I have to admit, for someone who's always had life planned out in front of them, it can be terrifying, but I'm learning to embrace going with the flow and seeing where life takes you.

If I hadn't, I sure as hell wouldn't have taken the leap with Madden, and we wouldn't be where we are now.

I've made the most of my time on the road, though. When we stay somewhere for more than one night, I drag Madden away with me to explore new places. The best part is I brought my camera with me and have captured every moment of it along the way.

On the days we're stuck on the bus and the guys are writing new music, I pull out my laptop and headphones and dive back into the story I've been working on.

Madden's been encouraging me along the way, urging me to take the leap and have it published, but for now, I'm just enjoying writing and letting my creativity flow.

When we're at their show later that night, I'm still replaying every second of our morning together through my mind.

Madden stands behind his drums, his headphones on, tapping his foot on the floor. He spins his sticks between his fingers above his head.

The crowd is wild tonight. I love watching their excitement every time they step on stage, doing what they love.

"Cedar Rapids, I want you on your fuckin' feet and your hands in the air," Brix roars. "It's because of you this song has been sitting at the top of the Billboard charts for the last fourteen weeks in a row."

The lights go out, and we're left staring into a sea of lights from the crowd, screaming and chanting, "Rebels," through the sold-out arena.

The girls are next to me, bouncing on their feet.

"Hell yeah, baby!" Ivy shouts. Kyla joins in, cupping her hands over her mouth, chanting along with them.

I can't contain the pride expanding in my chest, especially when I glance over to see the beaming smile on Madden's face.

He takes a seat on the stool, kicking them off with the song behind the album title, *Come Hell or Havoc*.

Tysin and Trey follow behind him on the guitar. It's a faster tempo, and Madden puts every ounce of energy into it, his head banging in time to the beat of the music.

Something is so fulfilling about watching the person you love live their dream.

Even though I can't see the next step in front of me, when it comes to my career, I'm learning to love the journey.

I know Madden will be there every step, no matter where the path leads or what twists and turns come our way.

"You fuckin' killed it, baby." I grin, shouting to Madden when the guys wrap up their last song.

Madden ripped off his shirt halfway through. He tugs it off his shoulder, using it to wipe the sweat from his brow, and stalks toward me, lifting me in his arms.

"You're sweaty." I scrunch my nose, pushing him away. "You need to shower."

"You're damn right I do, and you're coming with me." He grins.

"Will you two get a damn room?" Tysin balks from behind us.

Madden lifts his middle finger in the air, stomping down the stairs. He ignores my attempts to get down, hauling me over his shoulder.

"We were interrupted earlier." He lands a swat on my ass, and I squeal. "Now I'm coming to claim what's mine."

EPILOGUE

MADDEN
THREE MONTHS LATER

"Look at the color of the leaves." Brielle stares in awe out the window.

A cool breeze whips her hair around. She holds her camera up, quickly snapping photos.

This right here is what life is all about for me.

We wrapped up our tour a couple of weeks ago after spending the past four months on the road. It's been a whirlwind, to say the least. It's hard to believe when we packed up the bus and left for our first show in New York, we weren't together.

I don't want to think about what it would've been like without her next to me. The thought alone has put a lot of things in life into perspective.

"I swear, it looks like something out of a magazine." She sags against the seat, flipping through the photos she's taken, each one making her smile bigger.

While out on the road, we spent a lot of our downtime going out and exploring. I guess you could say the days of me hitting up bars and clubs after a show to drink and pick up women are long behind me.

When we weren't visiting the local tourist stops, we were talking about what our life would be like after the tour ended.

The guys and I all agreed after this tour was over, we'd take a break and enjoy some downtime. Something we haven't done in a few years, not since before we first signed with our label.

I've been planning this trip with Brielle since before we got back home.

I think she thought I was crazy when I suggested we go out on the road again, only this time just the two of us. It was risky traveling alone, but we knew it was something we wanted to do.

Over the past week, we've driven through Tennessee up to Nebraska, through South Dakota to where we are now in the backroads of Montana.

"Have I told you how sexy you look in that flannel jacket?" She presses the button on her camera, stuffing it back into the bag.

She reaches over the center console to wrap her hand around my forearm and leans in to trace her lips along the side of my neck.

I hiss, tilting my head to the side to give her better access.

We've been on the road for most of the day, and at this rate, I'll need a pit stop if she keeps this shit up. We're not too far from our destination, though, so I try to chill and stay the course.

It's taken a lot of planning for this night to come together, and I don't need her distractions ruining it now.

"What do you say we pull over in the middle of these woods and you fuck me in the back seat?"

I clench my jaw, flicking my eyes over to her. They lock on her lips when she slips her tongue out to wet them.

She knows all the ways to tease me, and dammit if she's not driving me fuckin' crazy right now.

"We're almost there," I mutter, my voice breaking.

Shaking my head, I turn my eyes back to the road and squeeze the steering wheel so tight, my knuckles turn white.

It takes everything in me not to take her up on it, but she won't let me go so easily. Not when she knows what she's doing to me.

"How much longer is 'almost there' exactly?" She drags her hand over my chest, unzipping the jacket to rake her nails down to where my hard dick threatens to bust through these jeans.

We pass a sign signaling Whitefish is only a few miles away. Judging by the GPS, we're about twenty minutes out.

Twenty minutes is a long time when Brielle is dead set on tempting me in every way she can to get what she wants.

I grip her wrist, knowing if she keeps rubbing her fingers over my pants, those twenty minutes will seem like two hours.

I trace my lips along the back of her hand, and she exhales a sigh, and mutters, "Fine," under her breath, leaning her head on my arm.

"We're almost there, baby, and I promise to make up for it all."

Judging by the sound of her gasp when we pull up a little while later, I think I lived up to my word.

She barely waits for me to put the car in park, unhooking her seat belt before reaching for the door handle and jumping outside.

"Why didn't you tell me this is where we're staying?" She stares wide-eyed at the tree house I rented for the weekend.

The little oasis is built around two trees located back in the woods. It snowed a little last night, which set us back this morning, but made for a beautiful view with the snow-covered trees surrounding us.

"C'mon." I smile, linking our fingers and nodding toward the wooden bridge leading to the house.

"We're supposed to walk across this to get inside?"

I burst out laughing. "Unless you want me to carry you over my shoulder, that's the plan."

She smacks me on the arm and takes off in front of me. I'll come back later to grab our bags.

There's a light on inside. I hand a key left hidden for us outside over to Brielle, who unlocks and opens the door, revealing the white rose petals scattered across the floor with candles lit throughout.

She steps inside, her eyes struck in awe as she stares around the room. It takes a moment for her to register what's going on. She spins around to look at me and slaps her hand over her mouth when she finds me on my knee waiting for her.

"Madden," she cries, tears filling her eyes.

"Yeah, baby." I nod.

She drops her hands, letting the tears flow down her cheeks. The sight of her crying has me choked up, and suddenly, the speech I've been reciting in my mind the entire drive here flies out the window.

All I want to tell her is I love her and ask her this one question. Two simple words.

"I love you, Brielle." My voice breaks.

She folds her hands against my cheeks, her body trembling when she crashes her lips on mine. My face is wet from the tears streaming down hers.

"Marry me."

She gasps, her eyes screwing shut. She straddles my bended leg, wrapping her arms around my neck, crushing my hand holding the ring between us.

"Is that a yes, baby? Will you marry me?"

"It's a hell yes." She grins, nodding her head in amazement.

She leans back enough for me to show her the ring again, another round of tears streaming down her cheeks.

"It's perfect." She brushes her finger over the diamond.

"I've never seen anything more beautiful in my life," I agree, never taking my eyes off her.

I slip my hands around her thighs, carrying her through the house to the bedroom overlooking the woods.

This is what sold me on the place, the bed facing two French doors leading onto a balcony nearly thirty feet high in the forest around us. When the night falls over us, the lights hung along the exterior will gleam in the darkness.

I set her on the edge of the bed, lifting her chin.

"I should call my parents," she whispers. "We both know how quickly word can travel. I want them to hear it from me."

"They already know."

Her brow furrows. "I asked your dad for his permission anyway. They knew what this trip was all about, and before you ask, he gave me his blessing."

"Is that right?" She smirks.

"He may have asked what made me think a rock star was good enough for his daughter. You know, the usual hassling."

"What did you tell him?"

I kneel on the floor, and she lets her legs fall open, dragging her nails along the collar of my shirt.

"I told him I'll love, honor, and protect her every single day of my life."

I run my hands up her thighs beneath her sweater, slipping my fingers into the waistband of her leggings.

"I may have left out how I'll also worship every inch of her beautiful body too."

Her stomach quivers, and I grin, dragging them down her legs along with her panties.

The cool room causes goose bumps to break out over her skin. I saunter across the room to the small wood-burning stove and fire it up.

When I turn to Brielle, she's teasing me again, her legs spread open with her hand brushing over her clit. The sight of the ring on her finger while she torments me is not a sight I ever want to forget.

"Take the jacket off, Madden."

I tilt my head to the side. "I think someone has forgotten who calls the shots."

I obey her wishes, unzipping it the rest of the way and shrugging it off. I reach for the back of my shirt, ripping it over my head too.

Her breath hitches when I unbuckle my belt and pop the button, leaving them open, then stalking toward her.

I shake my head when she reaches for the zipper, trying to finish what I've started. She drops her hand and lifts her sweater over her head, tossing it at me, hitting me in the chest.

"Mmm," I moan. "Now that's better."

When I kneel on the floor in front of her again, she stares down at me through narrowed eyes.

"The only thing I want you wearing all weekend is that ring on your finger."

I don't take my eyes off her when I lean in and trail kisses up her thigh. She finally gives in, collapsing on the bed, and I drag her closer to me, burying my face between her legs.

"This is what you get for teasing me the whole way here."

She brushes her finger over her nipple, tweaking the bud before continuing her path south to rake her nails through my hair.

"I guess I got what I wanted after all." She giggles.

She gasps when I flip her over onto her stomach, landing a hard smack on her ass.

This time, I don't wait any longer, lifting her ass in the air while I quickly unzip my jeans and shove them down.

I plunge into her in one hard thrust, and she throws her head back and moans.

I lift her hand and kiss the ring on her finger. With my chest pressed to her back, I grip her chin and growl into her ear, "I guess I did too, and now you're mine."

She sighs. "Forever."

Thank you so much for reading MADDEN!

Still want more Madden and Brielle? Don't worry, I'm not done with these two yet.

Turn the page to find out how you can read their bonus epilogue. Don't miss a sneak peek at Torn, a brother's best friend small town romance.

I hope you enjoy!

BONUS SCENE

Dear Reader,

I hope you enjoyed Madden and Brielle's story as much as I loved writing it.

I couldn't get enough of their love and wanted to give you a glimpse into their lives, so I wrote you a sexy and heartfelt bonus epilogue exclusively for you. All you have to do is visit the link below or scan the QR code with your phone, sign up for my newsletter, and you'll get access.

www.authorbrookeobrien.com/bonus

If you want to stay up to date with my sales and new releases, you can follow me on Bookbub at: www.bookbub.com/profile/ brooke-o-brien

Brooke

Torn

A TATTERED HEART DUET #1

USA TODAY BESTSELLING AUTHOR
BROOKE O'BRIEN

Prologue

MAVERICK

It was never my intention to fall in love with my best friend's sister. I was thirteen when I moved down the street from Dean Blake. He had come into my life at a time I struggled to cope with the world around me. Our friendship came without any pressures, it was easy. He didn't ask questions, but I think he knew what would happen if he did.

I closed off the door to my heart a long time ago. I didn't want to feel. The pain that comes with letting the emotions in is more than I could ever bear. Even through it all, I still remember the way I felt when I met his twin sister, Ryan. It was like a jolt to my heart, forcing it to beat out of rhythm.

Ryan was all legs, chocolate brown hair flowing in the breeze covered by her backward snapback. The first thing I noticed was the intricate detail of the designs covering her skin, like vines wrapping around her arm.

If the sweet and innocent look on her face was any indication, she was too young to have tattoos of her own. I was drawn to the outward shell she presented to the world because I recognized it for what it was. A distraction from all the parts you want to keep buried deep. She was like a mirage of walking contradictions, which I knew to be true the moment she opened her smart mouth.

The passion she withheld under the surface was like a beacon of light shining in the dark night. Her fiery personality was the first thing to trigger a spark in the hollows of my heart.

All these years I've spent keeping my distance from her, out of fear of facing my feelings and the consequences that could follow. The hard part is, I know she feels the connection between us, too. The pull that keeps us tethered to each other, despite never allowing her to get close enough.

She's turning eighteen in two days and the resistance I've been struggling to keep hold of is starting to wear thin. Nothing good can come from going down this path because no matter how much my heart aches for her, it's inevitable I'll leave her heart torn in two.

Chapter One

RYAN

"Roll the window down, it smells like sex in here!" I shout, waving my hand in front of my face. Sticking my head outside, I take a deep breath and turn my head toward my best friend with a shit eating grin on my face.

"Says the virgin," she mutters, rolling her eyes as she turns up the music to drown out any smart-ass reply I could fire back. I know she can hear me as I tell her to fuck off, which prompts her to wave her middle finger in the air at me while keeping her eyes on the road.

Papa Roach blares through the speakers, as I slide back into my seat adjusting my hat as I do. I can feel the energy from the music run through my body as I nod my head to the lyrics.

Nadia is my best friend, my A1 since day one. There's not much I wouldn't do for her and I knew it to be true from the day we first met.

We were in eighth grade, riding the bus to school, when Kara Parker thought it would be fucking funny to pick shit out of the garbage and throw it at me from where she sat in the back. She only messed with me on the days my twin brother, Dean, would opt to walk to school with his friends.

She knew better than to pull that shit around Dean.

Nadia had been sitting in the seat across from me. It was the first day we had ever talked to each other. After watching a pop bottle cap whiz past our heads, she turned toward me with her face hard as stone as she said, "You ready to put this bitch down?"

My response mirrored the same devilish grin she flashed me. She's been my ride or die ever since.

"Did you talk to your mom about staying over at my place tomorrow?" she asks, shouting over the music. Nadia's parents take on the role of parenting from a distance. They leave her money on the counter and make sure there's always food in the cabinets. Otherwise, they're hardly home, which makes it the perfect place to crash when we plan to hit up a party or two on the weekends.

"She hasn't responded to my text message yet," I mutter, clicking the button on the side of my phone to check for a response. "I'm going to call her and see." Leaning over, I turn down the radio as I click the call button.

"Big Papa's Pizzeria."

My brother's immature greeting has me rolling my eyes so hard I'm surprised they didn't pop out of my head and roll across the floor. The worst part is the annoying laugh that follows finding his lame joke funny.

"Put Mom on the phone," I snap, cutting off his obnoxious laughter, running my fingers over the frayed hole in my jeans.

"What's in it for me?"

"Staying alive. Now quit being a prick, dick licker, and put her on the phone."

"You wanna talk to your mom with that dirty mouth?" Dean laughs. I can hear the light chuckling in the background, and if I had to guess, Maverick is there with him.

Figures.

"Seriously, D. I don't have all night. If I don't talk to her now, I'm going to be home late."

"You better hope that's not the case. After the last time, you know you're going to end up grounded. Happy Birthday to you."

I can picture his smug face as he sings the last part to me and I seriously want to junk punch him.

"Alright, Dad. Noted. Now put her on the fucking phone."

I can hear the light rustling on the other end before my mom's overly chipper voice filters through the phone.

"Yes, Ryan," she says with a sigh.

"Hi, Mom," I reply, my tone extra sweet which has Nadia laughing. "Is it cool if I crash at Nadia's this weekend?"

"Not tonight, Ryan," she replies curtly. "You can tomorrow since it's your birthday, but it's not necessary to stay over two nights in a row."

"Can I stay out a little later tonight then instead? It's a Friday night and we were going to meet up with some friends."

"You've been late once already this month, even after I extended your curfew. You have until ten o'clock to be home, Ryan. By the looks of it, that gives you seventeen minutes. I'll see you soon."

Nadia glances down at the clock as the line disconnects.

"Ry, we're not going to make it in time," she says, voicing my thoughts. I don't say anything because she's right. My house is at least twenty-five minutes away on a good day.

"Shit," I groan, running my hand over my face.

Nadia does her best to get me home in time, but when we hit a train on Rockford Drive, I know it's no use.

"Look on the bright side," Nadia says, peering over at me out of the corner of her eye. "If Dean is home, that likely means Maverick is crashing at your house tonight."

Maverick is one of my brother's best friends, which is both a blessing and a curse. He and Dean never go anywhere without the other. Dean is the annoying, obnoxious jock who likes to have all the attention on him. Maverick, on the other hand, is the complete opposite and sometimes I wonder what prompted their friendship.

Don't get me wrong, Dean's my twin brother, and he's a great guy. I don't know what they have in common besides skateboarding. Whatever it is, they are nearly inseparable. Maverick usually ends up staying over at our house, which I appreciate because it means I get to see him more.

"Like that matters. He acts as if I'm not there. I swear you'd think he hated me or something."

"I don't think that's true." Nadia laughs, shaking her head. "I think he's very much aware you're there. He just knows Dean would lose his shit if he knew he saw you as anything but his sister."

Which brings me to why it's a curse. Any chance of Maverick seeing me as more than his best friend's sister goes out the window. I know he would never do anything to put their friendship in jeopardy.

I can keep a secret and what Dean doesn't know won't hurt him.

Nadia whips the car into the driveway, pulling in behind Dean's beat-up Ford truck. The thing has seen better days, but he refuses to replace it.

"Text me when you can and let me know the damage," she mutters, clearly concerned our plans for tomorrow could be ruined.

I push the door of the car open and lean the seat forward, pulling out my skateboard from the backseat. I sling my backpack over my shoulder and readjust my hat on my head.

"Wish me luck," I groan, as I move the seat back in place.

We say our goodbyes as I head toward the front of my house.

My mom is in the kitchen loading the dishwasher when I enter the house. She doesn't bother to look at me, which I know can't be good. Kicking my shoes off near the door, I prop my board against the wall.

I spot Dean and Maverick lounging in the living room. Dean has his leg draped across the coffee table and a grin on his face, knowing what's about to come. Maverick grimaces and I know this can't be good.

"Welcome home," my mother says, the force of the dishwasher closing draws my attention away from him.

"Ryan, this is the second time you've been late this month. Before you even try to argue, I want to point out your birthday is in less than two hours, and I know you have plans with Nadia."

Dropping my bag down on the bench near the door, I slide the hat off my head and toss it on top before facing my mom.

"I'm sorry," I sigh, knowing nothing good will come from me saying anything more. "I'm going to bed."

I walk through the kitchen and into the living room. The urge to junk punch Dean has returned when I see the arrogant smirk on his face.

"Keep it up, fucker," I mutter under my breath, careful to not let my mom overhear us as I flash him the finger.

"What's that?" he retorts, turning his head to peer over the back of the couch.

Spinning around, I find both of their eyes on me. Seeing that my mom has since made her way out of the kitchen, likely retreating to our parents' bedroom, I don't hold back.

"I said keep it up, fucker. I should be the one laughin' at you, sitting at home like a bum on a Friday night," I snap, sounding bored as I lean against the wall.

There are about seven minutes separating the two of us. My parents were expecting to bring home two baby boys when I was born. What they didn't expect was for the second child to be born a girl. My name is evidence of that.

Dean turns around, facing the TV and lets out an annoyed grunt, "Fuck off, Ry."

My eyes bounce from Dean to Maverick and I'm surprised when I find Maverick's are already on me. They shine bright with amusement, as he bites his lower lip in an attempt to hide the grin lining his mouth. Crossing his arms over his chest, he runs his hand over his jaw as he glances over to make sure Dean isn't paying attention.

The thick muscles are tanned from all his days outside without his T-shirt on. His dark-brown hair is longer on top. The wayward strands give the appearance like he has ran his fingers through them one too many times.

The sleeves of my white T-shirt are cut off, giving it more of a muscle-shirt look. You can see my black sports bra from the side and a hint of my sun-kissed skin underneath.

My heart starts to pound as I relish the thought of him struggling to take his eyes off me. Taking two steps backward, I keep my eyes trained on him. I think back to my conversation with Nadia in the car when she said it's Dean that's holding him back.

The bold side of me wants to test her theory and see if it's true.

Standing outside my bedroom door, I keep my eyes focused on Maverick as I grab the hem of my shirt and pull the cotton material over my head. I roll my shirt into a ball before tossing it in the direction of my dirty clothes but not bothering to check if it made it.

I watch as Maverick's jaw clenches as his eyes travel over the length of my body, resting longer on my chest than necessary before finally bringing his eyes up to meet mine. He leans forward, pressing his elbows to his knees. Even then, he doesn't take his eyes off me.

"D, I'm gonna use your bathroom quick and head out. I should've been home a little while ago."

I can hear Dean mumble out a response, but I have no idea what he says. I'm too lost in the look on Maverick's face to pay much attention to what is going on around me.

Bracing his palms on his knees, Maverick moves to stand. He's so tall, standing over six feet. He's athletic, but whereas my brother is stockier from his time in football, Maverick is lean.

I can hear my heart pounding in my ears as he stalks toward me with a slight tic in his jaw. The closer he gets to me, the more my body comes alive with his presence.

"A little bold of you. Wouldn't you say, Rebel?"

It isn't the first time I've heard him use the nickname, but the tone in his voice is deeper. I can feel the words roll through me, crashing over me like waves as he stands close leaving only an inch between us.

I'm not able to think properly as I stare up at his gray eyes. They're so dark, it's almost like a storm is brewing in their depths.

Raising his hand up, he runs his knuckle along the soft skin of my shoulder as I force a step away from him. I need to gain some semblance of sanity, but the move causes his lip to curl in a small grin.

"You have nothing to say now? I didn't think that was possible." His quiet chuckle does crazy things to my heart.

"Aren't you supposed to be leaving now?" I retort, hating how he can look so unaffected knowing the way he's making me feel.

"Yeah, I am. Are you sure it's what you want though?"

He presses the palm of his hand against my hip as he moves to step closer in the narrow hallway. I'm standing so close to the wall, I know there's plenty of room for him to pass by.

His thumb lightly traces my exposed skin, as he takes a step around me. His body is pressed against mine, bringing us closer than we've ever been.

The move forces the air out of my chest and I know he can feel my body tremble beneath his touch.

"I didn't think so," he whispers against the shell of my ear.

As soon as he passes by me and the bathroom, he glances back at me. His eyes travel down to where my chest heaves with every struggled breath before looking back up at me. Flashing me a wink, he turns and walks down the hallway and out the front door without another word.

Holy shit.

Do you want more Maverick and Ryan?
Check out Torn today at
www.authorbrookeobrien.com/tatteredheartduet

BOOKS BY BROOKE

A Rebels Havoc Series

Brix

Sins of a Rebel

Tysin

Trey

Madden

Men of Blaze

Personal Foul

Reckless Rebound (Cocky Hero Club)

Tattered Heart Duet

Torn

Tattered

A Heart's Compass Series

Where I Found You

Lost Before You

Until I Found You

Now That I Found You

Where You Belong

Standalones (In order of publication)

Wild Irish

Learn more and purchase your copy at:

www.authorbrookeobrien.com/booksbybrooke

ACKNOWLEDGMENTS

To my boys–I love you more than the universe. Thank you for thinking I'm cool and for being proud of mama for writing books, even though it makes me cringe to think about you telling your teachers. We'll just pretend that doesn't happen.

To my AMAZING beta readers – Thorunn, Kristen, Summer, April, Candyce, and Donna. Thank you for reading Madden and Brielle's story before anyone else, for your honest feedback, and for helping me make their story better. I'm so grateful to you! <3

Jenny Sims and Rox LeBlanc – Thank you for your hard work on this project. You both have been so wonderful to work with and learn from. I wouldn't want to do this without you on my team!

To the fantastic bloggers and my Rebel Hype Team, thank you for being a part of this one. I'm excited to hear what you think of Madden and Brielle. I hope you know how grateful I am for every one of you.

My Rebels Readers – I love being able to connect with all of you in my Reader Group and across social media. Thank you for your love of this series. It's changed my life and I'm so thankful for you all!

Anna B. Doe – I can't tell you how much I appreciate your friendship and our chats. Thank you for always keeping it real with me. I always got your back and support you!

Thorunn – We've grown close so quickly, and I can't tell you how much it's meant having your friendship and support throughout writing Madden and when planning what comes next. Thank you for always being a listening ear and sharing your opinion. It means a lot to me!

April – Thank you so much for being you. We've grown so close over the past few years and I'm thankful to have you and your sense of humor in my life. There's never a dull moment when we're together. I love having you as my book friend and my real friend.

Kristen – Thank you for always being honest with me, no matter what. I can always count on you to keep it real and raw with me. Even when I think every word I've written is shit, you're there to bring me back to earth. I love you!

Kate Jessop and Lyssa Cole – Thank you for your friendship and support, for checking in with me, and letting me bounce ideas off you. Your friendship and support mean the world to me.

ABOUT BROOKE

USA Today Bestselling author Brooke O'Brien writes steamy and swoon-worthy new adult romances. She's best known for her sports and rock star romances.

Brooke believes a love worth having is worth fighting for, and she brings this into her stories where her characters risk it all for love.

When she isn't writing or falling in love with a new book boyfriend, you can find her spending time with her family, cheering on her favorite sports teams, listening to ASMR, or binge-watching the latest true crime documentary. She loves rockin' a comfy hoodie with leggings and believes the best days include a good nap.

Brooke loves connecting with readers and hopes you'll join her on her social pages or reader group to stay in touch. To follow Brooke and join her newsletter, visit authorbrookeobrien.com/follow.

COPYRIGHT